Holding the CARDS

JOEY W. HILL

ELLORA'S CAVE
ROMANTICA®
www.EllorasCave.com

An Ellora's Cave Publication

www.ellorascave.com

Holding the Cards

ISBN 9781843604006
ALL RIGHTS RESERVED.
Holding the Cards Copyright © 2002 Joey W. Hill
Designed by Syneca.
Photography by olly/shutterstock.com

Electronic book publication 2002
Trade paperback publication 2004

With the exception of quotes used in reviews, this book may not be reproduced or used in whole or in part by any means existing without written permission from the publisher, Ellora's Cave Publishing, Inc.® 1056 Home Avenue, Akron OH 44310-3502.

Warning: The unauthorized reproduction or distribution of this copyrighted work is illegal. Criminal copyright infringement, including infringement without monetary gain, is investigated by the FBI and is punishable by up to 5 years in federal prison and a fine of $250,000. (http://www.fbi.gov/ipr/)

This book is a work of fiction and any resemblance to persons, living or dead, or places, events or locales is purely coincidental. The characters are productions of the author's imagination and used fictitiously.

The publisher and author(s) acknowledge the trademark status and trademark ownership of all trademarks, service marks and word marks mentioned in this book.

The publisher does not have any control over and does not assume any responsibility for author or third-party Web sites or their content.

HOLDING THE CARDS
ಐ

Dedication

Control is temporal, but some bonds will last forever if you submit to the blessing of their existence upon you.

To Mary, who deserves joy in every form.
To Ben and Gil, who contributed considerable inspiration to this work.
To my husband, always.

Chapter 1

ಲ

"Good grief, Lisette, don't worry so much." Lauren tossed her duffel bag into the front of the boat and began to tie the waterproof tarp over her belongings. "I used to camp by myself in the Blue Ridge all the time during college. And you said I'd be perfectly safe there, that the only reason you all lock your doors at all is to keep out the occasional sticky-fingered fisherman." She straightened, eyes twinkling, and pointed. "There's the island. I'll be a dot, but a very visible dot, when I reach the dock."

"But Thomas could take you over in the Whaler. You know, boating like this, by yourself, it's not safe. And I feel so bad, because I had hoped—"

"Don't start again," Lauren took her friend's hand. "I'm glad you've been asked to go on a book signing tour. Strange as it sounds, and as much as I enjoy your company, I think I need the time alone. I'm going to lay out on the beach, cook myself dinner, and read books until I sack out at night." Her chin tightened. "This is my gift to me."

"Well, just do me a favor and give my machine a call once a day, okay? I'll check it from Toronto. I know Josh will be there, but I'd still feel better knowing—"

"Whoa, back up, rewind. Josh?"

Lisette waved away Lauren's narrow look. "He's the caretaker, carpenter, fix-it person. He keeps a little crofter hidden on the island. His phone number is in my kitchen if you need him. If he's not on the island, it forwards to his cell. And don't worry," Lisette grinned. "I'm not setting you up for a D.H. Lawrence novel. He's gay. He has a male 'friend' that comes down a lot and works with him on some of his projects.

It's real obvious, they're both drop-dead gorgeous. They won't bug you."

Lauren sighed, the corner of her mouth quirking up. "I don't know. I get a private tropical island all to myself for the weekend, nothing there but a handful of million-dollar retreat homes of world-famous artists and writers. I have to lay on the beach and watch two good-looking guys in tool belts who aren't the least bit interested in hassling me. It sounds wretched. I'm booking a flight back tonight."

Lisette smiled and then surprised Lauren by pulling her into a tight hug. "I knew you'd bounce back," she murmured into Lauren's hair. "You always do."

Yep, she was like a rubber ball, just bouncing off of every wall. Lauren embraced her friend, but her control slipped, and she held on longer than she intended. Lisette waited just long enough, then eased back with a teasing smile as if she hadn't noticed anything amiss.

"It's probably good I mentioned him," she added. "He's a little strange, and he might have startled you when and if you do meet him."

"Strange, how?" Lauren snapped on her inflatable PFD.

"It's hard to describe. If you get a chance to talk to him, you'll see what I mean. I think he's stayed on the island by himself too long." At Lauren's raised brow, Lisette lifted a shoulder. "It's like he's so used to silence, he has to think about how to form words. He'll look at me as if he's said something and he's waiting for an answer. Then he realizes he didn't say the question out loud. It's fascinating."

"I sense a character about to be born," Lauren said.

"Honey, that's a done deal. You remember *Gazing at Sirius*, Jeremy -"

It was twenty more minutes before Lauren pulled in the dock lines and turned the JY16 toward Goat Island. Lisette had to assure herself Lauren had the charger for the cell phone, which was at the bottom of her bag, and hug Lauren several more times.

The wind was coming in perfectly across the starboard side of the boat as Lauren situated her feet under the hiking strap, and sheeted in the main and the jib. She had not sailed in some time, and the eager leap of the craft thrilled her as it took her out of the cove.

She looked back and raised her hand. Lisette waved and waved until distance and the movement of the water reduced her to a tiny figure.

Sailing had taught Lauren patience, the expectation that things go wrong. It tended to balance that with an ironic tranquility, the peace of working with nature to reach a goal. It was a view of life she had internalized, and was reflected in who she was professionally, as well as sexually.

She had graduated with honors from Duke University, and then fought her way to the top of their grueling medical program. She divided her residency between rural clinics in the North Carolina tobacco towns and the busy emergency room of the university hospital. A prestigious pediatrics practice in Atlanta accepted her immediately upon passing her boards. Now she was almost thirty, with an established base of patients, and two published papers to her credit.

Her family received appropriate and thoughtful gifts from her on birthdays and holidays, and she had a small group of loving childhood friends. She was healthy and happy with her life.

Lauren raised the dagger board, letting the counter weight of her body against the sails do the work of balancing the boat, and the craft responded with another burst of marvelous speed. She lifted her face to the wind and closed her eyes.

Yes, she was happy. But she was somewhat different than her close friends and colleagues. On Friday nights, when she bid goodnight to her co-workers, some would go to the bars and restaurants that catered to unwinding professionals, while others went home to the spouse and children. Lauren went home and prepared for a far different type of evening.

* * * * *

She would begin by pampering herself for an hour in her clawfoot tub, filled with scented bubble bath and surrounded by pillar candles. When at last she stood up, she would let all the bubbles slide down her skin like creamy silk before reaching for a towel. She bought her towels from a bath-and-body shop, where each towel was rolled and tied with a satin peach ribbon and a sprig of lavender. Each Friday night merited a new towel from the shop. She would dry herself with gentle presses and strokes of the absorbent cotton, awakening nerves that had to be encased in steel during the week.

When she laid aside the towel, she sprinkled her body with a light dusting of silver glitter. She applied her favorite perfume, an exotic sandalwood scent, to her throat, wrists, and inner thighs.

Her outfit of the night might be a thigh-high skirt and short jacket, severely tailored and woven of soft linen to follow the curves of her body like a second skin. She might wear a shell of shimmering black stretch gauze with a pearl embroidered collar beneath the jacket. The demure lapels and conservative pearl embellishment would frame the shadowed but distinct curves of her breasts, visible through the transparent fabric. Thigh high boots that laced up the side with satin ribbon might be chosen. It was entertaining to watch a man take a zipper down with his teeth, but to watch him work to pull out the same bindings that she might use to restrain him later...that was delightful. She could feel the hot touch of his mouth through the lacings, a sensation zippered boots could not provide.

Her long blonde hair might be swept up on her head, with just a few tendrils down to caress her neck. She would paint her lips with a delicate pink lipstick, and line her eyes with a charcoal pencil to deepen their impact.

At last ready, she would be off to an evening that could last until dawn, in one of Atlanta's upscale fetish clubs. There she might wander the "dungeons", and be mesmerized by a performer slicking oil over the taut muscles of a manacled young man and disciplining the aroused submissive with a riding crop.

Lauren had been aware of being a Dom sexually since college, thanks to an adventurous first boyfriend. She used the shortened insider term often instead of Dominatrix. She liked the word, but knew it had become a caricature in people's minds; a woman with a God-complex dressed up in leather and thigh high boots, wielding a whip and a smirk.

It was a part of her life that friends such as Lisette did not know about, for exactly that reason. Lauren was not ashamed; she simply knew that most of them would have the same view of it as propagated by television, a comedic farce of leather and chains.

Subconsciously, Lisette did understand, Lauren knew. In the alpha-male heroes and submissive-yet-feisty heroines of her romance novels, Lisette instinctively created characters that danced around a fragile triangle of control, trust and sex, and a few million readers just as instinctively responded to it.

There was an intimacy to a relationship between a Dominant and submissive that pulled on the elemental need for unconditional love and trust. So while she did not share her preferences with those closest to her, Lauren desperately wanted to find someone to share them with her, as well as a lifetime of love, marriage and all the rest. It was not just the submissive who had needs. The Dominant had vulnerabilities that were comforted and healed by the faith and pleasure of the submissive. They were two parts of a whole.

* * * * *

The salty spray of Caribbean waters misted her skin and Lauren did not turn her face away, hoping it might also wash away some of her thoughts.

Maybe she was meant to be alone. When a woman got to be nearly thirty and was delighted to be going on a retreat by herself, it said something. Maybe the energy for making a relationship work from scratch just ran out as a person got into three decades of living. So much was soaked up by the career, the commitments to family and friends. When the first thought upon meeting a guy was, *do I really have time for this relationship shit?*, it was a pretty obvious indicator. Everybody wanted love and a Mr. or Mrs. Forever, but only if he/she fit seamlessly into their life without disrupting the pattern already set by tenacious individuality.

The touch of Jonathan's hands and his moist mouth invaded her cynical thoughts, and her skin shuddered, the response of gnawing sensual hunger. She could find something to feed the body, but would she ever find someone to feed the heart? There were no emotional vibrators out there.

Maria, a third generation American-Spanish waitress and performer at Lauren's favorite club, had tried to get Lauren to do performances, even become one of the dungeon regulars. But she wasn't looking to fulfill someone's fantasies for one night. She missed the intimacy; she missed Jonathan. Cold, calculating Jonathan who had turned out to be…not hers.

Lauren shook out of the thoughts as she ducked under the boom for the smooth swing of the tack. She could do this, focus on a skill she had neglected, enjoy the fading sun on her shoulders. If she didn't know Lisette would stand there until she reached the beach, she would have stopped the boat midway and watched the sun melt into gold fire on the water.

Lisette's defection had been fated. For several months, her friend had been at her disposal for long, tearful phone calls and last minute trips by plane to hold Lauren together. It was time to start manufacturing her own glue again.

Lauren couldn't see the houses, even as she drew closer to the island. They had been designed to blend into the maritime forest. Though Lisette's had a clear view of the beach, Lauren could not make it out at all through the green canopy, a thick weave of palms, knotted sea-swept oaks, and uncut understory.

Everything was postcard colors, from the crystal blue of the water through which she waded, to the white crystals of the beach onto which she tugged the boat. She found the piling driven there for tying the vessel against high tide's grasp and made it fast. Just to ease Lisette's mind, she sat down, just out of the water's reach, pulled out the cell phone and left a message with her friend's answering service.

Lauren replaced the cell phone and eased back onto the sand, absorbing the silence. Only the soft whisper of wind and surf, and the gentle movement of the sails of the tied boat, spoke to her.

It was as if she had stepped into an alternate universe. How often did a person get to be genuinely alone, not just the privacy of one's house, but in absolute quiet, both within and without?

Lauren closed her eyes and stretched out her arms, feeling the rough grains of sand shift and trickle over her biceps as she slid them through the sand like a bird's wings. She nestled her head into the soft stuff and chuckled at the image of herself rooting with the joyous pleasure of a canine.

She arched her back and pressed her hips deeper into the soft mattress that smelled of the sea. The sun kissed her lips, warmed a path along her bared throat.

Without warning, the memory of Jonathan's hands was upon her. She remembered his lips touching, sucking, and caressing. Her body arched harder in instinctive reaction, wishing...wishing he had offered the intimacy that the eager touch of those lips and the caress of those strong hands had seemed to promise. The distant eyes were a mocking contrast to the expert lovemaking. He did exactly and only what she bid him to do. Even a dominatrix couldn't command a heart to love her.

Lauren's hand lay on her thigh, and she slid her fingers up, beneath the loose shorts, under the elastic of her panties. Damp, just from the thought of him.

At times when he knelt before her, she would consider him with cool eyes and crossed legs that revealed nothing. He would have to persuade her to uncross her thighs by tracing his tongue along the delicate anklebone, up the ridge of the calf, along the back of her thigh. When at last she relented, she made him sit back and watch her slide one knee off the other to spread open her legs. She would take her time. The flickering light thrown by the candles in their room would advance like a sunrise into the dark tunnel between her thighs as she drew back the snug skirt. When it was high enough, she would give him permission and he would surge forward and plunge his tongue into her.

He lapped, made intricate swirls, and she came again and again, but she wanted to beg, plead with him, to demand that he offer her more than his flesh. His soul was what she craved. In the end, she *had* begged, and he had left her.

A cloud covered the sun, leaving her skin chilled with its absence. She was crying, dammit. Goddammit.

Lauren erupted from the sand, cursed, shouted, kicked the boat, grabbed up handfuls of sand and flung them about her, screaming out her frustration at the silent island, a primal wordless cry.

Get out of my head. You're not fucking worth it.

She brought her clenched fists to her chest and bent her head over them, as if the heart beneath was an infant that needed protection. And it was, in a way.

"Sadistic bastard," she muttered and snatched up her pack, refusing to give in to the familiar spiral of terror that she would always be like this, always destined to end up alone because of who she was.

* * * * *

"Maybe this game is what's the matter with me," she had suggested to Maria.

The waitress had chuckled and laid a hand over hers, her long nails painted a burgundy color as liquid as wine.

"Everybody plays a game to find that special someone, sugar. This game isn't your problem, and even if it was, you can't get it out of your blood. I've seen people like you try to go vanilla. They think they always fuck relationships up because they're into kink. It's like a person who wants kids, convincing himself he can live without them to be with that special lady who doesn't want kids at all.

"You're not planning on strapping some boy's ass until you're both in dentures, though that's a part of it. You need to find out what's driving your game. You and Jonathan were playing the same game on the face, but in reality you were as different as Monopoly and Tiddly-Winks.

"Figure that out, and you'll know exactly what you want. Then when that lucky boy shows up in front of you - blam - it won't be just his fine ass that will be all yours."

* * * * *

Josh sat on his heels just inside the tree line, his arms crossed loosely over his knees. He had observed the woman's approach, admiring her easy handling of the sailboat in the stiff breeze. He had watched, at first amused when she flopped herself down on the sand. He got less amused and more intent as her body responded to the sensual offering of the natural world around her. When she arched and stretched in the sleeveless polo shirt, the muscles of her thighs contracting, raising, her hand finding herself, he had thought for a moment he was having some type of prurient daydream, a common phenomenon when a man spent his days on a deserted island. Then she had exploded into rage and he watched her tantrum, his eyes widening at both the immediacy and strength of her fury.

The infrequent visits by the residents didn't perturb him. They were artists, naturally reclusive and devoted to their respective crafts. It was the reason the island had drawn them, and though their temperaments might be volatile or celebrated when in contact with the mainland world, here most were quiet, at peace with themselves, gods busy in their workshops with the creation of their newest worlds.

It looked like this latest visitor had not come to create, but to vanquish demons. It would be an interesting process to watch, and maybe, to help her.

It was an unexpected thought. Josh straightened, unsmiling, and went to find Marcus.

Chapter 2

The house was so Lisette. Wrapped up in the lush stillness of the maritime forest, the combination of stone and natural wood siding made the home a part of the green and brown world around it. Half of the house's square footage was built inside the steep hillside. Though the architecture was impressive, the house was not ostentatious in size.

Lauren found the inside the same. Quality, not quantity, was the guiding force that had furnished the interior. The kitchen area was decorated in a warm blue with white counters and clean stainless steel that invited culinary experiments. Barstools pulled up to the white counters invited observers to gather around, chat and drink wine.

The spacious refrigerator and deep pantry had been stocked with groceries, bottled water and basic condiments. By the mysterious Josh, Lauren assumed. She had escaped responsibility in every sense.

She carried her bags into the living area, which had deep carpeting, a cozy horseshoe of couches with recliner options and inviting chairs and ottomans gathered around a beveled glass coffee table. The glass was held up on the tail fronds and slender hands of a mermaid carved out of a pale bleached wood. A stereo cabinet was tucked discreetly in a corner, so nothing distracted from the panoramic view offered by the wall of windows before the sitting area. There was a sliding glass door out to a deck that overlooked the lush ravine below, canopied by the graceful arms of the trees, which, if one raised the gaze, framed the distant, panoramic view of the ocean.

It made the decision of what to do with her first afternoon easy. Lauren took time to put away some of her things, but as soon as the essentials of settling in were handled, she stripped down. She wrapped herself in a towel and stepped out onto the deck, her eye on the hot tub she had turned on to heat up while she had unpacked.

The tub was surrounded by a Japanese rock garden and a forest of exotic plants. Keeping them alive was another task of Josh's, she assumed, since Lisette's busy schedule only allowed her to spend a couple months a year here. Lisette had told her the plants were potted in an array of interesting cast-off pieces offered to her by another island part-time resident. Art appreciation was an avid hobby; there was not a gallery or museum floor in Atlanta, or on any of her other travels, that had not been imprinted with Lauren's footsteps. She recognized the "cast-offs" as the work of a potter whose work went in New York galleries for four figures.

While she soaked, Lauren looked down and watched the myriad of wildlife that roamed, unconcerned, through the ravine, and the birds that flitted from branch to branch in the trees. An hour or more passed in that simple fashion, and after a time, her thoughts left her alone, so that she could simply gaze at the world around her, and be a quiet part of it.

Her growling stomach finally made her decide it was time to rise. She tucked a towel around her breasts and gave some thought to dinner. She had bought wine and goat cheese from a native vendor at the small airport, and there was a small box of Belgian chocolates and the makings for a green salad in the fridge that looked tempting. Savoring that meal and plunging into the first of the ten novels she'd downloaded to her handheld electronic reader sounded perfect.

She put her hand on the sliding door and pushed. Lauren frowned, shoved again. She glanced down. In dismay, she saw that the door had a safety rod. Made to lay down in the track of the doorframe to prevent the door from being forced open, it had apparently fallen into place when she had come out on the deck. It effectively trapped her there.

Well. She looked about, expecting there might be some way out of her predicament. There were no stairs off the deck, and no windows within her reach. Annoyance was her first thought. She couldn't imagine why a "sticky fingered fisherman" would scale up a tree to the deck.

There was no reason to panic. If she had to, she could pick up one of those cast off pots and smash it through the double paned glass window of the sliding door, but she certainly didn't want to take that tack until she'd thought all other options through.

She sat down on the edge of the tub and took another swallow of her wine, considering her surroundings more carefully.

Lisette had kept the large trees around the deck relatively unpruned. Lauren could only imagine what it had been like to construct the house within the span of the branches. It had to have been an architect's dream and a builder's nightmare. She suspected there were contractors on the mainland who could not pass a Lisette Delamar book without shuddering. However, the arms of one particularly impressive specimen reached out and over the deck, so close that a terra cotta birdfeeder had been anchored there. Lauren stepped to the rail.

The crotch of the tree would require about twenty-five feet of downward climb to reach, but the branch that could take her there was solid, with the circumference of a telephone pole. Once reaching the juncture, it would be a bit trickier, because it was about fifteen to twenty feet above the ground, and the tree's roots clung to the steep incline, giving the trunk the one hundred and ten degree angle of a woodpecker. However, she might be able to work her way down the trunk on that leeward side.

Just like sailing, she hadn't climbed a tree in some time, but she climbed the rope at the gym. She climbed it with furious intent, combating her gender's frustrating upper body weakness with a passion that she knew suggested she was fighting other, more personal weaknesses with her workouts.

No time for personal angst. She could do this. She rewrapped the towel about her waist and knotted it on the side, leaving her breasts exposed like a bleached *National Geographic* native. She was isolated here, and it wasn't likely the towel would hold firm tucked around her bosom. However, the terry cloth would provide her legs some protection from the rough bark.

She did a couple of stretches, touched her toes, and twisted back and forth. The hot tub had already loosened her up, so with a fortifying swig of wine, she was ready to play Jane. Or maybe Tarzan. Jane would be waiting for Tarzan to come rescue her, never realizing he was banging some Amazon and couldn't be bothered with some whiny city girl.

She smiled at the thought and stood up on the rail. The branch was now level with her waist. It was simple to lean over, grasp it with both hands and slide herself onto it like a horse's back. The bark scraped the tender underside of her breasts and rasped over her left nipple, leaving a red mark on the white skin.

She looked down into the green abyss of the ravine, which was thirty or a hundred feet down, depending on the side of the branch from which she fell. She rethought the idea of going back and breaking the window. It was an acceptable option if the alternative was plunging to her death or certain maiming in the forest below.

Nonsense. She was a strong, healthy woman, capable of climbing down a tree. It wasn't much higher than the rope. She didn't look down when she climbed the rope. That was the main difference.

She managed to wriggle down a good ten feet before her foot touched a branch, an offspring of her present perch. Unfortunately, in its quest for sunlight, this branch had curved upward, so she would have to maneuver around it, an obstacle in her road. Lauren sat up, bracing her hands on the bark between her thighs, and let her legs swing. Her bare back rested against the upward curving branch, forming a chair, and she relaxed a moment, or tried to do so.

Why was she in such a hurry? She didn't have dinner on the stove, wasn't expecting company. Lauren swallowed, remembering when she *had* expected someone.

She and Jonathan had lived together only a month. From the first day, he had balked at anything that smacked of the "how-was-your-day-dear?" rut, as he called it, describing it in disparaging terms as the innocuous brushing of lips, the sacking out on the couch in front of the TV after exchanging less than two sentences.

So to keep him happy, she ordered him to come home from work earlier than her, every night. He was to put away his briefcase, lawyer's suit and tie, and make her dinner. He would then kneel by the door, eyes gazing at the floor. He would be wearing nothing unless she had specified something in particular. She would come in, dressed impeccably in her skirted suit; hose and heels take his hand and raise him to his feet. He wasn't to lift his gaze. All subs tried occasionally, they couldn't help themselves, and those brief, forbidden glimpses were full of such naked hunger a Dom could not help but be aroused by a single look.

Not Jonathan. He never had a problem with that, unless he wanted to be punished. He would serve her dinner, and then she might make him kneel under the table and serve her another way while she drank her wine and caressed his hair, even as her body flushed with pleasure and she gasped at the touch of his lips or clever fingers.

Lauren broke into a sweat, and tears pricked her eyelids. She had come here to get away from these cursed memories. She told herself it was just a physical thing. She was feeling deprived. It was the way the tree rubbed her through the towel as she sat, swinging her legs. As the thought occurred to her, she lifted herself up so that the lips between her legs brushed lightly against the cloth-covered bark. Goose pimples ran up and down her skin. What was unpleasant on bare skin was not so unpleasant when covered with a thick cotton barrier. Oh, yes, tree climbing definitely had its up side.

She had gotten so she could get herself off with anything. When she finally came, the combination of intense physical pleasure and unbearable emotional anguish left her limp in mind and body. In those dark moments, her subconscious rose to the surface and laughed at her conscious mind's proud insistence that it was just the fulfillment of a physical need Jonathan had taken away from her.

She wasn't a liar. Not to herself or to anyone else. It was just a way of coping. She knew it was more than just having him naked at her door. It was looking around the corner and seeing his briefcase sitting in their bedroom, the evidence of existing together, sharing everything. In reality, all they had ever shared was sex and the game. Why had it been so hard to see that?

No-brainer question. Because she had wanted so much *not* to see it.

What cruelty made you give your heart on a platter to someone who didn't want it? It was so painful to have them politely dismiss it. *No thank you, none for me please.* She'd almost rather a lover attack her heart with knife and fork, consume it in three bites and throw it back up later. At least that was action, passion.

Lauren shook her head. She would rather have her heart hacked up like a hairball than left intact and unaccepted. There was a mental image. She needed to get a grip and stop thinking so damn much, or she was going to drown in pathetic metaphors.

Lauren contemplated the ravine below, all the mysteries of life moving among the foliage. The cycles of birth, life, death, beginning and ending in every moment. There was a majestic hush over it all, each sound resonating like music on a scrolled page. The calling of the birds, the rustle of the leaves in the wind, the soft snap of branches and staccato tap of animals moving along the paths known only to them. So different from the human world. Humans knew nothing of harmony with the world about them. They were so dedicated to enhancing their single note; they couldn't begin to figure out how to make a song.

The cool air of twilight touched her with questing fingers, as if just noticing her. Lauren closed her eyes and felt it stroke her hair off her nape and shiver down her torso, learning what manner of creature she might be. She concentrated on the stillness, seeing if she could somehow, by bringing that stillness into herself, make it dissolve the memories that refused to stop haunting her. She had to come to terms with them, and with herself.

She became more conscious of her breathing, and could almost sense that there were others who breathed with her in the impending night, creatures with liquid brown eyes and twitching noses, and musky soft fur that smelled of earth and animal.

Lauren slowly opened her eyes, not sure how long she had been lost in the meditative state.

Long enough that the air had gotten colder, and the sun had disappeared into the horizon, though it still illuminated the sky. She sighed, looked down, and found she was no longer alone.

Chapter 3

෨

A man stood below her tree, watching her with intent brown eyes, like the creatures of the forest. No wet black nose, but his lips were definitely twitching.

Lauren yelped in surprise. Instinct had her arms flying up into bat position to cover her breasts."How long have you been standing there?" she demanded.

"Awhile," he lifted a shoulder, studying her in a manner that was indeed animal-like. Humans didn't have such disconcertingly intent focus in their gazes.

"Why didn't you say something?"

He seemed to mull that over. The unexpected silence stretched out between them. "I didn't have anything to say," he said at last.

This had to be Josh. Since he was gay, he wasn't about to turn into a rutting beast and grapple up the tree to ravish her. Oh, screw it. He was a grown man and she was sure he had seen someone's breasts before hers. She hated the pathetic picture she imagined she made, so she forced herself to settle back against her natural backrest and readjust her arms to an akimbo position, so she wasn't flaunting herself, but she wasn't cowering either. His glance seemed to follow the movement of every muscle.

"Do you intend to be around awhile?" she said, exasperated when he said nothing further, just continued to study her. His hair was a variety of rich browns streaked with blonde. It fell in uneven lengths to his shoulders, just grazing the top of his tanned shoulder blades. He wore just a pair of jeans, so a great deal of that tan was exposed, as well as some intricate and stunning tattoos. Celtic designs manacled his biceps and wrists, and there was a dragon pattern on his flat belly just above his navel. It was beautiful work, and yet it did not quite fit him, which was a strange thought, since she had just met him.

"When you're safe, I'll leave." The simple and sincere statement shut down her ire and replaced it with embarrassment.

"I'm sure I'll be okay," she assured him, though she felt no real assurance of that herself at the moment. "What makes you think I didn't climb out here intentionally?"

His gaze dropped to her bare upper torso, then slid over to the deck where the hot tub still gurgled and the closed sliding glass door reflected the last light of the day.

"Fine," she said crossly, as if he'd called her an idiot outright. "Just...look somewhere else if you could. I mean, it's not like this—" she glanced down, "really does anything for you, but it's easier to concentrate on getting down if you're not staring at me."

She felt embarrassed. Josh wished she could see herself as he was seeing her. She was perfect. She sat on the limb with her upper body straight, no attempt to hide the slope of her bare breasts, now that she was over her surprise. The towel knotted at her hip gave him an unimpeded view of one leg from hipbone to ankle. With her hair piled onto her head, tendrils of it wisping around her neck, she was both delicate and powerful, inciting a strong dual desire to protect her, and serve her every wish.

It was likely his prolonged isolation that made her so potent. If he saw her on a street corner, amid a bunch of other people, wearing jeans and a sweater, buying a paper, he'd give her no more than a passing appreciative glance. Maybe. Regardless, thinking that didn't change his primitive reaction to her. There were no props like that here to protect the senses.

He politely shifted his gaze a couple inches, and his position a couple feet, as she began to attempt descent again.

He wanted her in his peripheral vision if she began to fall. He wondered why she thought so little of her body that she thought he wouldn't be affected by it. This woman's figure was worth days of perusal. She had built up her strength while making sure her body stayed stylishly trim. He could see and appreciate that in the flex of her biceps and shifting long thigh muscles. He was obligated to wonder what it would feel like to have those muscles flexing against his hips. He could appreciate the curve of buttock her movement along the branch revealed. But Josh was first and foremost a breast man, and it was that which anchored his peripheral vision.

Hers were firm and heavy, the delicate shadows of blue veins offering the tongue a path that he wouldn't mind tracing. He also wouldn't mind heating up the nipple in his mouth, feeling it go from the tight wrinkled point caused by the friction of the bark, to full hardness. He could imagine his lips and tongue soothing each red abrasion on the sensitive skin.

Her bare foot reached the crotch of the tree and Josh gave her another moment or two to figure out the obvious, that her only choice was a fifteen-foot drop. The trunk of the ancient tree was far too large to shinny down unless she was part monkey, and the angle too steep, though she'd done admirably well so far.

He moved back to the base and looked up. He was rewarded with an unencumbered view up the towel, her legs open as she braced one foot in the joining point of the tree and positioned the other foot higher, on the branch she had just traversed. The vision jolted him, the pink lips of her sex exposed by a neat shave. It was easy to imagine what those lips would look like, glistening with arousal, inviting him inside.

He jerked his gaze up and made himself focus on the tendrils of blonde hair, tickling bare shoulders he'd love to mark with a light swipe of his teeth.

"You're a handy man," she said. "A fix-it guy. Don't you have a ladder or something?"

"Yes," he nodded. "My ladder is a mile away. If I go get it, you'll get impatient and try to come down by yourself. I'll find your body," his gaze shifted below them thoughtfully, "in that ravine, and Lisette will be angry that I went to get my ladder."

Her chest started to heave with a touch of ire, distracting him. He raised his gaze back to her face and held it there, though the effort was making his eyes water.

"What if I promised not to move?" she said impatiently.

He liked the way she spoke, softness over steel, like she could order a man off of a cliff and make him want to do it. Realizing she was waiting for an answer, he lifted a shoulder.

"I don't know you," he said. "So I don't know how good your word is."

Lauren stared down at him. Her entire escape to this island, at the moment, was taking on the appearance of an episode of Keystone Cops Go to Hell.

She had envisioned herself having a flawless weekend of solitude, getting in touch with the inner Lauren, finding that calm, capable woman she knew was still in there somewhere. In short, she had imagined herself taking long contemplative walks on the beach, staring out at the waves, the heroine of a New Age self-discovery memoir. The woodland animals, feeling her amazing tranquility and strength, would approach her without fear and seek her touch.

This was her vacation, dammit, and she was going to get on the ground, get into the house with a cup of hot chocolate, and read one of her books. She wouldn't start with a romance, one of those books where women ended up in ludicrous positions half-naked in front of strange, handsome men. Like that ever really happened.

Well, hell, if he wasn't used to the proper social niceties, pretending everything was okay when it wasn't, then she needn't work at it. Her legs folded up to her chest and Lauren sank into the crevice of the tree, the bark scraping yet another area of exposed skin, adding to the list of abrasions she would have to address later. She turned her back on him and leaned her head up against the branch. She shut her eyes tightly, but the bitter tears fought free anyway, a knot of them jamming up her throat. Resolve number one, not to cry a single tear while she was on this island, was in shambles for the second time in less than two hours.

She massaged her temples and jerked around as a warm hand touched her shoulder. She would have knocked him off her perch if he hadn't been prepared for her startled reaction to his climbing ability. He had one hand braced on the branch she had descended.

Lauren had a momentary impression of wide shoulders and penetrating gray eyes studying her tear-streaked face, then she was brought into his arms, his hands pressed against her bare back, his arms gathering her close and holding her surrounded by the shelter of chest and knees.

It wasn't an embrace that said, "I'm the big, strong man holding the feeble female". It was a gentle, firm hold that offered her comfort, offered himself up as the tree she could lean upon for a moment or forever, however long it took.

She stiffened at the absurd thought and he brought her closer, like she was a child curled in a fetal position. His careful, tender hands stroked her back, her hair, as he muttered soothingly to her. Lauren's head fell forward, her forehead coming into contact with his chest. He put his head over hers, accepting her.

This wasn't Jonathan. This was a total stranger, someone she didn't know, couldn't possibly trust…

Lauren's arms shot out and she grabbed his lean, muscular bare back in both hands, dug in her fingers and held.

Josh was very conscious of her bare body pressed against his, the gentle pressure of her breasts, the nipples sliding against his chest as she hitched with those careful, silent sobs, but he wasn't a total cad. Well, not completely.

He tipped up her chin with one finger and settled his lips over hers. Warmth, wet and friction.

She stopped in mid-sob, made a surprised noise, did that quick little panic jerk, then literally melted into it, her arms sliding down to his waist, her body settling against his, her side pressed against his tightening groin.

He couldn't say what made him do it. He didn't know her, she was upset, she should react by screaming and tossing him out of the tree. Marcus said he was losing his ability to live in civilized society, that he was just starting to react in whatever manner his animal instincts dictated.

Maybe he was right. Something about her said the kiss would be welcome, that it was essential he communicate how much he wanted her, right from the beginning. If they were on the level ground, he might have displayed it in an altogether more reverent fashion. A gentle kiss laid on the knuckles of her bare toes. He would brush his hair against her calf, an intentional caress as he raised his head for a brief look into her blue eyes, showing her his desire to please, and protect, and cherish.

It was a strange thought, the type of thought he had never had before, but one that felt right as he thought of her again, sitting proudly in the tree gazing down at him, like a tribal goddess. His hands slid up to smooth shoulders and into her hair. He discovered spun silk, delicate ears, and a neck so fragile he could snap it with one hand. Good God, he wanted her, here and now, forever, and he didn't even know her name.

Lauren's first thought was that he was the best kisser, gay or straight; she'd ever had the pleasure to experience. Her second thought was a revelation that uncoiled in her stomach and sent tendrils out to tug at her vitals. Just as homosexuals often knew another homosexual just from picking up vibes, so a Dominant could pick up the scent of a submissive. She felt it in Josh, but there was an oddness to it, almost as if it had been brought into consciousness and then buried again. He had powerful hands, but they were hesitant. Not hesitant as in awkward, but as if he paused at the door, waiting for the invitation because he couldn't enter without it. That was normal for a sub, but there was a wounded quality to it.

Normally, that would send Lauren in full retreat. D/s, consensual as it was, involved a far more deeply emotional level of sexual interplay than most people engaged in, even those who had been partners for many years. Getting into it with someone excessively damaged could be dangerous.

Sweet baby, what happened to you, she wondered.

"Is this a private party, or can anyone join?"

Lauren jerked back, and Josh kept her from overbalancing with a sure grip on her shoulders. "Marcus," he explained to her.

Lauren looked down at the man standing negligently at the base of the trunk, his face reflecting amusement. Her jaw dropped.

Her high school art teacher had told her class that Michelangelo's David was considered one of the most perfect depictions of the male form. Her high school art teacher had never seen Marcus.

Marcus was six foot even, his body layered in smooth muscle as if it had in fact been sculpted by an artist's fine touch. He displayed himself well in the same outfit as Josh, just a pair of jeans. She assumed they had both spent a sweaty day working on one of the houses. His dark hair was fine and flowing as her own, falling carelessly over a high forehead and to his shoulders. His sensual lips, curved in that mysterious smile, made her imagine all the places they might have been, and his green eyes were full of secret thoughts.

He was more than riveting, he was familiar. She was in the middle of the Caribbean for the first time in her life. No one should look familiar.

"Could you use a hand? In the getting down department, that is?"

"Yeah. Can you see if Lisette has some rope in her workroom?"

"White knight, here to serve. Be right back."

Josh nodded and looked down into Lauren's face. "Think you can climb down a rope if I get you started?"

Lauren was trying to keep up with all the shifts and nodded dumbly to this latest suggestion. Josh touched her chin with a light fingertip, a trace of a shy smile flirting about his lips. "Er... he's the one that wouldn't get anything out of looking at your body."

Lauren swallowed. "Lisette also told me... you weren't house-trained."

He gave her a knowing look, but said only, "She had one out of two things right."

Marcus emerged from Lisette's basement workroom and tossed up the end of a generous coil of rope. Josh tied it to the branch and then set his hands at Lauren's waist, his palms hot on her skin. The knot of her towel had tightened during her climb, so now the terry cloth rode low on her hips. His long fingers lay inside the circle of it, grazing her hip bones. She was sure he meant his touch to be a steadying thing, to help her take a firm grasp of the rope without having to worry about her balance. Unfortunately the effect of that warm, intimate touch had the exact opposite result.

Jonathan's face flashed through her head, along with the memory of him sitting on the top stair to their second floor, dressed for work. It had been shortly before their breakup. She knelt between his knees, desperate for just a simple hug, the desire to be held. He had put his lips against her ear. "You are so fucked up, Lauren."

He had said it soothingly, reinforcing what she had come to believe about herself. Rather than feeling insulted, she had felt vindicated. Like having a doctor diagnose her illness, she felt an overwhelming sense of gratitude at having it acknowledged.

Lauren's skin crawled with the memory and her chin tightened. She knew how to climb down a damn rope. She was one of three women at the gym that could do it.

She seized the rope and swung herself carefully into a descent position, blocking out for a moment that she was giving the man below, gay or not, a great view of her ass, and the one above quite a display of tits. Well, happiness and joy to them both.

"Focus," her personal trainer at the gym had told her. "That's the key to getting to the top, and back down again. Never think that getting down is easier. That's when most accidents happen in climbing, because it's harder to control your descent. Psychologically your mind thinks it's made it."

Her current surroundings and situation were nothing like the gym, so perhaps it was understandable that the reminder of that lecture came *after* she lost her grip on the rope.

Lauren had time for a short shriek before she was falling, flailing through the air and then landing against another warm body. Marcus was knocked off balance by the weight of her hurtling body hitting him. They thudded to the ground in a twisted tangle of limbs and muttered curses and rolled several yards down the steep incline before he managed to catch onto a protruding root and bring them to a halt.

Lauren attempted to extricate her limbs from Marcus enough to turn and find out if he was all right. She found he was trying to do the same, but they managed it. Josh was coming down quickly, no hesitation, she noted sourly. She comforted herself with appreciation for the ripple of tense power across the shoulders and down his back, the way the jeans rode lower with his arms above his head and stomach muscles contracted tight. That's the way they'd be if his arms were tied at the wrists to a suspension bar, pulled just high enough to keep him on the balls of his feet, so his buttock muscles would be firm and clenched.

Whoa, where had that thought come from? A silly grin twisted her lips. It was a tasty image, though. She shifted her focus to the one who had broken her fall. Marcus had pushed himself up on his elbows, and his lip was cut where her elbow had landed. "Are you all right?" she reached out to it, at the same time he offered a solicitous hand to that same offending elbow and said, "Are you okay?"

He managed a crooked grin. "We must be, if we're both more concerned about each other."

"No," she said, smiling back. "You're male, and so you can't admit you're in terrible pain, and I'm female and so naturally would always ask about the well-being of others before my own."

"Another woman with an overabundance of therapy," he observed, turning his hand into a position to offer a courteous handshake, despite her current lack of clothing. "I'm Marcus."

"Lauren," she shook his hand and then cocked a brow at Josh. "And I think we met in the tree."

"Which explains why you flung yourself out of it," Marcus noted dryly. "Perfectly understandable."

Josh shot him a deprecating look, then turned his attention back to Lauren. She noted with some amusement his determination to keep his gaze fixed on her face. "Are you sure you're all right?"

"I think so." Lauren found her knees a bit unsteady as she rolled to them. She put her hand to the forest floor to push herself up. A pair of male hands supported her at either elbow, and she gazed down at her half-naked torso, stained with dirt and leaves.

"Well, this has been an adventurous day," she murmured to no one in particular, though she thought she heard Marcus chuckle. She was going to adjust that towel, as soon as she could discreetly turn away from the two men.

She put her weight down on her right foot and gasped, grabbing at Josh's arm to keep her balance. Sprain. Probably not a bad one, but just one more delightful thing to add to the day's charm.

Marcus squatted and ran his hand along the back of her calf, down to the injured member. "Already swelling," he confirmed.

She had been sucked into some parallel dimension, where every tawdry cliché from a cheap romance novel was going to be played out. If everything went true to form, one of the men, probably the one she found most irritating yet mysteriously irresistible, would swing her easily up into his arms.

"Okay, then," Josh nodded, hooked her arms around his neck, bent and scooped her up. "We'll take you back upstairs and get that wrapped." He lifted a brow at her snort of laughter. "What?"

"Nothing," Lauren shook her head. "Nothing at all."

Chapter 4

At least this parallel dimension had its perks. Being carried up a hill in a strong man's arms was decidedly pleasant, though unsettling, since her right bare breast was pressed into his unshirted chest, and she felt every shift of his fingers along her spine and thigh.

"You could have at least let me adjust my towel," she said.

He glanced down at her, and with her arm occupied in holding on, there was nothing she could do but endure the heated perusal.

"Why would I want to do that?" he grinned.

Her eyes narrowed.

"He's always been this way, Lauren," Marcus commented. "God knows I've tried to beat it out of him."

Josh snorted. "Like a little prissy fairy like you could beat up anyone."

"If you're going to act like a homophobic Neanderthal," Marcus remarked, moving ahead to open the side door of Lisette's house, "I'm not going to play with you anymore. Do you need some help?"

Josh's grip on Lauren tightened and Marcus clucked. "You see," he informed Lauren. "He doesn't share."

Josh's face suffused with color. He looked as if he might defend his actions with some excuse, but in the end he said nothing. He shouldered by Marcus, jabbing him in the chest with his elbow.

"Ow," his friend said mildly, and shut the door after them.

Outside, where her options were limited, being half naked had been embarrassing but not fatal, just part of the whole ludicrous situation. Carried up the stairs and into Lisette's living room, furnished with every comfort of the civilized world, Lauren felt a keen urge to have the floor open and suck her in. It was so much easier when she was in control, with all the right trappings in place. Even though she knew they were just trappings, and the real control came from within.

"Put me down, we're in the house," she said, struggling a bit to underscore the order.

"I don't think it's going to do you much good to stand on your feet," Josh observed. "Where do you want me to put you down?"

"Over there," she snapped, pointing at a comfortable chair. Her robe lay on the ottoman, next to the cursed sliding glass door that had started the whole incident.

Josh nodded. "Marcus, go see if Lisette has an ice pack and some bandages."

"I don't need—" Lauren closed her eyes and fought the desire to scream as he sat her gently in the cushioned embrace of the chair. They had helped her. There was no reason to take them off at the neck because she felt helpless.

"Lauren," Josh's fingers touched her jaw and she opened her eyes. That lean, half-bare body curved over hers. His eyes were on her face, not on her naked breasts or the low riding towel.

"Shit happens," he said quietly. "We're not teenagers here. We all know what we look like under our clothes. You were in trouble, we're neighbors, we helped. There's no 911, nothing but the three of us to take care of one another. If you're going to look at this in any way, think of it as a good story to tell Lisette later. Don't beat yourself up over it."

"Easy for you to say," Lauren managed, trying not to look away, a cowardly way to deal with the overpowering sense of invasion his sincerity caused. "You weren't the idiot that —"

"You're not an idiot." Lauren jerked at the hand that came down and clamped on hers. Josh squeezed her fingers. "You didn't know the door would lock behind you, you didn't know if someone would be coming to give you a hand, so you took the initiative and tried to help yourself out. That took guts. Okay?" His tone softened on the last word, and he released her fingers to touch her face again, one light brush, tentative.

Lauren studied him, swallowing at the sheer…energy she saw behind those marvelous gray eyes. She had read a book, or maybe it was a sci-fi movie she had seen, where an entire galaxy was enclosed in a pendant. What she saw in his gaze reminded her of that. His proximity, his words and those eyes were all dragging her under. She struggled to stay above water. "You're being too nice about all this," she said.

"You're right about that," he said, surprising her. "If you'd stop being so pitiful, I could drop the whole chivalry thing and stare at your tits."

Lauren choked on a laugh. A smile eased across his face, stopping her breath. He rose, moving out of her personal space, physically at least. "I'll see what we can make for dinner," he said.

"Dinner?" she squeaked at his back as she snatched the robe and worked her way into it. "I don't need… I don't recall inviting you to dinner," she wiggled the towel out from beneath the robe and belted the latter just as Marcus returned.

"But you were going to, because we rescued you," Marcus pointed out. "Besides which, Josh is a terrific cook. Here," he knelt before her with a first aid kit and a brush. He opened the kit and unrolled a bandage. "First I'm going to rub this with a wet cloth, and get a bit of the forest off…"

* * * * *

Lauren found herself at the mercy of a miracle, two nurturing men. Marcus cleaned and wrapped her ankle and then applied warm and cold compresses to it, exercising consideration to both her physical and mental discomfort. He dropped the arrogant wit in favor of comfortable questions about her visit to the island. Her history with Lisette, how she had gotten here, and then how she had learned to sail so well. Pleasant small talk.

Josh cooked and threw a comment or question into the conversation now and then. Mainly he listened, with the same intent focus with which he chopped, sautéed and transformed grocery items she would have nuked or eaten raw into a culinary delight. The aromas drifted into the living area with the dim glow of the kitchen track lighting, rousing her hunger and relaxing her body, as the cloak of night took over outside the sliding glass door.

"Now," Marcus picked up the brush when he was satisfied with the skin temperature and level of swelling on her ankle. "Let's get you tidied up for supper."

Before she could utter more than a sound of surprise, he was freeing her hair from its banana clip and pins and spreading it out behind her to take the brush through it and unsnarl the tangles.

"No protests, my dear." His voice dropped an octave. "If I recall, you enjoy being served."

Lauren's gaze jerked up to him. The sensual mouth and soft fall of hair was the type of face a woman did not forget. Even as she had the thought, it was there, the vague familiarity sharpening onto a distinct memory.

"I remember you. You were... sitting with another man. A younger man." Her eyes danced at Marcus's quick, wicked grin.

"Close your eyes, dear," he suggested. "And just lay back and enjoy."

*****

It had been during a pediatrics seminar on asthma and allergies in New York City. She had slipped away after the official dinner and visited a club recommended by Maria.

The place had been called *May I Have This Dance?*. IT had a hundred dollar cover charge to step into grace and elegance with a kink flavor.

Men dressed in black tie. The women wore formal wear heavy on corsets and long flowing skirts reminiscent of the Victorian era, and four inch stiletto heeled boots that were not. Diamond chandeliers sparkled, dimmed so they threw moving circles of light onto the ballroom dance floor but allowed the shadows to keep their secrets. Near the orchestra, bubbles drifted out onto the floor like schools of fish and dispersed among the diners like fairies alighting on flowers, touching a shoulder, a lock of hair, kissing a face before vanishing into moisture.

There was gallery seating, for those who preferred to watch the floor and sip a cocktail. Lauren had chosen that option. The mid-thigh sheath of black fabric shot with silver sparkles was somewhat inappropriate, in her estimation, for such a fantastical landscape. She wore seamed thigh highs beneath the dress that revealed a hint of their lace tops when she crossed her legs, and silver high heels fastened to her ankles with a swag of slender silver chains. It was fetish wear only to those who recognized it as such, in case she met one of her colleagues in the lobby of the hotel, on her way in or out. She hadn't even meant to go out, intending to skip Maria's suggestion. But something about a hotel room on a business trip, its odd combination of loneliness and temptation to indiscretion, had driven her to explore the boundaries of her world in a new place.

Marcus, though of course she had not known his name then, had come in from the bar. He had caught her eye, as he would any woman's, and she watched as he opened the door for the young man with him, guiding him through with a solicitous hand to his elbow. Marcus was wearing a tux with a swallow-tailed coat and white silk bowtie, his dark hair falling back onto his shoulders in perfect ebony waves.

She watched how he spoke to the waiter, while the young man looked about him uncertainly. She suspected it was his first time in such a place. He also had that anxious, anticipatory air of someone awaiting a Master's bidding, not sure what that bidding would be, and aroused by the very thought of what it could be. It was in Marcus, too, the studied, casual way he spoke to the waiter while keeping a proprietary hand on his companion's back. Behind the casual expression was something more, a still fascination, another form of anticipation. How would his companion react to what he would ask of him?

The waiter led them to the table directly beneath Lauren. Marcus pulled out the chair for his companion, seated him, then sat to his left, his arm laying along the young man's chair back, his fingers playing absently with the boy's nape. His companion was looking about, drinking it all in, his smiles quick and easy, and Marcus chuckled often during their murmured conversation.

They fascinated her, and at first she was not sure why, did not question why her gaze could not leave them. Marcus ordered for them both, and the waiter brought them drinks.

The young man picked up his napkin, but Marcus's hand closed over his wrist. "Leave it, Thomas," he said.

His words reached Lauren, a murmur rising above the undercurrent of noise around them. Marcus laid the boy's wrist on the table and his own hand dropped, a palmed caress of the boy's inner thigh that suffused his face with color. "I want to be able to see what I do to you."

Thomas nodded, settling his hand around the wine, but it trembled slightly. Yes, Lauren decided. They had played at home a good deal, enough that they knew one another's signals, but this was likely Thomas's first debut in public as a sub. It was enough to rivet any Dom's attention, watching a

Master acclimate a sub to serving his pleasure before the eyes of strangers, though of course in a place like this, "stranger" was a relative term.

It was not just her thighs that tightened at the interchange, but something in her throat, her heart. That dual sense of belonging, in the way of being equally possessor and possessed, the intimacy of it. She saw it in their tender play with one another and it made her miss Jonathan keenly, or rather, what she had wanted to have with Jonathan, and never had.

"I've a gift for you," his words drifted up, penetrating her pain, and Lauren gazed down upon them again.

"Your company is gift enough," Thomas said, touching his glass to Marcus's.

Marcus chuckled. "And here I've no hip waders for such flattery." At the other's cheeky grin, he fished something out of his jacket and laid it on the table.

Lauren leaned forward. It was an elegant gold chain, something a well-dressed man might wear, its simplicity and gleam speaking of its quality, but it appeared long for a man's neck.

Marcus leaned forward, and his voice dropped, husky. "It goes around your waist, my love, and you will feel its movement with every twitch of that delectable ass of yours. It will ride on your hip bones, reminding you of how my hands feel there, digging into your flesh when I'm driving into you, whispering your name, telling you to come for me." He lifted it, held it at eye level. "It symbolizes your willingness to be bound to me, obedient to me, for it is not my will alone that holds you, but yours."

The young man grasped Marcus's hand, the gold between their palms.

"Tell me you understand," Marcus murmured, his eyes on Thomas's, "And tell me in the way you have been taught."

"I understand, Master."

"And do you willingly belong to me?"

"With all my heart," the man's voice was ragged with emotion.

"Good, then," Marcus leaned back. "You will stand, remove your coat, tie and shirt, and unfasten your pants so I may place my collar upon you."

Thomas grew pale, but Lauren suspected she knew where the blood had gone by Marcus's appreciative chuckle. He eased forward again. Without any self-consciousness, he fondled his sub's groin, stroking the tightly packaged treasure there. "Keep your legs open for me," he said, so soft, but the steel of it thrummed through Lauren's own thighs. Her hand was tight on the rail, perspiration making her grasp slick.

Such behavior was expected in a D/s Club, but unsettling for a novice. The boy was not used to this intense level of play, she could tell, and he was mesmerized and terrified by it, ready for it before he knew he was ready for it. Embracing it.

"Are you mine, or not?" Marcus said, his voice an octave more stern. "Or do I need to whip you, to remind you who your Master is, and how quickly you should move to obey him?"

Thomas pushed back his chair, muffling a groan as Marcus's skillful fingers gave him a hard stroke. He stood.

"Keep your eyes on me, pet," Marcus settled back with his wine, "and it will not be so difficult. Or, perhaps you should watch the lovely Mistress in the balcony, who is being pleasured by the very sight of you."

Thomas's gaze shifted up and met Lauren's. She let an appreciative smile toy on her lips, keeping her eyes steady and expectant upon him, though it startled her to know Marcus had known she was watching. Marcus lifted his glass to her and she inclined her head, but they both instantly turned their attention back to Thomas.

He bit his lip, shrugged out of the coat.

"Slowly," Marcus barked, attracting the attention of two nearby tables. "You wish to please me, do you not? You have a beautiful body. Let them all enjoy watching it, but know it belongs only to me."

A subtle message of where the line was drawn, Lauren noted with approval. Thomas let the coat fall to the chair and undid the tie, careful this time not to rush, his eyes back on Marcus.

"It took me forever to tie this damn thing," he joked awkwardly.

"I will help you put it back on, dear heart. Or perhaps I'll run it beneath your chair and tie your wrists so you are helpless to me during your meal, and I will feed you, and stroke your cock at my leisure. Would you like that?"

Thomas stopped, his fingers hovering at the collar of his shirt, and met his Master's eyes. That silent moment, determining what he could bear and what he wanted. What he wanted was becoming rather plain, despite the generous cut of the elegant trousers.

"I thought as much," Marcus said, his gaze following Lauren's and discomfiting Thomas further. "Perhaps that is what I should do. But for now, the shirt, please."

Thomas darted a glance about, saw he definitely had the attention of the nearby tables. His fingers fumbled the first two buttons, but then he took a deep breath, met Marcus's gaze and held it, letting it encompass and steady him.

It was always absorbing to Lauren, the way a man undressed; particularly when he was wearing formal wear. The way the crisp white shirt pulled over broad shoulders, how the starched button side curved like water along the contours of firm pectorals. The surprising delicacy of the wrist bones contrasting, in his case, with broad palms and long, capable fingers. Total male, total art. The dip of the head, the unconscious tense hold of the jaw as he worked the buttons free, the exposed nape. She wished she was standing close enough to inhale him, the soaps or colognes he used. Gay men knew how to enhance their own male scent so well, garnishing it with musks that underscored their masculinity, the blatant sexuality of it. Regardless of sexual preference, men were inherently primitive beings, and Lauren enjoyed them all the more for it. And watching a beautiful male such as this was like watching a work of art be formed under a Master's hand. It was an accurate description of what she was watching.

He shrugged out of the shirt, so nervous he forgot about the cuffs. When he realized he was stuck, his arms trapped at his sides in the sleeves, he made to slide the shirt back onto his shoulders to remedy the situation.

"No," Marcus stopped him. "I'll do the rest."

He reached forward, slid the belt tongue from its loop and through the buckle. His elegant wrists brushed the top of Thomas's erection beneath the pants, and Thomas sucked in a breath. A smile played on Marcus's lips, acknowledging Thomas's torture, his internal war between embarrassment and desire. He worked the belt free of the tooth and then unhooked the trousers, lowering the zipper no more than an inch or two, just so the fine summer wool would drop lower on the young man's slim hips. He appeared to be wearing black briefs, perhaps thong or Brazilian cut, and his abdomen was well defined.

"Put your hands at your sides," Marcus instructed, noticing how Thomas had his elbows bent, his hands reflexively clenched up near his waist. Marcus's gaze flicked over the neighboring tables, and up to Lauren.

"Is he not beautiful?"

There was a heated murmur of assent, and the back of Thomas's neck, exposed by his closely cropped hair, flushed even redder under gazes of appreciative desire.

Marcus nodded, and sat back to take a sip from his wine glass. He studied his companion, allowing Lauren and the other diners a leisurely perusal. The waiter came back, refilled

Marcus's glass, not looking at Thomas, though he stood between the two men for a moment. Thomas waited, suffering and aroused, while Marcus took another drink, sat the glass back down, touched a napkin to his lips. Then he lifted the gold chain from the table and leaned forward.

He ran it around Thomas's lean bare waist, adjusting the length so it indeed rode low on Thomas's hip bones, and left a fine double strand about two inches long hanging below the fastening, which appeared to be a flat engraved disk.

Thomas's head bent, nuzzling Marcus's fall of hair, his fingers clenching with the obvious desire to touch."There, now," Marcus slid the chain around, adjusting it so the dangling tips lay in that indentation where the spine ended and the vulnerable separation of buttocks began. "Once fastened as I have fastened it, it can only be unlocked by a key," he held it up for Thomas's inspection before placing it in his pocket. "But it is not unbreakable." Marcus's eyes were steady. "Should you ever desire to cast away your bindings, then you need only break the chain and leave it where I can find it. You understand? And there will be nothing messy between us. I will accept it as your farewell, and wish you nothing but joy and happiness. The engraving on the lock is simple," he palmed the disk, his fingers caressing Thomas's heated skin, and held the gold oval up for his inspection. "Mine."

Things had become very still at the surrounding tables during Marcus's speech. It was the point in the game they all knew, shared and sought. It was that moment when, even if there were a hundred others in the room, it was just the two of them. Thomas suddenly leaned forward, pressed his lips to Marcus's. It was a touch of lips only, as his arms were still bound by his shirt. Lauren saw the curve of spine, the slope of his buttocks in the loose ride of the pants. Thomas lifted his head, adoration shining from them. "Yes, Master."

"Well, then." Marcus cleared his throat after a moment. He stood up and adjusted the shirt back on Thomas's shoulders, buttoning it down the lean chest, his fingers caressing, his face only an inch from his lover's. He was not touching him in any overtly sexual way, but the act of redressing him, not allowing him to tend himself, was expressive in its eroticism. Lauren felt damp all over, in and out. His hips brushed Thomas's aroused crotch with casual indifference, but not inattention.

Marcus refastened the trousers, belted them, and then began to work on the tie. Thomas raised his now free hand, closed it gently over Marcus's wrist.

"You promised to tie my hands and feed me, Master," he reminded him. "And I desire nothing more than to be yours in all ways." His eyes, his body, the light but insistent touch, all communicated his aching need to please his lover. An ache Jonathan had never had for her.

Lauren sat back, her heart breaking, and spilled her tears into her wine.

Chapter 5

ಶಿ

"Did he ever break the chain?" she asked softly.

The answer was a long moment in coming.

"When it was time," Marcus said.

She reached up, touched his hand against her hair. She did not know him well, but she knew the flood of pain that could exist behind such casual words. When love was real, not puppy love, not lust, not a crush, it became an internal organ that grew behind the heart and buried its roots there. When it was torn out, even the act of taking one's life to end the pain required too much awareness. Numbness was the only way to survive it, and it took months, maybe even years to grow the courage to allow the anesthesia to wear off and see if the pain was still excruciating.

Her hand slipped away, and she plucked at her robe. Though she had sensed Marcus had a Dominant sexual personality, and he knew the same of her, if not by sense then by personal knowledge, was he picking up the same warning signals from her that she had detected in Josh? Careful folks, you may be getting into a damaged vehicle here. Don't press the "go" pedal faster than this one's guardian angel can fly and, by the way, her wings may be clipped. Or she may be at her therapy session and off the clock.

She was losing her grip; she tightened her fingers on the chair arm to get it back. In her soft silk robe, with a glass of wine at her elbow, and Marcus turning her hair into the same silk stuff as her robe, she could relax. She *would* relax.

"Are you a hairdresser?" she asked.

Josh chuckled. Marcus snorted behind her. "I have thought about training to be one. Something to fall back on.

You know if my career as a New York art dealer earning over six figures a year in commissions ever falls through. There's always room for one more gay hairdresser, after all. I don't think you even have to have formal training - you can just show up in a beauty parlor and say, 'I'm gay!'" he ratcheted his voice up to make it effeminate. "They'll hire you instantly. Like being black and seven feet tall. Automatic NBA material."

Lauren tilted her head back. "I'm sorry. I offended you."

"You're not entirely sorry. You were asserting territory, darling, and I respect that." Marcus curled his hand in her hair so she was caught and held, looking up at him. "I didn't mean to pry," he said, more gently. "I apologize for being intrusive."

She nodded, a slight movement of her head, and he released her, but she continued to look up at him an extra moment, which was an apology in itself he acknowledged with a similar small movement of his head. He considered the brush. "I suppose you did have some context for asking the question. I have a sardonic wit I use liberally."

"Excessively," Josh put in.

"Only on Neanderthals with no sense of humor at all," Marcus rejoined. "Now, hold still another moment. Josh is ready to feed you and I haven't finished making you beautiful."

"She was already that," Josh pointed out.

Lauren smiled in his direction and was amused when he busied himself with the food again. Marcus leaned down to her ear.

"He is quite something, isn't he, our boy?"

He straightened and went back to general topics as he began to plait her hair into a loose braid on her shoulders. Lauren let his voice fade to pleasant background music that stirred the senses, like soft jazz, and watched Josh finishing the plates. There was something about watching a man involved in a task with his hands that could absorb a woman's attention. Perhaps it was the female subconscious connection to the earth, to creation and fertility. Those long fingers, taking things of the earth, carrots and snow peas, potatoes and onions, and transforming them with care into sustenance. His eyes, intent on his task as he sliced the potatoes into smaller pieces. A quick, careless brush of his arm against his forehead where a lock of hair caused an itch. The movement drew her eye to the ripple of muscle over his ribs, the soft hair beneath his arm. He shifted his hips, transferring his weight to his other foot, which was bare. He had removed his sneakers when they came in and tossed them carelessly by the door, like they were all home.

The two men seemed not the least bit uncomfortable to be cooking in Lisette's house, caring for her friend and entertaining one another with casual conversation.

"What does a caretaker of the homes of five famous artists and writers do, Josh?" she asked at last, taking a sip of her wine.

He glanced up, the corner of his mouth tugging in a half smile. "Just about everything. Repairs, home maintenance, water plants. They want the house to look lived in when they come. I also do things like this sometimes. If Mrs. Von Haugwitz doesn't want to cook herself dinner because she's at a crucial point in her latest sculpture, she can give me a ring. I'll let myself in and cook up dinner. I've given massages to Mr. Grimes because his back bothers him when he works with the scroll saw too long. That type of thing."

"So you cook, you're a masseuse, a tree climber, a carpenter and an HVAC man."

"And many, many other things. He has so many talents, our Josh."

Josh shot Marcus an obvious warning look. The undercurrent of tension felt flammable, so Lauren held her questions. For now. She took another swallow of wine and pretended not to notice their by-play.

Josh was certain the woman had no idea how she looked sitting there, her fingers toying with her wineglass. The pale pink silk of the robe outlined every feature of her body, from the point of her right breast to the long line of her thigh. The neckline parted to show him the graceful curve of the left breast as she stroked that glass stem with her slender fingers.

He turned away and took a bracing swallow of his own wine. Needles of sensation prickled along his back as Marcus passed him, sliding casual fingers along his spine, a little too close to his waist.

Josh shot him a narrow look that Marcus returned with a guileless expression. He snagged one of Lisette's imports from the refrigerator.

"She's about to drift off over there," Marcus murmured, giving Lauren a nod. Josh glanced over, saw the woman was in fact nodding a bit, her head turned toward the sliding glass doors, her body framed by the view of dark silhouetted tree tops and the ocean beyond, glittering with a rising moon.

He didn't realize he was just staring at the picture she made, until Marcus chuckled.

"More candles would be appropriate, I think. And cards."

Josh snapped back. "Marcus—"

His friend was already headed toward the back bedrooms. Josh stifled a curse.

Lauren roused herself with a smile as Marcus passed behind her and patted her head. "When do we eat?" she wanted to know.

"Now." Josh brought in a tray and began to lay out the feast on the glass table.

"Do you live here all year?" she asked, rubbing her eyes and straightening in the chair.

"Yes. Here, stay there. I've got a tray to put over your lap so you can keep that foot elevated."

He put the plate of food on the tile tray and bent to set it over her lap. She raised her arms to keep them from getting in his way and drew his eye to her breasts again. Josh concentrated on arranging the tray and tried not to think how much he'd like to spread open the robe and watch her eat with the silk framing her bosom like the work of art it was. The combination of ice pale pink and lily skin reminded him of mother of pearl on the inside of a shell, and he expected she would be as silky to the touch.

Maybe she'd even let him feed her with his own hand. Some of the soy sauce might slide off the glistening carrot and splash onto one of those breasts, and he'd have to put his tongue there and lick it off…

She glanced down his body, and her soft lips curved. "I guess Lisette was definitely wrong," she murmured.

Her gaze rose, and Josh saw the sly humor there. It alleviated some of his embarrassment, as he was sure she intended it to do. She was a kind woman, he could see it in her eyes, but her kindness was not of interest to him right now.

Hunger uncoiled low in his belly, and he picked up a carrot, daring to lift it toward her mouth.

"Stop."

He froze in mid-motion, and her steady blue eyes held his. "Ask me."

The warmth in her eyes contrasted with the coolness in her voice. That feeling in his belly spread, kicking up the pulse of blood through his thighs, the ache in his testicles. The way her lips formed the words, with just a hint of teeth, made him want to put his mouth on her, anywhere she wanted.

"May I feed you this?"

She nodded. "Since you ask so nicely."

He was wrong. She could be cruel, too, and he found it just as arousing as her kindness. Perhaps more, though that thought made him vastly uncomfortable with himself.

He brought the carrot to her lips. They parted, and his eyes sparked to flame when her eyes fell half shut. He stroked the vegetable over her bottom lip, making it glisten with sauce. He laid the carrot on her tongue when she opened her mouth, and the pad of his finger slid along the small bumps of her taste buds, traced the enamel of her underbite, and then withdrew.

"How do you all feel about French vanilla scent?"

Josh turned to find Marcus at the kitchen counter, lining up a charming mismatch of pillar candles. He was lighting them, and four already cast soft light into the room.

Lauren straightened and turned, bringing her foot to the floor. The confidence she had possessed only a moment before now seemed to evaporate. "I'm sorry," she told Josh, surprising him. "I didn't mean—I'm not—trying to play with you."

"Of course you are," Marcus blew out the match. "That's what we do. Except Joshua. He's afraid of games. He's Joshua the Monk, ensorcelled by the fair—"

"Shut the fuck up, Marcus," Josh exploded. Lauren jumped. He pressed his lips together, shaking his head as if reproaching himself for the outburst, but he shot Marcus another dangerous look, regardless. Then he knelt before her with an apologetic expression, firmly pushed her back in the cushioned chair and replaced her foot on its pedestal of pillows on the ottoman.

"—Winona." Marcus finished calmly, taking a pull from his beer and bringing the candles in on a tray. He placed them around the room, dimming the overhead so the room was bathed in soft light. "Do you give good massages, Lauren?"

She raised a brow. "I—"

"Josh has a muscle that knots in his shoulder when he gets nervous. It's quite painful. Will you tell him to sit down and have you work it out for him?"

"I am not nervous, I'm pissed off," Josh seized his wine glass up, but Lauren saw him flinch as the movement jarred his shoulder. She shook her head. She was being silly. They were all being silly.

"Come here," she leaned forward, taking the wine glass and placing it on the coffee table. "Come. Sit." She took his long fingered, unsteady hand in hers and tugged. "Sit down on the ottoman next to my foot. I'll work it out and then we'll eat."

"You don't need to do that," he grumbled, but when she tugged harder, he sat, presenting her with his back.

Lauren felt over the line of his shoulder and found the knot without difficulty. She had taken a couple credits in alternative healing, and had enjoyed exploring the more tactile healing practices, such as massage. She began to work it with gentle pressure, imagining it loosening and easing out, and let the work of her fingers be guided by that image.

Marcus sat down on the carpet so he could stretch his legs out under the coffee table and prop his back against the sofa. He was shuffling a deck of cards, and, as Lauren watched, he spread them out on the glass-topped table in a circular fan around the candles grouped in the center, which were wafting light vanilla fragrance through the room. Celtic harpstrings played their magic on the CD player, the notes combining with the effect of the candles to create a magical atmosphere, capable through the ages of lowering a woman's defenses.

Josh's back had been tattooed as well, but at the moment her attention was drawn to the unmarked area, the skin brown and stretched smoothly over muscle and bone. He was lean, the sign of someone whose body had been sculpted by labor, not a gym. She could well imagine what it would be like to knead and stroke not just that shoulder, but the ridges of the spine, the curve of the lower back, and rest her palms on his waist.

His skin felt warm beneath her touch and she recalled the slight sweatiness of his palm. Nervous, Marcus had said. Did girls make Josh nervous? A smile curved her lips at the thought. He hadn't seemed nervous in the tree. Maybe he only got nervous when he wasn't holding the cards, so to speak.

Like Jonathan? The unexpected thought erased her smile. No, she decided. Not like Jonathan. In a way, though he had submitted to her, he had held the cards all along. She had wanted love, and he had used her belief in that to almost destroy her. It was only when she realized love was not what drove him, and, more importantly, that she could not change that, that she had been able to break free. Of him, at least. The memories he had inflicted upon her were like a Bible imprinted on her soul that she kept searching to find an interpretation that would make sense to her. Well, at the moment, she wasn't in church.

"Do you like cards, Lauren?" Marcus asked. She felt Josh stiffen beneath her touch, but did not break her rhythm, soothing his shoulders down again.

"You should say no," Josh warned.

She had her own demons to fight, far larger and more wicked than any mischief Marcus could devise. She gave Josh a reassuring squeeze and cocked a curious brow at Marcus.

He laced his fingers on the table top, and fixed his gaze on them both. There was no trace of mischief left now, just a meditative thoughtfulness. As the silence drew out, it seemed to draw Lauren in, surround her along with the haunting percussion music in the dreamlike candlelit atmosphere. She could hear the soft roar of the distant beach, filtering through the cracked sliding glass door.

Oh, yes, Marcus had set a stage. She recognized it, but she enjoyed a man who would expend some effort arranging a seduction scene. For there was no doubt about it, Marcus intended to seduce. But seduce them into what?

So often, with Jonathan, she had been uncomfortable, stressed by the constant struggle to figure him out. Here she was warm, enjoying the feel of a man beneath her fingertips,

Holding the Cards

the sense of mysterious anticipation emanating off of Marcus, and the magical quality of her surroundings, a secluded home on a private island, two beautiful men in attendance...

Marcus was waiting, and she realized her inviting expression was not enough. While he would press limits with what Josh desired, he wanted her permission to continue on his course, and he wanted it verbalized.

"I like cards," she said.

Marcus smiled then, an easy, open gesture. "I thought you might." He settled his hands on either side of the cards, and his gaze shifted to Josh, though he spoke to them both.

"What would it be like, do you think, to pretend we were...no, not pretend." He tapped a pensive finger on the table. "What if we let down our defenses, all those social walls we create to fence in acceptable behavior and fence out anything else, and found the children in ourselves again? That sense of wondrous, unselfconscious adventure, when games were fun and yet utterly serious, the fate of the universe hanging on our shoulders until Mother called us home to dinner."

He had her undivided attention. She knew he had Josh's as well, though Josh was keeping his attention on the window, his hostile eyes focused on glass instead of his friend. "That time when we openly embraced our need for someone to love us, care about us, believe that we were essentially good people, worthy of being loved," Marcus said. "The time of our lives where, if we were privileged enough, we were equally capable of spending a day as heroes or watching butterflies. Think how it would be if we could do it, in our very adult bodies, recapture that which we did not appreciate then. The savoring of quiet moments that first time you did anything, that intense joy and faith in life, in who you are and what you could be to others. Think what it could mean to everything else in your life. You can recreate that in a place like this."

Marcus leaned forward, eyed Lauren as if he were a god about to impart one of the deeper mysteries of the universe. "A game, as you well know, can be a serious thing with a serious intent."

Her brow furrowed, her mind considering the layers of meaning, but he wasn't done spinning out all the fabric to it.

"When you were young, nobody played the game if they didn't want to play. And when you played, you trusted your playmates because they were, after all, your comrades-in-arms, those who would help you save your universe. So," he shifted, leaning back against the sectional sofa and stretching out his well-defined arms on either side of him. His dark hair brushed his bare shoulders and his jewel green eyes met Lauren's. "Would you care to play High Card Wins?" Josh rose, moving away from Lauren's touch, and taking his wine glass with him. "I can't believe you're pulling this shit," he muttered, draining it in two angry gulps.

"Are you afraid of a game, Josh?" Marcus asked.

"Yes, goddamnit," Josh slammed the glass down and the fragile stem of the expensive crystal broke against the etched glass of Lisette's side table, spilling the last swallow of red liquid across its surface. "It's fucking games that... Hell," he pointed a finger at Lauren, "That's probably what brought her running here. If people played a few less fucking games, maybe it wouldn't be such a screwed-up world. Maybe people could just love each other and not frigging wonder if it was all some goddamned cruel trick. They wouldn't begin to believe that when they die, rather than an afterlife, it will be one single moment of getting the big cosmic joke, that nothing meant shit, ever, and then bam! You're fucking dust."

Lauren registered the tears in his eyes a stunned moment before he spun away from them both, the habitual male defense to keep uncontained emotions screened from view. Her attention snapped to Marcus.

The art dealer's expression was filled with pain. She recognized what it was, because a physician was trained to mask that type of pain.

He was trying to heal Josh, without any roadmap of how to do it. There rarely was one. A physician was given a certain amount of knowledge to get started in the right direction, but when it came down to it, there were too many factors that could contribute to an illness. Sometimes the physician just had to follow intuition, hoping to ask the right question, get the response that would reveal the cure. Though Marcus had flinched, as she had, at the violence of Josh's reaction, there was no shock in his pained gaze. He knew more than she did about the simmering cauldron of emotions trapped behind those stormy gray eyes.

She had come here to hide for awhile, yes, and to face her demons. She had been in a situation that was utterly mortifying. She had been too paralyzed to act, from fear of a rejection that was already there, hammering at her defenses every day. However, something about Josh's bowed head, pressed against the glass of the sliding glass door now, moved her heart beyond those worries. She knew she had the tools to get over her heartbreak. Perhaps Josh didn't. He might need the help of comrades-in-arms to save his universe.

She reached out, laidthe dinner napkin over the broken glass to soak up the wine, then shifted her hand left and drew a card. Marcus lifted a surprised glance to her.

"A six of diamonds," she held it up for Marcus's inspection. "Josh," she pulled another card from the deck, "has drawn a five of spades."

Marcus studied her face a moment, then leaned forward and drew off the other side. "A two of hearts. The lady wins."

"So what does that mean?" Lauren asked, feeling Josh turn toward her.

"The rules say you may ask anything of us, Lauren," Marcus's eyes met hers, steady, "and we will obey."

A Master knew another Master, and knew what words would cause the knees to go weak, and a rush of liquid arousal between the thighs. Lauren drew in a breath.

A part of her was tight like a clenched fist, remembering the past, and how those games had turned out. Another part of her was curious, hoping for something. Hoping that even a modicum of what Marcus said might be true, that maybe strangers could succeed in achieving intimacy, in the right environment, where lovers had failed.

"Josh?"

He gave her a wary look, but she detected a strange element of hope. She wondered if her expression was an exact mirror of those two emotions. "I'm willing to play if you are. There's just us here, no 911," she reminded him, managing a shy smile. "I don't mind believing I'm a kid again if you don't."

"Who said he ever stopped being one?" Marcus observed. "I've been waiting for him to grow up for years."

Josh curled his lip at him like an annoyed dog, then returned his gaze to Lauren.

"If Josh wants to play," she looked at him, tense profile silhouetted against the glass, "I'd like…"

What would she like? The hundreds of possibilities overwhelmed her for a moment. She had shut off that part of her since she had broken with Jonathan, but her mind had catalogued the ideas and longings her listless yet conscious wanderings through her favorite clubs had suggested. The idea that two men might be at her bidding, particularly one moody, dark and beautiful creature like Josh, brought those possibilities leaping out of the closet. But would he play? The choice was his. She could but ask him to join.

"I want to feed Josh dinner," she decided.

Chapter 6

Josh turned toward her fully, his face reflecting his surprise at the deceptively simple request. She blinked at him, and patted the ottoman. "Come here and sit. Pick up your plate and hand me the fork."

He cocked his head at her, considering. Marcus was a silent presence in her peripheral vision. Giving Josh time to think was no chore, and she made good use of the moment, sliding her gaze over the bare broad shoulders, the smooth chest, that tantalizing slope of hipbone exposed by the loose fit of the jeans at the waist. She let her gaze go lower, examining with frank interest the way the denim molded his groin and long thighs.

She consumed the visual feast through all her senses, so it was no surprise to feel her breasts tighten, the nipples rise against the silk fabric of the robe, poured like water over her curves from the blessings of gravity. She knew without raising her eyes that his gaze would be drawn to that physical reaction. Unless his personal demons were too strong, her wary prey should almost be hers.

By the time she got to his bare toes, they were moving toward her, and a moment later, he was sitting on the ottoman, lifting the plate and handing her the fork. This close, he brought back the smell of the woods, and his faint musky odor, the same dried sweat of a day's hard labor that she had smelled when he had carried her.

"So," Lauren speared a tiny corncob and lifted it, "I know Marcus is a New York art dealer with a secret dream to be a hairdresser," she smiled as that one raised his glass with a devious grin, his composure recovered. "But what did you do before you were caretaker here, Josh?"

"I helped Marcus," he lifted a shoulder, and she knew he was being evasive from the quick flick of his gaze away from hers. It was not yet time to push, too early in the game. She raised a brow regardless, letting him know he was not fooling her, but she changed the flow of the conversation. "Marcus, tell us the most wicked story you can think of from your childhood."

"Before puberty, or after?"

Lauren slanted a smile at him. "Before."

She brought the glistening pale yellow vegetable to Josh's lips. When he had his mouth half open, she murmured "Wait."

She traced it over his top lip, moistening the curve with a light sheen of soy sauce, as he had done to her. "Now," she said.

His eyes were on her face, measuring, and she inclined her head. "Open your mouth wider."

He did, sending a jolt of electric energy through her vitals. She placed the food on his tongue, already wet from saliva that she hoped was not entirely from a hunger for food. His lips closed on the fork, the soy sauce she had left there compressing between them. The lubricated tines withdrew with the same silken ease of a man withdrawing himself from a woman's aroused body. As she anticipated, his tongue automatically touched on his top lip after he swallowed, collecting the sauce. His eyes never left hers, and she wondered that she could have every considered gray a cool color. It could become molten steel, simmering with the fires of the forge, anticipating becoming an instrument to serve the needs of its master, or in this case, mistress.

He was not a docile sub, which delighted her. The heat in those eyes could compete with the re-entry atmosphere of the earth, and she felt it building in the furnace of his body. He would become dangerous if pushed, and the anticipation of it shivered through her.

* * * * *

"This game is like a circus," Maria had told her once, during one of their many infamous "Corner Table Conversations", as Lauren had dubbed them. That was when Maria had a break and the two of them found a corner table in the shadows. Sometimes it was a time for Maria to hold her hand while Lauren had yet another post-Jonathan meltdown, but usually it was a chance to exchange wisdom and watch others together. The waitress followed the interactions of the other club attendees with the diligent attention of a NASA researcher.

"Are we that ridiculous?" Lauren asked, too swamped at that point with bitterness to hear the undertone.

"You're thinking clowns, honey." Maria said, her kohl rimmed eyes crinkling, the moist, full lips curving up. "Think of all the sensual, dark undertones of a circus. The life of the people involved, set apart from the rest of the civilized world in a mysterious society of their own. Those who walk the tight rope and run the trapeze, who must trust their partners completely. The delicate interplay between the animals and those who go into the cage with them.

"Like you," she ran a sharp-nailed finger lightly down Lauren's face, tracing the tiny tab protecting the entrance to her ear. "You're a lion tamer. Jonathan belonged in the poodle ring."

Lauren snorted with laughter, and Maria's teeth showed, but it was a half smile, most of her mind focused on a more serious point. "He was eager to please, never messing up, working for treats, regardless of whose hand gave them."

Lauren's eyes darkened, but Maria kept on. "You were looking for the lion, the one who obeyed because he knew the reward for obedience was you. Not some treat from your hand, but you, everything, body, mind and soul. He knows he's bigger and stronger, but he'll concede your dominance and lower his eyes because you make him want to do it. Even so, he'll still occasionally test you, because that's the nature of the lion. That's what you were wanting, and that's the only thing that's going to work for you."

* * * * *

Maria hadn't needed to tell her that finding that man would involve a game of high stakes.

She took a bite herself, and her eyes fell shut as a savory marriage of onion, pepper, soy and a mysterious dash of other spices awoke her taste buds. "This is marvelous. How did you make something this good in a half hour?"

"Well, technically, you can reach orgasm in less than a minute, and think how wonderful that is," Marcus, pointed out.

Josh grinned, and Lauren conceded the point with a wave of the fork. "I'm getting very little food here," Josh nodded to the plate.

Lauren snorted and slid another forkful of sautéed vegetables into his mouth. "Marcus, we're waiting for your wicked tale."

"A wicked tale," Marcus mused, took a chunk of French bread from the board on the table, and smiled. "The word itself calls it to mind. When I was seven, I had a dog named Winslow."

"Winslow?" Josh turned his head and Lauren bumped the fork against his chin, splattering his left pectoral with brown sauce.

"Oops," she took her index and middle fingers and wiped them over the spot, gathering up the moisture. Her fingernails scraped his warm skin. She caught one of the drips alongside his nipple and traced the curve as she scooped up the liquid.

Holding the Cards

The crinkled skin around it became taut at her touch and she brought the fingers toward her lips.

Josh reached out and manacled her wrist, pulling her fingers away from her mouth and taking them to his, drawing them into the warm cavern and sucking off the brown liquid, tracing his tongue lightly over the delicate skin between the two fingers. The movement of his tongue was not like the flick of a flame, but a slow pressure that rubbed each taste bud against the crevices of her finger joints like moist sand trickling over bare skin.

Lauren managed not to swallow her own tongue, barely. She began to draw her hand away. Her heart bumped up into her throat when he did not respond to the pressure, holding her slim wrist captured in his grasp for the space of several irregular beats before his grip loosened. Lauren tapped her moistened finger against his bottom lip reprovingly. "It's my card, Josh. I'm feeding you."

"It rather looked like that's what you were doing," Marcus observed dryly. "Do you want me to continue, or can I just enjoy the floorshow?"

Josh chuckled and Lauren smiled at the way it took ten years off his serious face. "No," she tossed her hair back. "I want to hear the story about Winslow."

"Winslow was a wonderful dog who unfortunately had a penchant for chasing cars."

"That dog's name was not Winslow," Josh shifted his intense gaze off her, allowing Lauren to take a deep, steadying breath without his scrutiny. "No kid names their dog Winslow."

"All right, if you insist on mundane authenticity, it was Petey."

"Like the Little Rascals?"
"Of course," Marcus sighed. "I suppose I was as monotonous and tritely cliched as all children. Petey was the best I could do."

"Does he always play the world-weary urbanite?" Lauren asked.

Josh nodded. "Only in front of guests. Once he gets used to you, you'll see his real personality. Iowa farm boy."

"No way," Lauren laughed at Marcus's woeful nod. "Your secret's safe with me," she raised her hand in pledge, then fed Josh another mouthful, her attention shifting back to the movement of his jaw, the flex of cords and muscle along his throat as he swallowed. "How did Petey fit into the most wicked thing you did in childhood?"

"Well, loving though woefully misnomered Petey finally caught a car. My father assured me and my cousins that Petey would ascend to the place where dogs may cheerfully chase cars all day long without fear of harm. However, four days after Petey's demise, I came to my father in great distress. Petey had not gone to heaven."

Marcus put down the wine glass and turned the stem with elegant fingers, the glass and burgundy liquid reflecting the candlelight. "'Of course he has, son,' my father assures me with great confidence, giving me that healthy backslap heterosexual fathers offer to ensure their sons need chiropractic care for the remainder of their lives.

"'No, he hasn't,' I insist. 'Come see.' For I knew my father had to see proof of what I was saying to understand. I took him to Petey's grave and pointed down at it. 'See? We buried him with his tail sticking up out of the grave so we'd know when he went, and it's still there!'"

Lauren choked on the wine she had raised to her lips for another sip and caught the juice as it tried to escape down her chin. "Marcus, that's terrible," she giggled, unable to help herself. She scrabbled for a napkin to prevent the escaped wine from running down her throat and staining her robe.

"Allow me," Josh leaned forward. Lauren followed the direction of his eyes and felt the wine trickle down into the hollow formed by her collarbone. He paused briefly, his cheek almost brushing hers, and looked sidelong into her eyes. She gave an almost imperceptible jerk of her head, a nod of assent, and his head dipped, his dark hair brushing her jaw line.

His eyes promised revenge for her earlier torture. There was playful mischief in his expression, as well as serious, sensual intent. It was a combination she found as thrilling as her first Ferris wheel ride, which had happened on a crisp fall night filled with sparkling lights, the smell of popcorn and funnel cakes. She teetered on the edge of womanhood that night, made even more ripe and confusing by the knowing, secretive gazes of the male carnies who ran the rides.

His warm lips covered the area, that clever tongue creating a warm, spiraling friction against her heated skin. Lauren sucked in a breath, which brought the top of her breast into contact with his chin. Sensation prickled to the tip and a light shudder ran from breast to thigh, making her toes curl.

Most men did not know what an erogenous zone a woman's neck was. Whether he did or not, Josh was giving it special attention, rubbing his lips up the side of the main artery, and Lauren had to keep her hands clenched at her sides to keep from taking him to the floor and devouring him whole.

Marcus kept his eyes on hers throughout the moment, like a naturalist in a secluded glade, unobtrusive and yet very present, enjoying the experience of watching the interplay of God's creations.

However, when Josh straightened, Marcus's gaze dropped from her face and followed the ridge of the other man's spine.

"Lauren," Marcus said, "I think you were deciding your next wish was that we play Monopoly."

"What?" She blinked at him hazily, feeling somewhat like a person who has misread an invitation and shown up at a neighborhood barbecue in formal wear.

His gaze slid back to Josh's bare skin. "Well, the high card belongs to you, and you just strike me as an obsessive

Monopoly player. I also happen to know Lisette has one in her closet. She plays herself, you know. Actually, four of herselves. A game will stretch on for days, in between her writing sessions. She says when things get too intense, when reality intrudes and locks up her creative mind with fretting about deadlines or editors, or other such drivel, she goes and plays a few rounds."

"And just how long does the game say I hold the high card?"

"How long did you say you were going to be here?"

Lauren decided that Marcus was altogether the strangest person she had met in quite some time, and that she liked him intensely. "Josh, Marcus," she shifted her attention between them, "I command you to play Monopoly with me."

Chapter 7

Three hours later, they all had had second helpings of stir-fry, Josh had made cookies, and crumbs were scattered as liberally on the floor as hotels on the board. And most of them were Lauren's. The hotels, that is.

This, despite Marcus's blatant cheating. Josh was not a tremendous threat, having a penchant for landing on the Go To Jail corner mark, and possessing pathetically poor judgment when it came to selling and developing his properties. Lauren had not had so much fun in…well; she couldn't remember when life had stopped being fun. Her mind wanted her to start the clock with the break up with Jonathan, but she wasn't sure that was true.

"Well, I guess we don't have to ask what you do for a living," Marcus said darkly, as he landed on Boardwalk, parking his pewter iron next to her three glossy red hotels. "You're a corporate raider."

She chuckled. "Worse. A pediatrician." She extended her palm. "Fifteen hundred dollars."

"That was going to be my next guess, right after loan shark," Marcus said. "I'm done. You've cleaned me out."

She had knocked Josh out of the game ten rounds ago and now he lay on his back on the floor by the table, his bare feet curved against the arm of the loveseat. His denim-covered thigh rocked back and forth with restless energy as he laced his fingers behind his head and watched them.

She picked up her wine glass, her gaze following the appealing way the jeans pulled along the inseam from his movement, and felt his eyes watching her.

It was late, and she had drunk a bit too much wine, but it was the relaxed camaraderie that was so intoxicating. The playfulness of the past three hours had lowered her guard. Like a slumber party after midnight, things became far more easy and familiar, affection for one's companions increasing exponentially. Similar to the old adage - everyone looked good at closing time, because otherwise a cold, lonely bed waited.

She had settled for loneliness, after Jonathan. In order to get the intimacy she craved, she had to deal with the demands and shortcomings of the guest invited to join her. She wanted the fantasy of a stranger spooning around her in her sleep, cradling her protectively against his body. Somehow they would know nothing and yet everything about each other, having connected far beyond the level of conversational inanities, those pathetic, required attempts to get to know one another in less than two hours over drinks.

It was the "required" that had turned her away from the opportunities that had presented themselves. "Had to" was what you did as an obligation, the price of admission, and putting a price on the rare gift of intimacy… well, it was no longer a gift then, was it? Gifts were offered from love, affection, inspired by your lover, an offering at the altar of their presence in your life. She didn't inspire that in anyone anymore. Right now, she corrected herself fiercely, unwilling to fall into that dark abyss.

The worry was there, though, that she was too tired to play hide and seek for love anymore. Maybe that was why the natural order of things was to marry and have children in your early to mid-twenties. It was something about the approach of thirty. You just ran out of whatever juice it was to play the games to get into a meaningful relationship. Once you reached thirty, all you wanted was to wake up and find love and a lifetime commitment beside you. The hunter instinct had dulled, and you were ready to reap and sow. Only the field was fallow, nothing planted and growing.

But she didn't have to worry about that here, did she? She held the card. Anything she wanted. She knew firsthand that some things couldn't be had, the most precious things, just by ordering them. But something in Josh's gaze pulled the hunter instincts reluctantly out of her heart, and she thought maybe she could…just for tonight…

She had stolen glances at Josh while he was playing the board game, brief snapshots that kindled her inner heat. His mane of sun-streaked hair tied back on his shoulders. The oddly out-of-character tattoos layered over sleek muscle. A silver earring, a simple loop in his left lobe, also not quite him. Still shirtless, just in jeans. At one point, he had rubbed his eyes a bit, and then pulled a pair of wire-rimmed glasses from his pocket to help him focus on the board. The unconscious lack of vanity, the boyish charm when he gave her a quick smile, the serious cast the glasses lent his expression as he studied his next move, had been at once sexy and endearing. It had been all she could do not to draw him into her embrace, hold his head to her breast as tenderly as a mother and then ravish him with the ferocity of a she-lion.

"You said," she cleared her throat. "That we should play this game like children. The fate of the Universe in the balance, and absolute trust in our companions."

Marcus was putting away the board, but he lifted his attention at her quiet words. He nodded.

Lauren looked back at Josh. His knee had stilled and he could have been a stag in the forest, watching her through foliage so thickly interlaced she could not see the shape of him, only the force of his presence by his liquid eyes, gleaming through the flickering shadows of the candlelight.

"I want you both to stay here tonight," she said, and she made herself look at Josh as she said it, for she sensed it was important for him, more than Marcus, to see her face. He was more afraid of the intentions of this game. "I want you to sleep with me, in my bed." Now she did shift her gaze to Marcus, to ensure he understood her. "And I mean sleep. I don't want to be alone. Will you do that?"

Translation: Do you understand me? Can I trust you? Will you play the game we all hope isn't a game? Can I believe, at least for tonight, that somewhere out there are people willing to comfort and nurture, love us and build us up instead of drain us, who won't rip our hearts from our chests and laugh at us?

It was as clear in those four words as if she had shouted it, if they had the proper sensitivity to hear it.

"A pleasure," Marcus agreed lightly. "Lisette has a king-sized mattress just down the hall. Josh has a bed of nails over two miles away, provided we don't fall off these excuses for trails into a ravine to die a slow, lingering death. A slumber party is the perfect end to a perfect night."

She chuckled, and eased her grip on the stem of her glass. Josh's quiet, steady gaze was an unsettling but satisfying answer on its own.

"Er, since you probably don't have any pajamas in our size," Marcus cocked a brow, "Does the lady have preference on sleepwear for her life-sized teddy bears? Or will just fur do, for those of us who have it?"

"Oh," Lauren considered the problem and lifted a shoulder. "Whatever you're most comfortable in is fine with me."

The double entendre was intended, if a bit juvenile, and the flash of humor in Marcus's eyes was as instant as the flame in Josh's.

Lauren felt shy suddenly, and tried to shake off the feeling. She levered herself up, removing her foot from its pedestal of pillows to test it on the floor. It was already feeling better and she suspected she would be able to walk competently, albeit cautiously, by the following morning. "Well, then, I'm going to hobble back to the bathroom, take a bath and get ready for bed. Just leave the kitchen, I'll take care of it tomorrow."

"No, don't worry about it, I'll do it, since I didn't have to cook," Marcus waved a hand at her. "Josh'll make sure you get to the bedroom safely."

"Oh, you don't need to —"

"I'm sure, but you'll agree it would be good for you to have an arm to grab if you lose your balance," he advised, taking her glass from her hand and giving her a wink. "Darling, if you have two men at your beck and call, do I really have to tell you to take advantage of them?"

"Well, I'm sure the two of you had more important things to do with your day than to rescue a crazy naked woman from a tree."

The two of them exchanged a look. "I can't think of a thing more important than that," Josh grinned. He rose and came to her side, scooping her up in his capable arms. "I like carrying you," he confessed before she could protest. "I haven't..." he stopped, and regret passed across his face, but he finished the thought. "I haven't had the chance to take care of a woman in awhile."

"And you like that?" she asked.

"I need that," he said simply.

Chapter 8

Josh carried her down the hall, being careful not to let her feet hit the wall as he turned the corner.

Lisette's bedroom was as welcoming as the rest of the house, dominated by a bed with a wrought iron headboard, sculpted with a design of leaves and branches that brought to mind the forest that surrounded the house. The quilted spread and plethora of tapestry pillows made it into a nest, an impression furthered by soft green Berber carpet, natural wood panels covering the walls and the lack of windows in the room. As in every other part of the house, the clay and wood offerings of her artistic neighbors created an intriguing journey for the eye. The lighting was purposefully kept dim to enhance the effect of a place to escape and put the heart and mind at ease. Lisette, with her infallible sense of wit, called it The Womb.

"I'll just leave you here," Josh crossed the carpet and turned on the light in the bathroom with a dip and slight upward jerk of his elbow. She could see the spacious bath with its sunken Jacuzzi tub, surrounded by porcelain, silk flowers and stone fountains.

Josh sat her down at the vanity and turned a brass handle on the Jacuzzi controls. It brought the fountains to life, the hot water flowing over their rock foundations and through brass sculptures to give the fairies and butterflies carved into their design life, with artful placement of light and its reflection off the moving water.

"Do you need me to bring you anything?" He nodded toward the fountains. "They'll fill up the tub in a few minutes, and you can use that control to turn the flow of the water into the separate channel drain, so the fountains will keep going but the tub won't overflow. It's programmed for 106 degrees."

"Really?" Lauren raised a brow. "And how would you know so much about how Lisette's tub works?"

Josh chuckled. "Get serious. I'm the one who programmed it for her. You know she can't even operate a blender without supervision."

Lauren grinned. "I know. But I was hoping to get a rise out of you."

"Believe me, you've done that more than once tonight." His eyes clouded. "I'm sure you know it."

Lauren's brows drew together on her forehead. "Josh, I'm sorry. I'm not...I mean..." She sighed as the tension in his jaw eased into impassivity, and she felt something slipping away. She almost lunged after it, scrabbling like a starving dog for a scrap, but she'd been in that hell before and knew where it went. "I've had fun tonight," she said, her fingers knotted, restrained in her lap. "But it wasn't at your expense. I just haven't enjoyed someone's company...just enjoyed, for awhile. And Marcus made it sound so easy to trust, like we've been doing. I guess, ..." Her words died, "I guess I wanted to believe..." She didn't seem capable of developing the cynical skepticism she had certainly earned the right to have. She should be pulling out the armor that this moment of withdrawal seemed to call for.

She looked up into Josh's eyes and was startled to see a vulnerability that did not match the bitterness of his words. That fragility reminded her of a child, waiting with his hands down for the next blow, believing somehow in the miracle that the next touch from a clenched fist would be a caress.

He dropped to one knee in front of her, covering her twisting fingers with one calloused palm. "You weren't wrong," he said. "I'm sorry. Forgive me."

She suspected they both had been slogging through a dumpsite of emotions for so long they were unbalanced to find they had stepped into a fragrant garden. They should probably just turn and retreat, not drag the stench and offal clinging to them into it. However, like all lost souls, they were desperate for the sunshine and earth that could be found in fertile ground.

How could she not forgive him? His warm skin over her knuckles was making her itch to touch. And he made it worse, the way his gaze lingered, hungered, but he made no further attempt to touch her. She understood the primitive nature of what lay behind his eyes.

"Hold still," she said softly, wanting to test it. "Put your hands at your sides."

Josh studied her, blinked once, that sensual mouth twitching at one corner. He took his hands from hers, lowering them to his sides as he knelt before her.

Lauren reached out and slid her knuckles along the curve of his neck, trailed her fingertips in the hair that lay on his shoulder. A breath shuddered out of her at the adrenaline that surged through her veins. Her palm flattened against his pectoral, just over his heart. She raised her gaze from avid appreciation of the line of his ribcage and flat abdomen, to the stillness of his face, the lion rising in his eyes. It was masculine power that could overwhelm her, but for now was held in check. She leaned forward, breathing along his jawline. She placed a gentle kiss, just a soft brush of lips, against the corner of his mouth. "Forgiven," she murmured.

She sat back, taking her touch away, and looked at him. A rueful expression twisted his firm mouth and he made to rise.

"No." She took his hand.

"You're killing me," he muttered, and she nodded, simple unrepentant acknowledgement of her power over him.

"Marcus said it was my card. Do you trust me?"

"How could I not? You're like…" he lost the train of thought as he stared into her steady blue eyes, and she loved him for it. "It's your card," he murmured. "I'll do whatever you want me to do." And the bleakness was back in his face.

"Josh, what did she do to you?" she said softly.

A sigh escaped his lips, just a breath, and she saw his eyes close. He bent forward on his one knee, laid his cheek alongside her calf, and brushed a kiss just above her ankle. Then, his back curving, he went lower, to the insole, his lips parting so he nipped some of her skin in the moist caress. He stayed there, without kissing her further, his jaw pressed against her leg.

Lauren lowered her hand and stroked his hair, somehow understanding that he would not rise until she bade him do so. Her eyes moved along the bare ridge of his spine, the way his hair beneath her fingers fell along his shoulders and forward, curtaining his profile from her.

"Lauren." It was a whisper. "I can't tell you —"

"Hush."

* * * * *

Josh wasn't sure if she said it in reaction to his statement or as an answer to it. But he quieted, compelled by a strange yearning to let her hold the reins. It created a nervous anticipation in him that intensified how much he wanted her. If she had thrown open the gates to him, he might have leaped upon her, filled his hands and mouth with her like a savage animal. But with that gentle command, that "hush", the wildness was reined in, even as it was stoked to a higher pitch. Being given the hope of touching her was almost more overwhelming than having her, in that perverse way that a small bite of the finest Belgian chocolate was more tempting than a one-pound bar of the same.

Whereas a moment before he would have fed upon her body like a lion tearing into fresh blood, now he ached fiercely for permission to press his lips alongside her knee, or even the bridge of her dainty foot again.

"Keep your eyes down," she said in that same soft voice, velvet-covering steel. She rose, using his bare shoulder to steady herself. He swallowed, audibly, as the silk robe pooled around her feet, the sash falling over his shoulder.

"If you look up, I will be very angry," she murmured. Her fingers ran beneath the hair at his nape, and he made a sound, guttural in its passion. "I won't let you sleep in my bed tonight."

His lids had twitched, wanting to test her resolve, but at that, they stayed locked down, keeping his eyes focused on her bare feet and the slender curve of her ankles. He wasn't sure if Marcus had anticipated her turning the game in this direction. He knew he hadn't, with her soft, vulnerable eyes and pink mouth, a mouth with lips he would have given anything at this moment to lick and suck until they were full and moist, the way the secret folds between her legs would be at the same form of ministration. He wanted... hell, he wanted to look at her, had to look at her.

"Don't test me, Josh," she warned, as if she could read his mind. She chuckled when he swore, inventively, and the music of it caressed his ears the way her hand was doing to his neck. If she had yanked on his hair or sharpened her tone, he might have laughed it off, sparred with her will, but it was the sheer gentleness of her voice, weighted with command, that kept him obeying. "I want you to close your eyes and stand up."

He complied and stood, keeping his hands at his sides, though his palms were so hot he suspected they'd burn her fair skin, turning it as red as if he'd laid her over his knee and spanked her round, sweet ass.

His whole body went rigid with cold horror. Jesus, where the hell had that thought come from?

He turned away from her because he had to open his eyes, had to break away from that line of thought, and get away. "Lauren, I can't... I have to—"

"Josh," her fingers circled his wrist, delicate as flower stems. He could have broken free with a mere pressure, but her soft touch was as effective as a manacle of iron. "It's my card." There was a hesitation, a slight, uneven inhalation of breath. "You won't do anything wrong, as long as you obey me. And I command you to stop thinking of anything other than pleasing me. If you think of anything else, I will make you sleep…naked, here on the cold tiles, until all you can think of is how warm my bed would be. How warm my body would be, wrapped around yours. Close your eyes and face me."

* * * * *

He could not know how it felt to stand there and watch him, his head hanging low in despondency. His back expanded with short breaths, his fists clenched to fight demons that she well knew couldn't be fought with fists, even those as capable and strong as his were.

She didn't understand what was compelling her at the moment. Seeing him fight with himself against the power of an invisible chain made her hot, aroused, and perversely overwhelmed with tenderness for him. Maybe it was the sense that he desperately needed someone to take the reins and make him face the pain that Marcus had merely hinted was haunting him. Or maybe this was revenge on Jonathan, pushing Josh to the breaking point, to bring out the emotion and vulnerability she could never summon from Jonathan.

No. No. Double no and hell no. She did not want to punish Josh. She would not allow Jonathan to turn her into Prometheus, manacled to a rock where uncertainty would eternally tear at her vitals, such that every man she met would be pushed to breaking to prove something to her that could never be proved. It felt good to be doing this. It felt right.

It always feels that way at first. The internal voice had poison in its nasty tone, and it had a quick effect. Her shoulders dropped, and she bit back a sigh. "Josh, you don't—" she began in a near whisper.

He turned to face her, his eyes closed as she had instructed. The rest of her words died as his hand reached straight out and caught her fingers, forming a link that prevented either of them from tumbling off a cliff of destructive memories.

"Good," she managed, re-centering herself. She cleared her throat. "Lift me," she said, "and carry me to the tub. I'll tell you when you're there."

"I don't want to trip and hurt you."

Lauren reached up with her free hand, drew her finger along his lined forehead, tracing her nail over each closed eyelid. "You won't."

She stepped closer, just a space away from having her bare breasts pressed against his slightly damp chest, and slid her arm up to his neck.

Josh bent, put his arm beneath her legs. His palm crooked beneath the bend of knee, his fingertips curved up just beneath the line of bone that marked her kneecap over the resilient yet sensitive cartilage that joined knee to muscle. He slid the other palm along her back, moving across the soft skin below her shoulder blades, trailing fingertips across the ridge of spine between. Her body swayed with an overload of sensory reaction to his touch and then she drew in a breath as he lifted her in that easy way that left her stomach pleasantly behind. It bounced back into place as if on a spring, with the same jolt of impact one had upon reaching the bottom of the hill on a roller coaster, resettling with a spasm of exhilaration.

For the second time in a day, she was naked, all naked this time, aware of the stroke of steam from the tub caressing her flanks, and moistening areas already wet. As if that part of her were a separate being, an aroused feline in truth, it was sharply aware of the proximity of his arm, pressed against the back of her thighs, the imprint of each finger along her knee cap, and what each of those fingers would feel like, imprinted on her slick crevices. The thought shivered through her body and he frowned, his eyes still closed.

"The water will be good and warm," he promised.

She smiled. "I'm not cold. Walk toward the tub."

She nearly moaned as his first step moved his skin against her bare breast. With impish intent, she shifted in his embrace, dragging the already aroused nipple across his pectoral as she settled. His lips twisted in a wry grimace, his acknowledgement of her torture, and his grip tightened on her, in a way that suggested he would like to hold her so, in a myriad of positions, his hands never full enough of all she could have to offer.

It was only three steps to the almost full tub, but he stopped after each, asking her if his path was clear to take the next step, to be sure he would in fact safely deliver her to her destination. The clouds of steam were getting thicker, floating up from the fountains, swirling about them from the quiet whirl of the fan vent, and Lauren inhaled it, that dewlike air, coming off rock and earth, as if they were by a hot spring in a mountain cave.

"We're here," she said, and was pleased when he stopped, but did not automatically put her down, awaiting her pleasure on the matter.

Lauren reached up and traced his jawline with one finger, caressing his nape with the other hand molded to his neck. Her knuckles drifted down his sternum and to the place where her breast and his pectoral met. With one fingernail, she traced the joining path of the two curves, letting him feel the shape of her against him, as if drawing it on the canvas of his own body.

"Don't open your eyes," she repeated, suspecting the order might need reinforcement. "Remember the punishment if you do."

"It would be worth it," he muttered, but he did not open them. She smiled, locking both her arms around him to draw herself up for a light brush of lips against the leaping pulse in his throat.

She gasped against his skin as he crushed her to him, holding her squeezed in his arms as if he could meld their skins together and make one inseparable organism if he held her that way long enough. His jaw pressed against her hair and she knew she did not imagine the tremor she felt run through the muscles there.

Again the thought ran through her, its passage like the drag of barb wire across her heart. *What on earth happened to you, you lovely man?*

She let him hold her that way for a moment more, tightening the grip of her own arms, to give him comfort. The sexual drumbeats receded to jungle sounds, and there was something far more gentle between them, something far more dangerous than the sexual vibrations.

"You can let my legs down, now," she said at last, breaking the spell. He complied, stooping slightly to release them, his hand following the length of her thigh so that when she stood, his hand trailed up her hip, his long fingers caressing the curve of her bottom.

"Drop your hands to your sides," she ordered, and he let out of whuff of frustration that brought back a startling memory. At her giggle, his brow creased.

"What?"

She studied his face, touched it to reassure him that she was not making fun of him. It would never occur to her to do so, not to this gift of nature. Her gift, for the time being.

"Well, I was remembering going to a dog obedience class with one of my friends. They had this exercise; I think they called it Sit-Stay with Stimulus. It was where the dog sat at his master or mistress's heel while the trainer and her assistants went up and down the line, approaching the dog, and crooning to them. You know 'you're such a good dog, look how beautiful you are,' to see if they would resist their master's orders and stand up or go toward that stimulus."

Lauren glanced down between them. She was standing nude before him, the heat of her body close enough to radiate onto his, and send the message clearly behind the closed eyelids that she was within touching, embracing — hell, a dip of the knees — fucking distance. Her gaze drifted down further. She suspected if she freed him from the constraints of his jeans, his arousal would be laying along the seam of her slightly parted thighs. And then it would be over. Even a Dominant had limits to what she could bear. So, regrettably, for now, the clothes stayed on, though she would have enjoyed seeing him kneeling by the tub naked, his cock jutting up above his folded knees, all four knuckles of either hand required to be pressed to the tile floor on the outside of his thighs, his head up. Lauren wasn't a big subscriber to the "head down and don't look the Mistress in the eye" school of Dominatrix. She loved faces, and all their expressions, and with a tucked down head, you missed a lot of information. Plus, it was actually harder for a self-conscious sub to keep his head up, which made it easier to earn the pleasure of punishment, if you made holding the chin up a requirement.

"That noise you just made," she injected warm humor into her voice, "reminded me of that class, the dogs impatient with the whole silly nonsense, but willing to endure it for the reward."

"Do the trick, get the bone," he said.

"There was that instant gratification, yes," she curled one lock of his hair around the curve behind his ear, following the sensitive shell of skin down to the silver earring and tracing the small inside loop of that with the tip of her finger. "But while most of the dogs did need the little reward treats to keep them focused, mostly they seemed happy to be pleasing their Master or Mistress, taking joy in their owners' pleasure in them. I liked that."

"Why?"

"Because it said there was something more between them, something that made them obey beyond treats. Maybe love.

Maybe sort of the for better or worse bonding that dogs seem to be so much better at than people."

His fingertips reached out, touched her face with unsettling accuracy. Lauren looked up at him.

"Don't be sad," he said softly.

She laid her cheek in his palm, and let him feel the attempt of a smile.

"Okay." She straightened, gripped his forearm for balance and stepped into the tub, grimacing, as she had to shift weight to the tender ankle. All pain was forgotten at the blissful embrace of hot water. She shut off the water as he had instructed, leaving the fountains running. Lauren picked up a couple of the sapphire colored bathbeads Lisette had in a dish in one corner and dropped them in with her, changing the texture of the water so it became a soft oil upon the skin, perfuming the air with rosemary and lavender.

"Mmmm," she lowered herself down further and rested her head on the edge. She looked at Josh, still standing, a bit uncertain in his expression, as if he was not quite sure what to be doing and feeling awkward as a result. She reached out and took his fingers.

"Come, kneel here beside me."

He felt his way to a position parallel to the tub and knelt just as he should, his legs folded under him, his thighs cradling his genitalia into a triangular, straining area of denim. He laid his palms flat on his thighs and she permitted it, because it did not obstruct her view of anything and it kept his forearm in stroking distance.

"You may open your eyes, but only if you keep your gaze on the floor. One flicker of those beautiful lashes," her finger brushed them, gently, but they quivered in response, "and I'll blindfold you with my robe."

She watched his eyes open, blink, and focus on the tile. He tried so hard to control the involuntary flicker toward his peripheral vision that his eyes teared up. He would steal a glance when she started to wash, she was sure. She was hoping for it. She tilted her head back and let the water from the fountain nearest splash down on her head, the back of her skull seated comfortably on a smooth ledge of rock. The water ran down her face, her throat, and pitter-pattered down her breasts, the rounded tops floating just above the water's edge, like the smooth curve of a dolphin's rise.

"Would you like some help scrubbing your ears, sweet love?" Marcus asked.

Chapter 9

Lauren raised her head. He leaned in the doorway, watching them both. "Nothing more relaxing to a lady than being groomed by a good looking eunuch or, in this case," he smiled enigmatically, "The closest thing to one."

His gaze passed over Josh, kneeling by her tub, his eyes down. Marcus's expression reflected acceptance, and no surprise. Somehow, Fate had brought together three who knew how this game was played. She knew it as a way to intimacy and to explore the deepest regions of her heart. Marcus seemed to have turned its practice into just another art form he admired. Her eyes strayed to Josh. It was a mystery as to how Josh knew the secret handshake, so to speak, and uncovering that mystery would become as much a part of the game as anything else.

For now, she knew she felt comfortable, and she had not felt that way in a sexual situation in a long time. She had not felt comfortable with Jonathan. This wasn't the same game she had played with him. The same field perhaps, the same essential rules, but not the same game.

It was a relief to realize that Maria might be right, that the game was not the problem. What had unbalanced her was the discovery that she was not playing with someone who cared about her, someone she could trust, and perhaps, even more painful for her to acknowledge, never had been.

She nodded to Marcus. "The cream colored wash cloth and the moisturizer soap in my bag on the counter," she said. "The one that smells like vanilla."

He nodded and retrieved the items, then came to kneel by the tub, next to Josh. Marcus's gaze passed over her naked body. He did not look at her with impersonal disinterest. He looked at her as a lover of art would, with appreciation for form, and she felt flattered to see approval in his eyes.

"What I like best about this is not seeing you naked, love," Marcus said. He began to massage the bar of soap in the washcloth, creating a rich lather. "Though you are quite beautiful. What I like is knowing Josh is kneeling here beside you and cannot see you." He held out his hand and she put her wet palm into it. He began to wash her arm, smooth strokes less than a foot from Josh's bowed head. "He can only imagine the way the cloth strokes the soft, pale skin on the underside of your arm, that area between the elbow and wrist as soft as a baby's skin." He turned her arm as he spoke, in tones that were slow and measured, like the caresses of a lover's tongue. "The way your breasts lie heavy in the water, the nipples full and soft from the warmth. Your legs wet and slick, your knees bent so the soap rolls down your thighs and melts into the bath."

A muscle flexed in Josh's cheek, sending a ripple along the tense jaw. His nostrils flared, taking in her scent like a stallion whose eyes had been covered with a scarf. Lauren ached, watching him. It was a state of delicious anticipation, her will torn between wanting to thrust her wet body into his arms and give him what he desired, see how he handled it, and taking him higher, seeing when the stallion would break free.

She was in control of the cards, so this could go somewhere or nowhere, and the choice was hers as long as Josh's choice was to submit to her will. But there were other factors at work here, and it was not that easy.

She knew how to whip him into a state of arousal akin to the grip of a deadly fever, a state that would make him believe he had no choice. While not the same thing as forcing him, it was problematic to her conscience. It was why a Dom often shied away from the damaged subs. It had to be the sub's choice throughout. If it wasn't, then you had crossed the line, and it was hard to see that line in a cloud of emotional issues, and to resist the temptation to draw on a sub's weaknesses. Power could corrupt a good intent. It was that simple. She had to be careful. Josh mattered.

She turned from the disturbing path of her thoughts to the man washing her. Marcus's squatting, splayed-knee pose made it obvious he was aroused by Josh's plight, and while the arousal wasn't for her, it did not make her less appreciative of the view. It was difficult to keep her eyes open, though, with his capable hands lathering her shoulders in a massaging motion that had her purring. He pushed her unresisting body so she lay with her head resting on the cushioned rim of the tub. Her eyes came back open, however, as he slicked the soap smoothly down her breasts. It was peculiar to have a man hold her breasts who had no interest in them sexually. However, since he handled them with such reverence for their form, she could not feel offended. In fact, quite the opposite.

As he traced them with his knuckles, weighing them in his palms, her heightened sexual awareness of Josh made the nipples rise under the light brush of his fingertips. She arched, expelling a trembling breath. Josh gripped the side of the tub, agitated by the possibilities beyond his sight. A smile touched Marcus's lips as he raised his eyes to hers and her own lips curved. The flickering candlelight of the bathroom played along Marcus's perfect features and deepened the dark shadows in Josh's expression.

"I can smell the desire for you coming off his skin," Marcus observed. "Lay back, dearest, and let me rinse you. You should see her breasts, Josh. They're perfect. Large enough that they quiver when she so much as breathes, glistening with the water and soap I've put on them, but small enough that they weigh comfortably in a man's palm, particularly a broad palm like yours, where those long fingers could reach up and tease her nipples."

Lauren swallowed and shifted, lifting the objects that Marcus was describing.

"They're stiff now," Marcus continued in a murmur, "large and dark red, filled with blood, just aching to be sucked."

The hot water passed across them and back, the stimulation of tiny needles. Lauren caught her lip in her bottom teeth and bit down hard to suppress a groan.

"I could take care of that." Josh's voice was almost a growl.

Lauren reached out trembling fingers and trailed them along the nape of Josh's neck, making circular patterns on the skin.

"No," she murmured. "Not yet. I like watching you want me."

At her touch, Josh shut his eyelids, clenched them into tight folds of skin. At her words, his fingers became fists on his knees, but he nodded once, a quick jerk. Tears sprang to her eyes, startling her. In all the time she had spent with him, Jonathan had never shown such an obvious desire to please, coupled with a rage to devour.

Passion. He had never given her passion. Josh was passion in human form, undiluted, protected on an island that was about sensation and the genuine substance behind it.

It was demoralizing, how the strongest woman could be reduced to insecurity in the absence of passion. She had not realized until now how she had begun to doubt her beauty and self worth. Passion was a flower with a fragile bloom, easily collapsed by frost. It was fortunate that it also had strong roots, able to survive in darkness for lengthy periods without dying away completely. Under the heat of Josh's passion, the flower was opening.

Lauren realized she felt like a goddess, her every movement sinuous and worthy of worship. She was fascinated by the beauty of her own skin, the soft touch of her hair on her shoulder blades, the long, graceful curve of hip and thigh. She was more than worthy of desire. She was worthy of begging, of adoration.

Lauren raised her face with an incoherent murmur as Marcus brought the sprayer to her neck. She moved her face through the water, drowning the tears.

Marcus chuckled, though his eyes were intent, showing he had not missed the emotions crossing her face. He conscientiously squeaked a strand of her hair to ensure it was free of soap, and managed a light touch of her chin at the same moment. Lauren gave a slight nod. She was fine.

"Ah, the unspoken fear of all men," he voiced the thought behind his laughter, "that a woman with a hot bath and a good shower head will have no use for a man."

Lauren smiled. "And a woman's greatest fear is that the cable company and La-Z-Boy will create the combination of channels and recliner options that will render her unnecessary."

"You mean they haven't already?"

Lauren snorted and splashed him with water. "I'm ready to get out of here. Marcus, will you bring me a towel?"

She rose, water pouring off of her, and stepped out of the tub, one hand braced on Josh's shoulder as Marcus went to comply. Josh's gaze stayed on her feet. She knew his eyes opened as she rose. Even looking at the floor, he would have enough of a view just above the rim of the tub to see a quick slideshow of wet breasts, navel, hips, and water gleaming off the ends of the neatly trimmed triangle of soft downy hair between her thighs. His lips parted, his tongue touching them, and it was easy to imagine him sucking every drop of water away. The image was so strong; it tightened the coil of longing in her body at each vital point and weakened her knees so her grip on his shoulder increased for balance. His muscles shifted beneath her touch and she blocked the sudden desire to lean down and press her lips to the bump of shoulder blade. She thought if she did, she might wind her arms around him and never let go.

She wrapped the towel around her and hobbled over to the sink. "I think I'll just get ready for bed now, if you guys want to go do the same," she managed, avoiding her own gaze in the mirror. She caught Marcus's nod in the corner of her eye. He shifted past her and touched Josh's elbow. Lauren raised her gaze to the mirror as Josh rose. He gave her a long look. She could not summon a smile to lessen the seriousness of his expression, so she just stared back at him until Marcus touched him again and he turned away, preceding his friend out the doorway. Marcus turned in the frame, pressed his own fingers briefly to his lips and sent the gesture to her, gentle approval in his gaze.

She wasn't sure if it was merited. A Mistress took away the places for a submissive to retreat, made him vulnerable to her by patient, tender eradication of all emotional shields, until there was nowhere he could hide from her. It worked hand in hand with proving to the sub that he could trust his Mistress at the very deepest level, making those protections unnecessary.

Jonathan had wanted a Mistress who would treat the "breakdown" process like an amused predator cutting off a rabbit's every path of escape. Perhaps if she had loved him better, she would have been willing to go against her own nature and provide him what he wanted. No, even then, she could not have done it. It just wasn't in her to be vicious. That wasn't the kind of Mistress she was, and for the process to work right, the Dom had to let go of her shields as well, perversely be as open and exposed to the sub as she demanded he be to her. She hadn't been the right Mistress for Jonathan, the right person, the right woman.

"Go on to the guest bathroom, I'll use it after you."

She heard Josh's footsteps retreating, and then Marcus was leaning in the doorframe, watching every shift of her expression with those brilliant green eyes. "You know," he commented. "You are very appealing, for a woman."

"That's because you get turned on watching another Dom at work, as I do." She pursed her lips, considered him. "I wonder if I'm being too unkind, if I shouldn't ease up a bit. I could be taking this too far, much too fast."

He considered that, studied the ceiling, then brought his eyes back down to her face. "However cliché it sounds, my dear, you know and I know that a Master is cruel only in order to be kind. It's a very, very important rule."

The silence drew out between them and she never let her gaze drop from his. "But I don't know him well enough. In a dungeon, there's room for mistakes. I've never moved this fast with any sub."

"Don't you dare lose courage on me now," Marcus admonished. He stepped forward, touched her face, but his expression was one of understanding, not condescension. "I have extensive experience with many rebellious youngsters," a slight smile curved his lips. "But I know, as you do, sometimes there's an instant click. You are doing very well with Josh. If you follow your instinct, I believe there is very little you will do wrong. And I am here, just in case."

She considered that, nodded. "Okay," she said, the one word quieting her worries, for now.

It felt good, the sense of support, but as soon as the door closed behind Marcus and Lauren faced the vision in the mirror alone, she lost some of her confidence. The dominant siren she had projected became a suffering, fragile-eyed woman with haunted features.

She had not sacrificed her whole being to Jonathan's bullshit, damn it. She ran her tongue over her teeth, picked up some of Lisette's perfumed body cream and dropped the towel. Watching herself, she spread the lotion over her breasts, rubbing it into the aureoles, over the nipples, watching them respond to her touch, already stimulated by the evening's events.

She had one or two friends with whom she was affectionate enough that occasional sex was possible, but it was mutually accepted that the emotional bond was based on friendship alone. It was something to be enjoyed, like a sport. Sports played well provided a synergistic lift when the game was in full swing, when you forgot everything but the momentum of that interaction, the playing. But you couldn't compare sex to racquetball or golf, or a good set of tennis, even under those circumstances. If anything, it was more akin to a sport that interacted with nature. Leaning back, hiking out as a sailboat surged up to ten knots close-hauled, the water bathed in the golds and reds of sunset that was more like it. You looked over at your friend and your faces reflected the shared ecstasy of that moment. That moment became part of your bond, deepened the friendship, but it was still just friendship. It was not the stripping of the soul, daring it to touch the bared soul of another.

Sex with someone who drew you down that path of vulnerability could make you believe that a never-ending love might lie at the end of it. That click Marcus was talking about, that too-intense feeling she had around Josh, a virtual stranger, was making her feet turn to ice while other parts of her exploded the thermometer. Maybe that was the problem, not the dysfunctional bullshit baggage she was carrying from Jonathan. Maybe she was just scared.

Didn't she keep telling herself she should stop thinking so much? Maybe she needed to jump off the hamster Habitrail of her mind and say fuck it. Or, fuck him, rather. Josh was a fascinating, attractive guy. What was wrong with a fling? Never mind her adamant insistence to Maria that one night stands were not her thing, that they sucked her soul dry. It wasn't what she ultimately wanted, but maybe it would be enough for just this weekend. Dissatisfied, she picked up the brush and blow dryer and went to work on her hair. Unfortunately, the drone of the appliance did not drown out her thoughts.

Her ex-psychotherapist had used the term D/s (once Lauren had introduced her to it) in a tone that suggested the doctor thought it was a disease. It had taken awhile, but Lauren at last had regained enough of her confidence to disagree, and dump the therapist.

Two committed people choosing to exercise their sexuality in a dominant and submissive fashion was not the problem. Everything in nature reflected the assertion of those characteristics. Every interaction between the beasts in the forest started with it, and animals were far more connected with what was "natural" than humans.

The problem was the all-too-unnatural dysfunctionality humans brought to the game. So what was happening here tonight? Was it a relapse or a healing, a symbolic return to her sexual self, maybe to all parts of herself?

There was a way to give herself a hint. She retied the silk robe, hopped to the door, and opened it.

"Josh?"

She heard a pause in the men's conversation, then his feet padded down the hallway. He came around the corner, a towel carelessly slung over his shoulder and his hair damp, the aroma of Lisette's sandalwood soap coming off of him.

Lauren lifted her hand to him and he came closer, taking it. He laced his fingers easily in hers, his brow lifted in silent question.

"Kiss me?" she made it a soft question. Lauren wanted to be sure he understood it was a request, not part of any game or strategy.

Josh stepped closer. Without a word, he set his hands to her waist, his warm palms covering the curves of her hips, heat through silk. He drew her to him and her fingers curled onto his hips as he brought his lips down to hers, the strands of hair on his forehead brushing her cheek.

Lauren melted at the touch of his mouth. She relaxed in his arms, all the way down to the bones, and she reveled in his strength, which increased consecutively in his arms, chest, stomach and thighs, to accommodate her loss of self-support.

His mouth opened hers and she moaned at the flick of tongue past her lips and teeth, the warm wet caress, the pressure of his body as he pulled her more against him.

When he raised his head, she was barely conscious of herself as a separate being. Her eyes cleared and she blinked up at him.

"Good," she breathed. "I like you. I really do."

His eyes crinkled with humor, and he cleared his throat. "That simple, then?"

"As long as we don't move from this moment," she gave him a rueful smile.

He cupped her cheek and Lauren rested her face in the strong palm, her chin on the rapid pulse in his wrist. "Please don't let me hurt you, Josh," she murmured. "I couldn't stand to do that."

"I'm not porcelain, Lauren. I won't break that easily."

"Someone has broken you before," she raised her head and closed her hand over that wrist. "Just as someone has me. Let's not shatter each other again, okay?"

He looked as if he might say many things, including the obvious truth that there was no way to prevent it if hearts got involved, but in the end he leaned in, kissed her nose.

"Okay," he said.

Chapter 10

Lisette believed in top quality mattresses fitted with cotton sheets and smothered in layers of quilts. It gave a guest the sense that she was burrowing into a nest, made all the stronger in a room decorated with so many soft textures and hues of nature.

Lauren did not give any specific instructions. It was simply assumed she wished to be in the middle. She had donned an oversized T-shirt and a silk pair of panties and now lay in the center of the bed, on her side, watching Marcus.

He turned the torchlights off, which left the room lit by the soft glow from several bowls of floating candles he had placed, strewn with flower petals, on the vanity and night tables. He casually shucked off his jeans and the silk boxers beneath and laid both over the chair. She wondered at his daring, but then realized that, from her surreptitious examination of him throughout the afternoon and evening, Josh wasn't wearing underwear under his jeans. Marcus was not going to let his friend be embarrassed by being the only one in the buff, and Lauren had no complaints with his generosity.

Marcus was equally beautiful beneath his clothes. Sleek lines of flank and thigh muscle suggested a home gym and daily Central Park jogging regimen. Her attention drifted low center and she concluded that those "rebellious boys" he chose to bestow with his attentions were amply rewarded.

She raised her eyes to his. Marcus gave her a wicked grin. "No drooling, love."

Lauren chuckled. Behind her she heard the rustlings as Josh stripped. She could have turned and given him the same perusal, but after the kiss, she was feeling a strange shyness about looking at him. Besides, there was a pleasant torture in hearing the metallic noise of a zipper, the sound of denim being pushed down bare skin.

He slid under the covers behind her and his heated body drew close to her back.

If she had been told she would be ending this day tucked into bed between two obscenely attractive naked men, she would have asked the informant if she could also book the space shuttle for a moon tour while she was at it.

Josh laid his arm about her waist. He did not fit his body to hers, but the invitation was there if she should choose to accept it. Marcus crawled in facing her. She felt his hand slide over Josh's arm so they were woven protectively around her. Josh did not draw back from his friend's touch, though the only place Marcus's hand could be resting would be on Josh's waist or the point of his hip.

Marcus had the faint smell of expensive cologne. It brought to her mind a chic night in a New York gallery, and an image of him dressed in a suit custom made in Hong Kong, finished with a silk tie and elegant cuff links. Josh was all musky male, earth and trees, evoking the vision of a native slipping through the forest, a shadow as lithe and intriguing as a passing wolf.

It was an unsettling contrast, and an altogether attractive one. Lauren slid one arm over Marcus's bare ribs, touching the light down across his abdomen with the tips of her fingers as she did so. She slid her other arm up to Josh's hand at her waist and tugged him closer. He obliged, sliding in and cupping her silk clad backside in the hot cradle of his thighs. He tightened the coil of his arm so his arm circled most of her waist, his fingers curved between it and the mattress. Her shoulder blades pressed against his chest. His head was just behind hers, his breath brushing the nape and side of her neck. If she tilted her head just a bit, she would brush her jugular against his lips. Her fingers trailed Marcus's bare spine, an idle stroking gesture, just indulging the pleasure of contact. Her forehead rested against his muscular bicep as he lay his angel's head on his crooked arm and smiled into her near face.

Their legs were a delightful tangle; Josh's couched up behind hers, one calf insinuated between her calves, his toes idly stroking her curled ones. Marcus's leg lay over both of theirs.

Lauren giggled. "This is like a pile of puppies," she said.

Marcus chuckled in the dim light. "You're a bit less fuzzy, love, and Josh… Well, he has practically no chest hair. I've often wondered, does he even have hair —"

Lauren squealed as the blanket above her kicked up in violent disturbance as Josh fended off Marcus's playful grabs over her hips.

"You've seen it often enough to know," Josh said evenly. "The only reason you come here is to see me naked when I swim."

"Yes, there are no good looking men in New York," Marcus said dryly. "I have to go a thousand miles to the middle of nowhere to get a look at a fine piece of ass. And a straight piece of ass at that."

Lauren shrieked as the blankets kicked up again. Josh punched at his friend and Marcus retaliated, launching a brief tussle. Lauren struggled to get her own blows in and succeeded in swatting them both. "Hey! Innocent civilian caught in the middle here."

Marcus grinned over her head. "Saved from an ass kicking by Mom."

"I know you were."

Lauren choked on a laugh at the suitably childish retort and seized Josh's arm, clamping it around her waist. She used the same hand to shove Marcus's head back down on the pillow beside hers. "Are you sure you two aren't brothers?"

"No, thank God. I wouldn't want to endanger my soul with the kind of thoughts I have concerning Josh's straight ass." Marcus's teeth flashed at Josh's snort, but he settled back in, laying his arm once again over his friend's on Lauren's hip.

There was a moment of silence, then Marcus's voice murmured just above the crown of her head. "We are brothers." Lauren felt him squeeze Josh's arm. "Family formed by circumstance rather than blood."

"Sometimes it's stronger that way," she said, and then they all were still, aware of one another, and not needing to say more.

The silence was a peaceful one, but as it settled over them like drifts of warm sand into hollows between rocks, Lauren's mind turned to the immediate physical sensations, and the input there was far from serene. The silk of the panties she wore with her oversized T-shirt was a transparent conductor of the heat of Josh's groin. The way they were nested against each other, his aroused member fit intimately into the silken channel of her labia and the crease of her backside, giving her a screaming urge to rub. His occasional slight shifts, which pressed him more firmly into that channel, were not easing that desire. There was moisture dampening the cloth between them, the perspiration created by flesh pressed against flesh, and her body's response, oiling itself for penetration.

She could part her thighs, slide her finger along the fragile line of elastic, pull the undergarment aside and let him pull her down on him. She had asked him to be here, to sleep with her, for the intimacy. She had enjoyed her power over him. Now that had opened a door deeper within her, as such play always did. She wanted to go beyond that, link her desire with his and let it overpower them, wrap them in its cocoon and let them sate themselves until the experience transformed them.

How could the emotional need vibrating from her in waves not be pounding against his senses? Her body was trembling with it. The men had to feel it. Josh had to know how close she was to giving in and letting him have her body to plunder at will.

His hand touched her hair, stroked, soothing her as she had soothed him. "Sleep," he murmured. "Just sleep."

The warm, non-sexual touch was a sweet, searing contrast to what was happening below their waists, and it gradually balanced the scale in her mind, bringing her back to a more level perspective. He could not give her what she sought in one fell swoop, like sitting down to one meal to nourish the body for a lifetime. It didn't work that way, though many people, including herself, had often made that mistake, thinking one gigantic fuck would answer all the needs hungering inside. He knew it, she knew it, but it was him who took the reins at this moment and slowed the wagon down. He knew how to be strong.

His perception of her needs was unnerving, considering less than twelve hours ago they had been strangers.

She took a firm hold of Marcus's arm at her waist, like the safety bar on a roller coaster, and focused on Josh's hand instead of his tempting cock. It took some time, but beneath his gentle touch, the dangerous intensity building within her eased, and at length she expelled it in a soft sigh. She rooted her cheek deeper into the support of Marcus's bicep and Lisette's pillows. With Josh's hand caressing her hair, she slid into sensual dreams with the two men intertwined around her.

* * * * *

Her dreams were a languid swim through warm liquid, populated by underwater plants of vivid colors, with fleshy smooth stalks that stroked her body like long, silken fingers. She swam through them and rolled lazily, feeling their touch all along her skin, naked in the substance of the womb.

A shadow fell upon her. She looked up. A man was just above her, outlined by the shafts of sunlight piercing the water's surface, far above them. No, not a man, not exactly. Her eyes traveled over his familiar face with gray eyes and floating hair. The water etched out every feature, from his bare chest and shoulders, and blatant arousal, to the long, powerful scaled tail that marked him as a merman and kept him vertical above her as she lay on her back, floating.

Lauren felt the whisper touch of the ocean garden again. The sea fronds wound themselves around her wrists and ankles, an inarguable pressure that drew her thighs far apart and spread-eagled her helpless before the watching sea creature. His eyes darkened further at the site of her exposed sex and, as she struggled, part alarm and part quivering excitement, he began to descend toward her. His tail propelled him with the casual ease of a shark, but there was nothing casual about his expression. It was the comfort of moving in one's own element. In that way one often did in a dream, for a moment Laurel stood apart from her dream self and recognized what was familiar about it. It was the way she often moved when in the clubs at night.

Her struggles only served to increase the intensity of his gaze, which roamed appreciatively over her jutting breasts and the flexing of her thighs. Lauren stopped, panting, as he came to rest between her legs, his aroused, impressive member at eye level. Instinctively, Lauren licked her lips and raised a hungry gaze to him. A smile touched his mouth.

He spoke, a soft crooning noise, almost like a dolphin or whale, and her bindings obeyed, wrapping high on her thighs and lifting her up, so her hips were elevated to his lips as the rest of her stayed lower, increasing her sense of helplessness.

His nose brushed her swollen clitoris and she screamed into the water. His tongue pushed in between the tight folds and she moaned. Though she was panting, the water was like air to her starving lungs.

His large hands, callused as if from carpentry work, came beneath her bottom and cupped the individual cheeks, separating them so his fingertips as well as the cool water and waving tips of sea life brushed the sensitive opening. More vines wrapped around her waist and thighs. Still more wrapped under and above her breasts, lifting them and binding them tightly, trapping the blood in them. She could no longer even writhe, only shudder with convulsions and tremble at what he was doing to her. She wanted to come, but she could not come as long as she could not move.

His eyes spoke eloquently, and she knew that his possession of her was not the toying of a shark with prey. It was a possession born not of a predator's hunger, but that of a lifetime mate laying a claim to her whole being.

He rose over her, hovering, and his lips closed over one tight nipple, unbearably sensitive because of the seaweed's constriction around her breast. She quivered and made soft cries. Spasms rolled through her body, small almost-climaxes that made her pleas incoherent, at least the words. Her need was as clear as the water around them.

The fronds drew her hips down, and he sank with them, descending so he was between her thighs. With his eyes on her face, his fingers slid to her hips and he thrust into her in one fluid stroke.

She came instantly, the intense sensation of being held still during his penetration equal to a bomb exploding in a contained space. The seaweed held her as she cried out, a long, low moan that rocked up to helpless screams. He continued to thrust with slow, tortuous strokes that prolonged her own orgasm until even in the breathable water she could no longer draw in enough for her lungs. Only then did he buck, unable to contain his own seed any longer, and she heard his voice, a haunting cry that reminded her of whales and other mysterious creatures.

He covered her mouth with his and gave her air, the ability to breathe and live above the water's surface. He filled her with oxygen and all the substances that made life worth living.

Exquisite. An elegant, passionate word, reserved for an untouched box of Godiva chocolates, the sparkle of a diamond in sunlight, and this moment.

She called his name, begging to touch him. She would have torn her soul from its shell and offered it to him for the opportunity. As if she had made a wish, the seaweed was abruptly gone and she lunged, wrapping her arms and legs upon him. She groaned in joy as she felt his arms come around her and cried out in renewed passion. The lazy movement of the powerful tail continued his thrusts within her, stroking her trembling tissues and heating them again.

She pressed her cheek and her heart against his. "Never let me go. Promise you'll never go," she begged, and her tears joined the ocean.

He held her with relentless strength, but took her lips in a gentle kiss, so different from his fierce possession of her body that it unbalanced her. The trembling of her body made the ocean floor vibrate, a shifting of plates signifying a change in the earth's surface, the alteration of the landscape of her mind, a wavering, and awakening.

Lauren's eyes opened. Her arms were wrapped around Josh, her nails dug into his back. The wet saltiness against her face had moistened his bare chest, and he was stroking her hair, murmuring to her, gentle crooning, like a lullaby, or a chant. It was early morning, according to the clock on the dresser. Marcus was gone, but he had put fresh candles on the night table to throw a dim light in the room that had no windows to let in the soft shades of dawn.

She had never had a dream of submission; her sexual dreams often had the same flavor of her real life, the drive to tenderly dominate. It left her unsettled, not so much the dream itself, but the underlying sense of drowning, the willingness to go under and submerge herself in sensual exploration. She had carried it with her, out of the dream into a natural extension of thinking about Josh.

She chided herself for her initial uneasy response to the dream. A Dominant needed a sub's devotion as much as the sub desired the focused attention of her dominance over him. When it came down to it, they were willing captives of each other, the lines of control and possession ever shifting because of it. But the dream, being the voice of her unconscious and subconscious self, underscored how much she wanted to establish that level of intimacy and trust, where safe rules and strictures were not needed, everything intuitive between her and a lover, whether in play or in reality. She wanted love and a forever with someone. Simple, natural, and unbearably painful, because of how complicated it was to find it. But dreams did not care about torturing the soul.

Sensing that she was awake, Josh moved his lips against her temple. He stole a kiss over her eyebrow, nibbling a bit at it, sucking it into his mouth. Lauren sighed and nestled closer, pressing soft cotton and swollen breasts into his chest. His hand wandered down her hip to the flank and she shuddered as his fingers curled around one cheek. He ran his touch along the satin leg band of the French cut bikinis and then slid his long fingers under them, using his knuckles to push the fabric back, and into the cleft of her bottom, like a thong. He gripped the top edge of the bunched panties and tugged at the rolled fabric, increasing the pressure on her clitoris.

Lauren lifted her eyes to his. He withdrew his touch, resting his hand on her hip. "It's your card still, Lauren," he murmured. His eyes promised her anything, a dangerous gift she could unleash or bridle at will, and the knowledge of it soaked her flimsy panties in a warm gush of response. She pushed the disturbing dream into her subconscious and took hold of the reins again.

"I want you to grab the headboard," she commanded. "And don't let go of it."

He obeyed, shifting to his back, the long muscular arms threading through the slats and then gripping the wrought iron spindles from behind. Lauren rose to her knees and pulled the covers back, exposing him to her gaze. His arms tensed as if he might move to cover himself, but he controlled the urge and merely flushed, a rush of blood to his cheeks. Lauren ignored his discomfort and took her time looking him over, the graceful hips and long thighs, the light dusting of hair, the thicker thatch at his groin, the sectioned abdomen and soft tufts of hair beneath his arms. The longer she looked, the more his limbs trembled, the more turgid his cock became, until it was all she could do to maintain her indifferent look and not drool.

"God, you are beautiful," she said softly.

He groaned, and the fire in his eyes became infused with something else, something that spoke of yearning, and regret. It was so similar a reflection of how she felt when she came out of the dream, shattered and aroused, it almost broke her now. It would have, if he had chosen that very moment to ignore her command, release the headboard and seize her to him. In the light of day, the game should probably be over anyway. He and Marcus should be going back to work on whatever they had to do. She would hobble around to see if there were the makings of a pimento cheese sandwich in Lisette's kitchen and savor a few of Josh's chocolate chip cookies while mulling over the events of the previous evening.

But it wasn't over. Josh himself had set the parameters, reminding her the card was still hers. It occurred to her that, for some reason, he needed her to hold the cards, as if he was afraid to interact with her if she wasn't in charge.

Not that she could possibly object. The male torso stretched out before her in mute, powerful submission was a perfect creation. He had no spare flesh. His thighs, arms and stomach were roped with wiry, lean muscle. The buttocks flexing with his slight, agitated shifts were tight as she could wish, and she had a sudden, amusing desire.

"Roll to your side," she commanded. "Away from me."

He obeyed, giving her a lingering look, a look of wild desire she recognized as the hungry stare she had fixed on the merman in her dreams. When it came from Josh, it made her want to suckle him at her breast, protect and care for him, and yet keep him at her mercy forever. It was an interesting thought, since he stood half a foot taller than she was and could probably bend steel between those luscious ass cheeks. She desired him. Lord, she wanted him like she'd never wanted anything in her whole life, but something held her back. This game, for lack of a better word, had to be played out. She did not know if experience or intuition was telling her that, or just her raging hormones, but for the first time since Jonathan, she was going to try to trust herself again.

She reached out and scraped a fingernail down the curve of a buttock, watching it flex at the faint pain. Then she splayed her fingers out like a spider across his buttock, leaned down and bit him.

Josh jumped, and the muscle quivered beneath her touch, but he did not pull away, even as she tightened her grip and the pressure of her bite. He kept his fists locked on the headboard; those glorious back muscles rippling with tension against the pain. When she lifted her head, she saw it had not diminished the impressive erection in the slightest. In fact, it was brushing his belly, so filled it was with blood.

His ass now bore the imprint of her teeth. She bent back down to it, running her tongue over the marks, soothing the pain like a wolf's mate. He made a noise, somewhere between groan and growl, and his hands flexed on the board like he might let go, roll to his back and seize her up, thrust her onto his shaft and then pump his seed into her while she clung helpless to his powerful forearms.

But he did not. He closed his eyes and swallowed, controlling his need. Watching him do so flooded her vitals with the sweet sensation of power, power made even more potent by the fact he was submitting to it by his own choice, if not entirely of his own volition.

She knew he was damaged, and eventually, they would have to get to the bottom of that. Her glance strayed over the marks she had left on him. No pun intended.

"Roll on your back again," she said. "But keep holding the headboard."

He obeyed and stared at her, his gray eyes steel that heated her skin with a flush of prickling desire. Lauren slid forward, rose up onto her knees again and straddled his neck, putting her thighs along either side of his tense jaw. His nostrils flared, taking in her scent, and she nodded.

"Would you like some of that for breakfast, Josh?" she murmured. "Unh uh," she moved back as his mouth opened. "You have to ask for it. What do you want?"

"I want you," he rasped.

She shook her head. "More specific, Josh. And you have to ask. You can't demand it. Or maybe I'll go sit in that chair way over there in the corner and take care of it myself." She passed her finger lightly over the damp impression of her panties, which revealed the arousal beneath.

"No," he jerked his head off the pillow and fastened his mouth over her swollen clit, plunging his tongue into her, through the soaked silk. Lauren jerked back with a gasp as her body vibrated in the clutch of a near orgasm. For a moment, she fought her own will, which screamed at her to put herself back in proximity of that clever tongue and finish it.

Then she looked at Josh's face, the way he glared up at her, smug satisfaction in his eyes. She was making him feel vulnerable, and he was reacting as a new or damaged sub sometimes did, shielding himself. He didn't want to feel vulnerable. She had to make him understand that he was required to be open and exposed to her in all ways. She wasn't going to permit him to withdraw from her and make this into nothing more than a kinky fuck between two strangers.

Lauren grasped his hair in her hand and jerked his head back, wrapping her fingers into the thick mane and tightening her grasp, intending to cause him pain.

"You do that again, and I will go over to that chair, lick my fingers and fuck myself with them while you watch." She did not permit any kindness in her voice now, nothing but cruel denial. "I'll spread open my thighs over the chair arms, so you can see everything, and when I come, you'll see the way it sucks at my hand, instead of your tongue. I won't rub my scent over your face and make you mine. Now," she eased forward again, her throbbing center only a breath away from his panting mouth. "Ask for it, and be specific. And you look at me when you ask."

You won't hide from me, Josh.

"Please let me eat…" it was fascinating to watch his thoughts chase each other, look for the words he thought she might like best. She revealed nothing, keeping her expression aloof and stern, though her tissues quivered from his rasping breaths, less than an inch away.

"Please let me lick your pussy," he said, stumbling over the awkward word, his eyes pleading. "Please. I want to make you come."

"You don't make me do anything, Josh, but you will eat me until I come, because I won't let you stop until you do."

His body jerked as it trembled, and she recognized the nerves overtaking passion. The uncontrollable shaking came when a sub felt his true vulnerability to a Mistress's will for the first time, an anxiety that came with relinquishing control to someone by some compulsion that defied issues of logic, strength or bindings. It puzzled her, because she *knew* he knew the game. But overriding the confusion was a more unsettling emotion.

His quivering brought tears to her eyes. Lauren bent, pressed the softest of kisses to his damp forehead, swept back his hair with gentle fingers. Then she straightened, took the head board in both hands, and slid over his mouth.

He did not lick. He devoured. With the noise of an animal, he plunged his face into her musky wetness, tongue stabbing into her flooded passage, lips and teeth pulling her aching labia and clit into the hot cavern of his mouth, the soft growls bringing extra vibration to the sensitive nerve endings.

Usually, her orgasms began as a lazy spiral that built with the rhythmic rocking of her body. His mouth was on her three shuddering breaths, and her spine snapped back, her head falling onto her shoulders, as a climax harder and more intense than the peak of the best orgasm she had ever experienced seized her body. She rocketed over a crest that she had never imagined could be so high. It occurred to her, a flash of a thought, that she might not survive the fall. She could have cared less.

He released the headboard and held her fast by the forearms when she would have toppled. His desire to protect made her forgive his disobedience, even though he took advantage of the moment to shove her harder against his mouth, his teeth scraping her shuddering, slick skin.

She screamed, too overcome to be self-conscious. She didn't even remember who Marcus was as she ground herself against Josh's face and felt each spasm jerk through her.

There was no finesse to it, just raw, fast response. She came down like an ejected pilot of an exploded plane, adrenaline still roiling through her veins, her heart pounding, fingers clenching and unclenching against her palms. She made soft, keening noises, her reaction to his mouth, tongue still busy with gentle lavings, soothing and stimulating all at once.

It was quite awhile before Lauren had the strength, or will, to slide back. She collapsed into his embrace, and her gaze fell on the imprints his fingers had left on her forearms. She noticed with puzzlement that her limbs were shaking, though she felt only muzzy languor.

The earth was shaking, not her. She tried to clear her hazy mind and realized that Lisette's house was rumbling on its foundations in sporadic bursts. Each tremor was preceded by a thud that sounded as if it were directly beneath them.

Passion cleared from Josh's eyes and he swore, amusing her by giving her a hard squeeze on the ass and an apologetic, desperate look before he rolled away. He snatched up his jeans and leaped out of the room, not a bad view all the way around. Lauren turned over, snagged her robe and followed him, more slowly, since the room was still tilting in a pleasant way. She was pleased to discover she could walk better this morning, though her slight limp and wobbling progress were no match for Josh's athletic strides.

The orchestrator of the morning's events, in an indirect way, was standing out on the deck, staring down. Lauren approached the living area just as Josh stepped out of the open sliding glass door, zipping up his jeans and buttoning them.

"She won't listen to me," Marcus informed him.

Marcus's gaze passed to Lauren as she came out. "You've got healthy lungs," he commented.

"Leave her be," Josh said, leaning over the rail. "Isabel? I'm right here. Look…look up - Isabel!"

Lauren blinked as an earsplitting trumpet sound vibrated along the boards beneath her feet. It sounded like an elephant. It couldn't be an elephant. She approached the edge of the deck. Marcus smiled at her, easing her discomfiture, and curled an arm about her waist to draw her forward.

She blinked. She was looking down at an elephant. A small, white elephant, but most definitely an elephant.

The elephant's crinkled dark eyes shifted to her and the creature made a curious crooning noise. Apparently she was much happier now that she could see Josh. With some alarm, Lauren realized the earthquake had been caused by his devotee pushing her head and considerable weight against the pilings of the house.

The bright sun and the reminder that he had other responsibilities, albeit in a form she would not have expected, returned her to reality. She needed to push off the effects of the mind-boggling orgasm and not make too much of it. She wouldn't push him. It had been a night of fun, was all, and now they all had things to do. His words this morning about continuing the game were probably just a case of male morning horniness.

"So," she propped her elbows on the wood and ignored the peculiar sinking feeling the idea gave her, "Are white elephants native to this island?"

Josh chuckled. "Here," he said, "You shouldn't be standing."

Lauren caught hold of his shoulders as he lifted her up to sit her on the wide railing. He kept his hand braced against her back, his fingers splayed over the curve of her hip, an automatic gesture to keep her safe that made her stomach flutter in emotional reaction. So much for casual. His posture put his body close to hers, so close she could still smell the scent of herself on his mouth.

"Isabel was in a movie," Josh said, looking down at the elephant, now stripping a six-foot sapling of leaves. "They injected dye into her skin to turn her white."

"I remember that movie," Lauren recalled. "That fantasy thing, like a Conan type...what was the name of it?"

Josh shrugged. "I don't see many movies. Regardless, when the movie was over, they didn't need her anymore." A shadow crossed his face. "The dye poisoned her blood."

Lauren, dismayed, looked back down at the elephant. Even while eating, Isabel kept one eye on Josh. The eye, clear and bright, nevertheless possessed that ancient look of wisdom and mystery that pachyderms have, a reminder of their existence on the planet significantly earlier than humans.

"They think she has a couple years before organs start shutting down and she'll be in pain. They were going to go ahead and put her down. I was in a position to take her, and so I brought her here, on a barge."

He shrugged. "She likes to know where I am. I forgot to tell her I wouldn't be in the usual places. Of course," he smiled at Lauren in an open, affectionate way that erased some of her tensions, "I didn't know I was going to end up staying here at the command of a beautiful woman."

Lauren looked over the edge, pleased to feel his grip on her tighten. "Seems to me," she observed, "That you're at the command of two women. And one of us just decided Lisette's banana plants are fair game."

"Hey!" Josh called out sharply. "Isabel, no! Ah…son of a—" with another apologetic look, he scooped Lauren off her seat on the rail and set her down on the bench in a move so effortless it caught her breath. He took the rail himself, swung out to the tree she had used for her descent the day before, and shimmied down the trunk.

Marcus chuckled and set down his coffee cup. "So, beautiful lady, what's your pleasure today? We can leave you to your own devices, to hobble around the house as best you may, or we can take you on our adventures."

The idea of being stranded in Lisette's house held little appeal. Lauren overlooked the fact that she had intended to do just that, nurse her hurts and wallow in dejected solitude for the weekend. Of course, she had put a more positive spin on it than that when she got in the boat yesterday.

Still, she hesitated to answer. Where did the events of the past half hour leave them? *Did* they just shrug it off, resume their separate schedules, or was there something happening other than a night of sex games?

Stop being a moron. She had never been a woman to doubt her own appeal to the opposite sex. She knew when attraction was there and when it wasn't. A D/s relationship did not evolve this quickly unless strong desire was driving it. She put a hand on her fluttering stomach. Strong might be an understatement for what she was feeling for Josh. She was shielding herself precisely because she sensed there was far more than the physical involved. She was being a coward.

"I'd love to go with you," she admitted. "But you're not here to entertain me. I don't want to impose. After all, you took care of me all afternoon and evening." Her cheeks flushed at the double meaning of that remark.

"True," Marcus quirked a brow at her expression, and laid his hand over where Josh's had been on her waist, increasing the heat that lingered there. "This morning Josh planned a swim for eight a.m. You've put him behind schedule already."

Lauren chuckled. "I intended to take a nap on the beach about one o'clock," Marcus continued, "after we checked in to see how the Salerno's hot water heater is doing. We installed it earlier this week. After that, we usually go sit up on the Knoll, the highest part of the island. Josh brings a book and I do some wishful amateur sketches. We go through a six-pack of Heineken while we watch the sun go down over the waves. And that would be the end of one of our busier days. So you see," he ran his knuckles down the side of her face in an easy, affectionate gesture, "we asked because we like playing with you, and we don't want playtime to be over. I would have expected Josh to tell you that, first thing this morning," he lifted a brow, "but perhaps his mouth was otherwise occupied."

Lauren punched his stomach. "Worm."

"Regardless," he caught her fist, raised it to his lips, "We're three children on a deserted island, and we've designated you queen. Josh wants you to keep holding the High Card as long as you wish to play."

"It doesn't feel like a game to me, Marcus," Lauren said, loosing her hand from his grasp and hooking her fingers under her legs. The rough wood of the bench rasped against her skin. "Sometimes it is just playing, and that's okay. But this doesn't feel that way." She drew a deep breath, let it out. "And I don't want it to be just a game. That sounds stupid, doesn't it? I just met him what, less than twenty-four hours ago."

"No. I'm glad to hear it." All teasing left Marcus's emerald eyes. "It's not a game to him, either. You're the first thing that's gotten a rise out of him, physically or emotionally, for months."

"You're putting a lot on me," she said, staring down at the subject of the discussion.

"I'm putting nothing on you," Marcus responded; with a trace of flint that jerked her attention back to him. "I'm trying to tell you as subtly as possible without abusing Josh's trust that you're dealing with someone who has locked himself in a cage, as if he's afraid he's a danger to others."

"So you won't tell me what happened to him?" she said.

He shook his head. "It's not my story to tell. And," he admitted, frustration tensing his angelic features, "he hasn't told me all of it. I know about his divorce, but something happened, something more. He was always very private about his life with Winona, everything, even sex, but I sensed something was wrong in that department, in a lot of departments. There was an unhealthy energy between them and…" Marcus stopped himself. "Regardless. Whatever happened, he's got it jammed up his ass like a railroad spike."

Lauren winced. "Visual."

Marcus lifted a shoulder. "I've got good intuition about people, Lauren. I have to know when a talented artist has more temperament than commitment. I have to know when one is close to the breaking point and needs breathing room, and when one needs stroking versus goading. I like you, very much. You're strong."

"We're all Sampson," she murmured. "Find our weakness and we'll shatter."

"Only if you happen to hook yourself up with Delilah, instead of the faithful and loving Ruth. On the other hand," the corner of his mouth tugged up, "Sometimes shattering is the best excuse to rebuild yourself on a better foundation."

He shrugged at the surprise on her face. "I think you and Josh have a gift to give to each other. It may be a small gift, just a step in the right direction, a couple days of simple pleasures and reminding each other what that feels like. Or, it may be a gift of life altering size. Either way, if you lose courage for it or the pleasure to pursue it, know what you're dealing with and don't crush him with your pain. I love Josh, very much. He is my friend, he is a brother, and he has a beautiful, intelligent spirit that is struggling to heal itself despite his best efforts keep the wounds open."

She nodded. Marcus's love for Josh as a friend, combined with his nature as a Master, would make him automatically protective. Hence, the frequent trips to the island to check on his well-being. She felt her regard for Marcus grow. Not all Masters were like that. But it was also the kind of Mistress she was.

"Marcus!" Josh called, holding onto Isabel's trunk like a harried parent trying to keep hold of a child on the verge of a tantrum. "Stop trying to impress Lauren with your jaded New Yorker routine and toss out a handful of peanuts."

"I'm actually trying to convince her that you would like her to spend the day with us, despite your dark, brooding personality. Perhaps you could take some pains to reassure her." Marcus shot her a look that seemed to say, "Ball's in your court, darling," and stepped back through the sliding glass door.

Lauren peered down as Isabel jerked Josh several feet sideways and he grunted, a sound of discomfort. "Everything okay down there?"

"Nothing that a 2x4 wouldn't cure," he muttered as she wrapped her trunk around his waist and whuffled at his palm, trying to get past him to the banana plants.

Lauren chuckled. "Doesn't she realize she could just stomp over you?"

Josh looked pained. "Now that you've told her."

Lauren giggled and a smile crossed his face, so shy and hopeful it wrenched her heart. "You will spend the day with us, won't you? I mean," he grimaced, "I'm sorry, Lauren. I'm sure you have your reasons for being here, and they don't necessarily include company. We shouldn't be—"

"Why don't you let me decide what you should and shouldn't do for me, Josh?" she said, her decision made in that moment.

She pitched her tone low, but her direct, imperious gaze made the implication clear. She felt the air between them heat and her lips curved. "Didn't we get that straight, earlier this morning?"

He gazed up at her. The shy smile was gone, but what replaced it was no less potent. "Yes, you did," he murmured.

She nodded, and lifted an eyebrow.

"Well, then," he played with Isabel's trunk and slanted a look up at her, the expression of a mischievous boy. "If it pleases you, I'd very much like it if you joined us today."

"It pleases me," she said, and let it be at that.

Chapter 11

While she cleaned up and changed, Marcus put together a packed lunch. Josh left them to go to his home and get the two men a change of clothes, which she discovered meant a pair of clean cut-off shorts and an extra shirt in case the day turned colder.

Gauging the day and where they might go, she changed into a sapphire blue bikini and a pair of shorts. She had expected to be quite alone on the island, and so the bikini allowed for maximum tanning area. She didn't care to bake bronze like some women did. She had no desire to resemble a Shar-pei pug by age forty. However, she did like to maintain a light golden coloring. The bikini top was a shelf bra style that raised her breasts up and together with padding beneath and on the sides. Besides displaying the generous rounded tops of her breasts and giving great play to their movement, the stretch of the garment molded over the jut of her nipples. The bikini's blue material had a sheen caused from sparkling threads in the weave, and was sheer enough that if a man tried to focus past the subdued glitter, he could see the dusky shadow of the aureoles. She expected at least one man would be trying.

Lauren brushed back her hair into a twisted chignon that exposed her delicate neck and would keep her cool. Right. Like that was possible with Josh around.

She put in a pair of silver hoops, and allowed herself the vanity of pale pink lipstick. She looked delicate; something a man would ache to touch. If she let him. Her lips curved. Therein lay the fun, seeing how long her mastery could hold out, how he would connive to get around it.

Playfulness mingled with healthy lust had never been part of her life with Jonathan. Was she rewriting history to help her heal? She frowned. Maybe, but there was more to it. Josh made it more.

Good God, she was beating this to death. She adjusted the strap to give her breasts an extra lift, turned from side to side to admire how the suit showcased them, and then headed up the hallway. Her ankle was feeling better, enough that she could give her hips a slight swing to offset the distraction of the limp.

Marcus lounged on the couch with a breakfast Bloody Mary. Josh sat restlessly on the counter, his bare feet just above the floor. His gray eyes ran over her soft pink lips, the exposed column of her throat, and down to her breasts. She managed to control a blush, just barely, as she felt the nipples peak against the material, a shiver of reaction that ran across the exposed tops of her breasts, down to the lower extremities beneath the shorts. His gaze seemed to follow her reaction, all the way down the lean muscles of her long thighs, to her toes, curling inside loose canvas sneakers with no laces. His eyes alighted on the ace bandage she had rewrapped.

His expression shifted from blatant male appreciation to a protective evaluation of her self-nursing. It caused an emotional tug on what lay beneath her breast, and that mental twinge plucked at the physical.

"So, I'm yours, gentlemen," she managed, looking between them. "Where do we go first?"

Josh slid off the counter and came toward her as Marcus gave a mysterious grin and slipped out the back door, Bloody Mary still in hand.

Lauren's gaze shifted to make her own thorough appraisal as Josh approached. She appreciated to the point of an audible purr the bare chest, the way the shorts cradled his half erect cock, the way the waistband of his cut off shorts slid along his deltoids, much the way she might like to slide her hands over them. She tilted her head back as he got to her, and gave him a raised brow and slight smile.

"You wore that swimsuit to torture me," he accused.

"Did I?" she arched her brow higher, considering, then nodded. "Maybe I did. Maybe I want you to be hard for me. Are you hard for me, Josh?" She kept her eyes on his, but as he leaned forward, she leaned back.

"That wasn't an answer, Josh," she reproved gently. "Put your hand on your cock, over your jeans, and show me how hard you are."

"Lauren," he said, a flush creeping up his neck.

She took another step back. "Do I hold the cards or not, Josh?" she asked. "Show me," she murmured. "I want to know how hard looking at my breasts makes you."

He swallowed and then, with a quick look toward the door, lowered his hand and cupped himself. Lauren followed the line of sight and smiled at the outline of his bulging groin cradled in his hand. The discomfort of it crept higher up his neck. She stepped closer to him, marveling at how much taller he was than she, how much more physically powerful.

She put her one hand behind his neck and her other hand over his on the source of his discomfort, keeping it there as she raised up on her toes. She pressed her breasts into his chest, shifting slightly to ensure the stiffened nipples would drag over his skin, and kissed him, a light brushing of lips, a brief touch of her tongue to his teeth. His other hand rose to her hip and held there, an anchor against the need that quivered through his muscles and communicated how much he ached to use that power advantage to crush her to him. But he didn't.

"I'm glad you wanted me to be with you today," she said, needing to give something to him. She needed to let him know she wanted him, too, to keep his discontent based in banked lust and not the brooding unhappiness that seemed to be waiting, simmering behind his extraordinarily beautiful eyes. "Show me your island."

He raised his hand, his fingers twitching once as they passed the side of her breast, but he kept the movement going until he rested his knuckles along her cheekbone, a feather of contact. She tilted her head toward the touch, then caught her breath as he scooped her up, taking her off her feet.

"You might get tired, transporting me this way," she teased, proud that her voice cracked only on the first note before she regained her composure. "I'm really fine to walk, just not fast."

"Not as far as we're going." He took her out the back door and down the steps. "We've got you a ride."

The light fresh breeze of morning in the islands touched her skin, bringing her the smell and sound of the ocean. Sunlight filtered over the tree tops, lighting the activities of the many island bird species. It was going to be a beautiful day, and her heart swelled with hope for new beginnings, cleansing, and forgiveness. Her grip tightened on Josh's neck, reflecting the sudden constriction in her throat, her reaction to the abrupt touch of happiness.

They turned the corner, and Lauren saw Marcus standing with Isabel. An oversized beach towel had been doubled and laid across the white elephant's shoulders to form a sitting area. Lauren grinned with pure delight, a reaction that dimmed somewhat as Josh carried her toward the elephant. Isabel eyed Lauren with at least a degree of the apprehension Lauren was beginning to feel as they approached and Isabel's much greater size became apparent.

"Now," Josh said smoothly, "she's a lot like a New York taxi driver. You can tell her where you want to go, and she'll eventually get you there, but she may take the circuitous route to get a better fare."

They reached the elephant and Lauren shrank back against Josh as the large pachyderm raised her head to give her a better inspection.

"Isabel, this is Lauren," Josh said seriously. "I'm supposed to take care of her, which means you have to help me."

"Josh, I don't know — "

"It's okay, Lauren," he looked down at her, tightened his hold. "You can trust Isabel."

He held her gaze for a moment more, and Lauren felt an unexpected peace steal through her. He wouldn't let anything hurt her. It was a dangerous, naive thought, one she was far too experienced to be having, but there it was, filling her, calming her.

Marcus stepped on Isabel's offered knee and swung up. Josh set Lauren with her weight on her one good foot on the elephant's provided step. He set his shoulder behind her knee, told her to reach up to Marcus, and then he laid his hand on her thigh, pressed on it to get her to sit on his shoulder. He straightened, and a gasp and a moment of weightlessness and she was there, seated before Marcus.

Josh swung up in front of her, ready with a peanut as Isabel lifted her trunk up to him to retrieve the expected treat.

"If it pleases the lovely lady," Marcus observed, "we might go to the beach first. Mornings are the best swimming times."

"It pleases me," Lauren agreed, running a fingertip along Josh's bare spine and enjoying the reaction of goose pimples along his flesh.

God, she had locked down her hormones for nearly a year, since Jonathan, and now she couldn't keep her hands off this man. Maria had warned her that celibacy for one of her sexual nature would result in an explosion of "felonious proportions". Lauren had laughed at her, until now.

However, Josh didn't appear to be objecting to her attentions. She recalled with a flush of heat the impressive evidence beneath her hand, matched by the heated steel of his eyes.

"Beach, Isabel," Josh requested. The elephant agreeably started down the steep drive to Lisette's home. Lauren laid her hands on Josh's waist just above the line of his jeans and observed that she had an excellent view of his ass because of the way they rode low on his hips. Definitely not the gross exhibitionism of an overweight plumber. More like the provocatively loose "modesty" drape around the hips of a young Roman god.

Isabel reached the bottom of the drive, but instead of continuing down the slope, she went right and onto a narrow trail that began to climb upward.

Josh's shoulders lifted in a sigh. "New York taxi driver," he reminded Lauren.

"I almost prefer her to take the circuitous route," Marcus chuckled.

His voice came from somewhere below her, rather than under her ear as she expected. Lauren twisted about to see him lying on his back, his long legs bent and swinging just behind hers to keep his balance. Lauren considered the way his posture strained the twill of his shorts over his groin and then, in the leisurely manner of a true sensualist, let her eyes graze up the equally appreciable ground of his bare, muscular chest. He was bronzed, not quite as dark as Josh, but still a nice compliment to his dark silky waves of hair.

He glanced down the line of his body at her, making it clear he knew what she had been doing, and grinned. He extended a hand. "Come down here. See why Isabel is smarter than the rest of us."

Lauren agreeably lay back; letting his hands on her shoulders guide her. She giggled as he snorted, caught her under her armpits and hauled her back about half a foot. "It may feel like a comfortable cushion at the moment," he said sternly, "But that's not the best place for your hard head. It makes a better neck rest."

Lauren nestled the back of her skull into the lower part of his abdomen, still smiling. She settled her hands on the armrests his thighs provided and followed the direction of his pointed finger.

A canopy of vines stemmed with broad leaves wove above her in various shades of green, from mint to a rich dark color that was almost grape. Spreading branches displayed splashes of color, the exotic blooms of a jungle environment. The rising sun sent streaks of light through the foliage to illuminate the pockets of light morning mist in the close air of the forest. One moment the early breeze shivered across her skin, and a breath later, a sunbeam stroked it away.

There was noise. No, that was wrong. Noise meant chaos, jobs, streets, cars, and too many people, all wanting something. This was a rhythm, like the movement of waves, a serene pattern expressed audibly, in the conferences of birds, the rustle of the tree dwellers, creatures foraging and chattering. Beneath the sounds, there was a hush, a cavern of noiselessness that Lauren associated with a Presence, something that lived quietly in Nature, but spoke only through its creatures.

It was like being in a church, she realized. It was spiritual.

"Come down here," she reached for Josh. He obliged, adjusting forward, so when he lay back between her spread thighs, his head rested just below her breasts. His hands, like hers with Marcus, slid down to rest on her thighs for stability. The base of his neck pressed against her crotch, and that pressure sent a pleasurable spiral through her belly beneath his head. She raised one hand from Marcus's leg and laid it on Josh's shoulder, stroking his hair and the side of his throat as Marcus did much the same to her. Marcus was a true Dom, assuming all within range of his fingers were subject to his fondling, but she wasn't complaining. He would have made a good sheik, she'd warrant. She liked the feel of his long fingers stroking her hair. She ran her knuckles along the ridge of Josh's shoulder, drew a circle on his pectoral, idly traced his jugular. It pleased her when he raised his chin to give her better access. She kept up the motion, all the while looking up at the world above them. It was a world that existed without self-analysis, falling into a natural pattern without question of that pattern, of the wrong and right of it. It was much how this felt, the three of them together, part of it, and at least for the moment, Lauren knew peace.

Chapter 12

ঞ

Isabel eventually decided to turn and head down from the higher elevations of the island. Lauren sat up at Josh's urging when they reached a clear spot, in order to see the panorama of ocean stretching out below them, the sun glittering off the waves.

Lauren slid her hands around him and scooted up close, outlining his hips and thighs with the lengths of her own. She was gratified when he laid his hands over hers on his chest and tugged her a bit closer, so her breasts were shelved against his bare back.

"Wow," she said, of the view before them.

His fingers tightened over hers and he nodded.

The ocean stretched below them, the perfect blue of postcards but even more vibrant. Its white foam was the same crystal sparkle as snow. As her eyes traveled to the horizon, the green-blue glass darkened into turquoise, sparkling in a dazzling tapestry of light, paying homage to the sun. It was perfection in the way only Nature could pull it off. The air brought her the smell of brine and seaweed, contributing to the view's arresting impact.

"Makes you wish they had never eaten that damned apple, doesn't it?" Josh murmured.

She pressed her chin to the point of his shoulder. "Do you believe that story?" she asked.

He lifted her head with a shrug.

"Sounds just like us," he said.

Lauren couldn't help but agree. Unable to accept Eden, man had to delve into its one place of darkness and try to prove his mastery.

She spent a great deal of time analyzing the art forms of power. She had learned that domination could and did sculpt the factors within one's control for pleasure, but mutual pleasure was the ultimate prize. If done right, the Master or Mistress reached a point where he or she could let go, and magic took over. Then there was no more need for games or thinking, just simple existence. That had been the miracle God gave Adam and Eve in Eden, dominion as a gift, not a tool.

"It makes a person feel…so small," she said. He brushed her cheek with his jaw.

"But in a good way," he echoed her feelings. "Like there's nothing you've done that can't be fixed."

"Or forgiven."

"Or healed," Marcus suggested. Lauren twisted to see him sitting up, his arms braced against Isabel's rump to prop him while he watched their interplay with as much aesthetic appreciation as Lauren had displayed when gazing at the view before her. "I brought sand buckets, by the way."

He had the face of an angel and the mind of Lucifer, she decided, with a quick grin. "Plastic shovels too, I hope."

"Of course. No trip to the beach is complete without them."

Lauren turned back and squeezed Josh to her, pressing her palms over his rock hard abdomen. He worked his fingers around one of her hands to lift it and surprised her with a tender nip on her knuckles. The moment needed nothing more.

Isabel raised her head and trumpeted as they gained the beach, like a bus driver announcing a stop. Marcus slid off first and Lauren slid down into his grasp, holding onto Josh's forearm and bringing her knee back over the elephant's back. Once having her, however, Marcus did not put her down, instead tossing her over his shoulder in a fireman's carry with surprising strength. He clasped his arms over her thighs to keep her struggling body in place as he backpedaled.

"Got to catch me to get her back, Josh," he cheerfully challenged the man still up on the elephant.

He pivoted and took off, more bloody quick on his feet than a New York art dealer had the right to be, proving he hadn't lost his Iowa farm boy roots, though an Iowa farm boy would have given her an advantage by wearing underwear. She could have caught the elastic under the loose, twisting waistband of his jeans and yanked the fabric up to constrict his balls and make it a more uncomfortable run.

Even without her sabotage attempt, Josh's long legs and athletic build, and the extra weight Marcus was carrying, were eating up the ground between them. Rescue was imminent; though she was laughing so hard she was afraid that would do her in first. Then Marcus feinted right and heaved her into the air. Lauren had time for a short scream before she landed with a resounding splash in a crashing breaker. The two men dived under it on either side of her.

She surfaced, snorting water and chuckles, and pounced on Marcus as he emerged, shoving him back under. His hands gripped at her swimsuit and she shrieked and twisted away, but not before he got hold of the back of her and, in a deft move, unhooked the fastening.

Lauren spun away from him, and backed into Josh. He caught her about the waist, not realizing her predicament, and his knuckles beneath the water grazed the bare undercurves of her breasts. His touch stilled and Lauren stopped breathing, stopped moving, waiting to see what he would do.

His hands left her rib cage, moved upward. She felt their movement by the flow of the water, like fish gliding around her, just above the surface of her skin. He found the floating fabric of her bikini top, while his cheek pressed against her temple. Lauren leaned back against him as he pulled the fabric back down, fitting it into place by light, maddening touches on the sides of her breasts. His grip slid to where the two portions of the clasping straps came out of the triangles and he pulled them around her, nudging her forward, and re-hooked the suit at the center of her back. His fingers lingered there, on the sensitive indentation of spine.

"Now, Josh," Marcus winked at her. "She might be a European girl. You never gave her a choice."

Lauren splashed at him and moved away from them both, turning so she could float on her back in the water. "This is incredible," she murmured, trying to take her mind off the raging inside her body and the unsettling mystery of the man causing it. "How can you bear to go back to New York, Marcus?"

"I use this place as my reward for good behavior. And since I am rarely good," he tugged on her foot and she kicked playfully at him, "I don't deserve to be here for more than a short time anyhow. However, keep in mind, dear heart, that one man's Eden," his gaze flicked to Josh, "is another man's self-imposed Purgatory."

"Surf with me until we're hungry enough for lunch," Lauren said, not wanting the shadow that crossed Josh's face to linger. "And no adult thoughts," she decided, shooting Marcus an emphatic look. "You're six, I'm seven, and Josh is five. We have no responsibilities, no past, no history, no baggage. If we had any white sunblock, I'd paint it on all our noses."

"And there are so many other fun places to put it," Marcus chided. At her quelling look, he grinned. "I'm a rather mature six year old. Do we get to make sand castles?"

"Absolutely." She dove into the next wave and then swam away from them like a dolphin. Her ankle still hurt, but in the buoyancy of the water, she felt unencumbered by the injury and more certain of herself. She spent the next hour playing tag, dodging under waves and enjoying impromptu splash fights until her ploy succeeded and they were all three laughing, red-eyed and relaxed as children in truth. Even the sexual tension melted away before the joy of pure play.

She couldn't outlast their energy, though, so when she was doing more floating than swimming, Marcus made the suggestion they retreat to the beach and open their picnic basket. Two wet men, bronzed and muscled in shorts plastered to their bodies, made an agreeable escort to shore. Per her request, they let her limp, testing the strength of the ankle, but they stayed close. Their readiness to catch her if she toppled one way or the other both amused and touched her.

Marcus had pulled the blanket from Isabel's back before she wandered back into the forest on more elephantine pursuits. Now he spread it out to form a table for bread, cheese, wine and grapes. There did not seem much need for conversation, all of them wet and panting from their exertions in the water, so they ate, gazing out to the sea with their own thoughts for awhile, and listening to the random cries of the few seabirds keeping them company on the beach. Lauren reflected that she had not felt so relaxed in a long time, and watched idly as Josh picked up a handful of dry sand and let it trickle over her calf, following its progress until he had created a small cone leaning against the relaxed calf muscle.

Marcus's attention was drawn to it as well, and a light came to his eyes that Lauren was beginning to anticipate, with a mixture of delight and trepidation.

"I'm ready to build a sandcastle now," he announced, taking a swallow of wine.

"Mmm." Her eyes were half closed behind her sunglasses as she turned her head to look at him. They had let the blanket be the table, but she had passed on the folding beach chair he had brought in a duffel bag. Instead, she lay stretched out comfortably on the sand, wiggling until its hills and valleys supported her concave points comfortably. "I'm taking a nap."

"Excellent." He rummaged in the bag and produced a large purple plastic sand bucket with a bright yellow handle. Lauren chuckled. "One of Lisette's?"

"No, my dear girl. I bought it at one of those tacky little beach places before I came across. You can't be at the beach without a sand bucket."

"You know," she said, "They have those molds now that are shaped like castles."

Marcus made a horrified face. "Cheating. As blasphemous as copying the Mona Lisa. Every work must be an original to be called art. It's like re-creating a movie or song someone else has made famous. I have more respect for an original piece of crap than I do for someone trying to ride on the coattails of someone else's success. At least they made an effort to create rather than being an artistic copy machine. It's just re-manufacturing, piggybacking the genius of the original artist. Parasitic art industry, not worth our notice."

He stomped toward the ocean.

"You know, he should open up more," she commented. "Express how he really feels."

Josh chuckled somewhere to Lauren's right. "I keep telling him that."

Lauren slanted him a glance over her glasses and grinned. "But not everyone can be as talkative as you are."

"Exactly."

"Here we are," Marcus returned with a bucket sloshing seawater. As he placed it on the sand, Lauren saw the bucket was a half-and-half mix of sand and water. Her scrutiny turned to wariness as Marcus dropped to his knees beside her.

"You said I could make a sand castle," he reminded her. "I'm partial to drip castles."

Lauren caught on and scrambled to a sitting position. "Oh no," she shook her head. "You'll get my swimsuit all nasty."

"So take it off."

The trap closed with an audible snick, reflected in the devilish challenge in his eyes. Lauren glanced at Josh. She couldn't see his thoughts behind his sunglasses and she reached over, drew them off with both hands so her fingers brushed the soft hair at his temples. His gray eyes were almost as opaque as the lenses. "Do you like to make drip castles, too?" she asked, eyebrow raised.

"I'm developing an interest."

The warm breeze from land whispered up the column of her spine, lifting her hair off her neck and spilling it forward, over her breast. His eye followed it, and her nipple tightened at his regard, hardening and lifting further at the responsive darkening around the pupil.

Lauren drew in a breath and looked out at the sea, that blissful scenic reminder that she was in a different place, could be whoever or whatever she wanted to be here. She didn't have to be afraid. After all, she was the one holding the cards. They had both said so.

"Okay," she said. "But you better not let me get sunburned."

Marcus chuckled and lifted her hair, giving her hands the freedom to work off the tie at the neck. "Believe me, dearest, I'm sure neither one of us wants to slick your bare body down with aloe vera gel at the end of the day."

"Mm-hmm," she said dryly. "Just keep in mind how much fun it will be, oiling me down while I'm screaming, 'Ouch!', 'stop that', 'No! Don't touch there!'" She felt Josh's hand on her back, unfastening the strap, and shivered as his fingers touched her skin.

She closed her hand on the front of the swimsuit as it came loose, but only to deliberately pull it away from her body and rise.

"If you'll allow me," Josh nodded at her bikini bottoms and shorts from his kneeled position. "I can take those off so you won't have to put so much weight on your other ankle."

Lauren pivoted partially toward him, to study his face and to give him her profile, her raised chin, the curve of her throat, the sun gleaming on the spherical surface of one bare breast. She nodded her permission.

He stood up on his knees, which brought him just above eye level with her chest, so close that his breath touched that bare breast and rippled across the skin, raising the fine hairs on it. He gazed at her breasts a moment, unmoving, content to look with silent, obvious pleasure at their weight and shape. His attention slid along the outer curve of the right one, from where it began its crescent just at her armpit, down to its fullest point, resting on her rib cage, the dark mauve nipple full and soft as a pussy willow bloom.

"You're beautiful."

"Mistress."

Lauren looked over at Marcus, startled by the serious, slightly stern tone. He squatted behind her, and cocked his head. "You should call her Mistress, Josh. As long as she holds the cards, that's what she is to you, until she gives you permission to do otherwise."

It was another step, and she waited, seeing if Josh would take it. She was fascinated by the myriad of thoughts moving behind his eyes. It was even more intriguing to see that Marcus's words affected him in a manner she could discern. His erection, already noticeably swelling behind his zipper when she had removed the top, was now full and tight, straining against the constriction of the wet jean shorts.

Her eyes lifted back to his face, and the flush on his neck. He swallowed. "You're beautiful, Mistress."

It was the most natural thing in the world to reach out and fondle his jaw, and push a lock of his hair back behind his ear, which of course made an interesting spectacle of her breasts before his avid gaze. She could almost see saliva gathering in the corners of his mouth with the desire to taste them.

"My swimsuit, Josh," she reminded him gently. "I'm waiting."

He tore his gaze away and put his hands to the waistband. He was able to easily slide his fingers over her bare hipbones and slide the clothes over her backside. He could have let them drop to the sand unaided at a certain point, but he took them down, a smart man who took advantage of the opportunity. He managed a light brush of her clitoris through the crotch of the damp swimsuit, smoothed his palms down her slim thighs and calves, caressed her ankles, even the bottom of her feet as she stepped out of the shorts, aided by Marcus's steadying hold on her waist.

His eyes lifted, taking a leisurely amount of time. His gaze was a warmer caress on her body than the wind at her back. When his face did rise to where she could see his expression, she was jolted by the combination of fierce hunger and pleading submission there. It almost broke her. Almost. It would have if Marcus had not been there, a steady third party influence that helped her get a grip.

She wanted to twist the rubber band a bit tighter. Balanced equally with the lust in her own body was the desire to prolong his, to draw it out to the point of explosion. What would it be like to get him so visually excited that she could whisper softly, "Come for me", and watch his body explode without any stimulation other than her cool command?

God, the idea sent a flood into the channel between her legs and made them tremble beneath his hands. She needed to lie down, now, before her need trickled down over his fingers and gave her away.

When she bent her knees to do just that, he guided her down to her back, his hands at once caressing and protective.

Despite feminist protestations of self-sufficiency, she could still be melted by a man who obviously considered it a point of honor to protect a woman, keep her from harm. The gesture of respect and care, coming while she was completely stripped, added a level of eroticism to it that weighted her down. She was unable to do more than just lay still, reclined under their attention and intent. She was content to watch the fire in Josh's eyes flare as Marcus scooped wet sand and ocean water into his palm and let it slide through his knuckles, just over her abdomen.

The impact of the first small crescent of sand was cold, and quivered through her, sweeping down her shoulders and raising goosebumps across her breasts. She remained still, watching Marcus. His brow furrowed in concentration as he increased the flow of sand to build up the dripcastle, covering her navel. He moved upward, increasing its coverage along her rib cage. Some of it slid down her waist in tiny rivulets of earth and ocean. Most stayed where he placed it, rough turrets of gleaming wet sand, a castle wrought by nothing but the movement of his fingers and the inclination of the sand and water itself as it came in contact with her flesh. There were flecks of glitter in the sand, so the sun made his creation gleam amid the hills and slopes of her body.

"May Josh play, m'lady?" Marcus asked absently, "Or must he just watch?"

Lauren pulled her gaze from his hands and looked over at the intent eyes the color of doves that were devouring every slight movement of her body in reaction to the sand. "He may play."

Josh reached over her, slipped his hand into the bucket. She watched his long brown fingers emerge, covered with dripping earth and sea water, and then hover over her hips. Her stomach drew in with her breath as he began to construct his own annex of the castle along the inside of her left hipbone.

"Your panting is ruining my work, my dear," Marcus whispered, as he leaned in and pretended to brush some sand from her temple. "Just close your eyes and relax. Let us enjoy you and this beautiful body of yours."

Lauren smiled and dipped her head in acknowledgment. She took one last deep breath, using it to pull the tension from her muscles and relax. She settled her head into the indentation of soft sand behind her, and closed her eyes behind the sunglasses. It took some effort, but she was a

Mistress after all, and knew the rewards of control. She was just out of practice. She shifted her focus to the lazy flow of sand and water across her skin, rather than the eroticism of how it was being placed there.

The sun warmed her where the damp sand did not cover, and because of the contrast, she felt every new addition to the foundation of her body. When her eyes opened to slits, Marcus was building a crescent of turrets along the undercurve of her breasts, trailing water down her sternum. Josh worked his way across to the other hipbone, and formed a triangular city, the three corners being her hipbones and her shaved mound. She knew, with his head bent close in concentration on his work, he must be able to smell her arousal, and see the cold slide of sand and salt water over her swollen clitoris. Her thighs trembled once, but for what reason, or for all reasons, she did not know.

She watched how Josh's hand moved, his fingers twitching in the same gesture they would have made if he were manipulating the labia in tortuous friction against the clitoris. His range moved from one thigh, back to the other, wrist dipping and twisting as gracefully as a dancer. Each passage across the channel of her thighs received a touch from the medium in his hands. She was so mesmerized by his intense concentration that she barely noticed when Marcus sat back to watch with her.

The cool touch of wet sand, its soft plop of impact against her enervated skin, began to set off a spasmodic reaction. Her muscles leaped at each touch, despite her willing them not to move. The sand's impact acted upon them like the charge of a small electrode.

The desire to part her thighs was beginning to climb into her belly. She wanted to let the cool waterfall patter upon her slick parts, but at the same time she did not want to interrupt his concentration. She was absorbed by his intent expression, the tension of his bottom lip, caught in his teeth. It stretched his skin across his face, further defined the high cheekbones, the straight nose.

He was so beautiful, so gentle, and yet at the same time he contained a dangerous, explosive sexual power. She felt like stirring the water, to see if she could tease the beast to lunging for her.

"You need a better view of what he's doing," Marcus said. "Here." He moved behind her and lifted her up by the shoulders, sliding his knees and thighs under her shoulder blades. It propped her up in a shallow, comfortable angle that did not disturb the work he had done on her abdomen and breasts, but permitted her a three dimensional view of Josh's efforts.

It was not a castle, as she had thought. Josh's work had produced thin spirals that curled along her thighs and pubic bone in intricate, non-touching designs that reminded her of a henna paste. His artistry had a Celtic flavor, twining, curling, and flaring. He had framed her sex as the central piece of his design, and the continuous touch of water had kept the clitoral lips glistening and erect, and made it appear as if a delicate, half-open flower bulb was the centerpiece of the work

He had not spoken or even looked at her face since he had placed his hand in the bucket, but Lauren did not feel ignored. His awareness of her was as immediate as the touch of the sand and sea. He was paying silent homage to her, wooing her, worshipping her and her sex with his artwork.

He stopped, staring at his work. She swallowed, but before she could speak, he leaned forward and placed his warm lips against the cold ones of her pussy. She felt the electrical charge of the contact jolt to her toes and prickle the hair on her skull, though he merely laid his mouth against her skin. The kiss was as chaste and reverent as any laid by a knight upon the pale knuckles of his chosen lady.

His eyelids lifted, but his lips stayed upon her as he met her gaze. As she watched him, he moved his mouth into a slow, sucking kiss, drawing the clitoris into his teeth, holding it up so she could see it. He flicked his tongue over it. Once, twice, three times. Her body arched, and a strangled moan came from her. He stopped, let it slide from the grasp of his teeth, and then breathed on her, the heat of his mouth washing over her quivering clit.

Lauren's hands gripped Marcus's knees. She could well imagine that tongue inserting itself in her vagina, the broad part of it unfurling and giving her pussy a long, slow, and thorough lick from back to top. She moaned as his breath rippled over her again, pounding the image into her mind, and she caught hold of her land sliding control with her fingernails, cutting into Marcus's flesh.

"Stand up," she managed.

Now the bitter fight for control shifted. Her tension increased, seeing in his expression a struggle with the powerful desire to override her command and simply plunge his mouth into her. He could take control and lead her where he wanted to go. They both knew it. At this moment, with his mouth on her, she had no power to stop him.

Perhaps Marcus might have spoken, and helped her take back the reins, but this moment was between the two of them, and she had the right to make the call. Lauren's breath clogged in her throat and while she could not say what hung in the balance, she knew it was important, a vital moment on which everything else might pivot.

Josh's eyes shifted away at last, his broad shoulders rising and falling in one shuddering breath that, thankfully, was no longer directly over her clitoris. Otherwise, the force of it might have pushed her to orgasm.

Lauren drew a slow, steadying breath of her own as he got to his feet. The leg openings of his cut off shorts had pulled up, exposing his thighs almost to where they joined to his hips, due to the size of his stiff cock. She could see the shadowed curve of one testicle behind the pale fringe.

"Take them off," she murmured. "And make yourself come. Finish your sculpture."

Marcus's hands convulsed against her shoulders, and she knew she had pleased them both. She felt her strength of will return, despite the strident pulse of need from between her thighs. She channeled it in the way she had once known how to do automatically, and used the power of the lust to drive them all.

"Do it, Josh," she whispered. "I want to see you do it over me. You can't imagine how much it makes me want you to fuck me."

His neck and chest were flushed in embarrassment, his eyes shifting like a nervous animal's. He gave her a half glance, a strangled chuckle. "Well, I'd be happy to do *that*, Mistress."

"I know you would. I can see you would." Her gaze roamed downward, caressed him with a heated glance that made him groan. "But it's not time yet, and you must obey me, mustn't you?"

Her eyes lifted back to his face, her brow arched. She knew the look she was giving him. There was a mixture of tenderness, and implacable sternness that clearly said, <u>you will do what I say, and you will trust me.</u>

The look was successful only if it was genuine, and if the foundation to trust the Mistress had been firmly planted in the sub. In the real world, it was too soon to establish a moment as intimate as this. Lauren was going on faith, and the extraordinary strength of the attraction she had felt between them from the beginning. Whether it was the fantastical setting, Marcus's facilitation, or something else, something too good to hope for or think about at this moment, it did not matter. Some moments were spoiled by analysis. She simply held his gaze, waiting.

Josh swallowed, nodded, and unbuttoned the jeans. He slid them down over his hips. His cock bounced free of the restraint of his clothes, enormous in its torment, full to bursting. Lauren shivered at just a thought of what a hot stream from it would feel like on her skin. His gaze followed the quiver, resting on her open pussy and she parted her thighs slightly, giving him more.

"Fuck yourself for me, Josh," she said. "Use your hand and imagine it's my pussy stroking you. But," his gaze flicked back up at her sharp tone, "You better ask my permission before you come."

God, she could barely breathe from the erotic sensation of her power over him. The surf roared and sparkled behind Josh, silhouetting his naked, tanned body. The miles of white sand stretched around them, and the palm trees rustled like feathers over skin. His long hair fluttered over his broad shoulders. His mouth was tight with craven need for her, and horrible shyness. He was so...everything.

She tilted her hips, so his uncertain eye was drawn again to how much she wanted him, cherished him. She wanted to see him spurt over her in a moment of wild absorption, lacing the beautiful sculpture he had done on her pelvis with further proof of his devotion to her.

"Come closer, down on your knees," she commanded, and spread her thighs to let him fit between them, giving his avid gaze a full view. "No, don't put your ass on your heels. I want you standing on your knees as long as they'll hold you." A wicked grin crossed her face, though the corners of her lips trembled with something more feral.

He had gorgeous thighs, muscular from outdoor work. His right calf had a serpent dragon coiled from ankle to knee. From the tender joining crease of pelvis to mid-thigh, a tattoo of a sword had been stenciled. The jeweled hilt was drawn just below his hipbone. A latticework of ivy and pale gold flowers twined around the blade, and at its point the greenery twined into a tight vee that curled up into a dime-sized upright pentagram, a symbol of the elements and protection, which anchored the work on the inside of the thigh, just below the heavy nest of testicles.

Once again, though the work was beautiful, she wondered at the artist who had not recognized perfection when it was plain before their eyes, needing nothing to adorn it. Her lips curved. If it were up to her, and at least for this weekend, it seemed to be, she would have him walk around naked all the time to admire.

He had a fine silken triangle of dark sable around his standing cock that she would dearly love to run her fingers through. But later. For now, she held herself still, and watched.

Marcus had slid out his legs on either side of her so now she was cradled between his thighs. She felt his blatant, impressive reaction pressed against her lower back. Lauren reached up a hand and pressed it to his jaw, and smiled at the absent brush of lips against her pulse, with a hint of teeth, but her eyes did not leave Josh. She was sure his did not, either.

"You let him touch you easy enough," Josh growled, desperation behind the snarl. "When I could touch you and mean it."

His words shot pure fire through her vitals, but she kept her expression cruelly bland. "Put your eyes on my pussy, Josh," she said. "Don't take your eyes off it. I want you to watch it grow wetter with every stroke of your hand on yourself, watch it drip on the sand, all for you."

He groaned. She knew he was not aware that his hand began to rub his shaft as she spoke, primitive instincts overriding the mind's embarrassment. She knew because he jerked, startled, when he realized it, but at her encouraging murmur, his hand settled to its work. That loose curl of fingers that showed how well men knew their bodies, just as women knew their own, the right pressure to stimulate themselves to orgasm. The pressure up his length that pushed the loose skin forward, creating friction against the velvet steel beneath. It worked his hips forward and made his breath quicken, get more harsh. Clear fluid collected on the tip of his cock and a drop fell, landing on the sand design, then another, this one landing on her clit, a tiny kiss that made the flesh quiver.

Marcus's hands moved, cupped the outside of her breasts, pushing them together so the drip castle he created tumbled in on itself. He spread the sand across her skin, rubbing the grit gently into her nipples, the rough texture stiffening them further. Josh's eyes flicked up to them, his tongue coming out to wet his lips.

"Stop," she snapped, albeit a bit breathlessly.

His hand froze on his cock, quivering with its longing to continue, his body vibrating. He was so close; she could feel it like a heavy haze in the air, the stillness before an explosion.

"Where is your gaze supposed to be, Josh?"

He dropped his attention to its proper place, while beads of sweat rolled down his shoulders.

"Tell me."

"Your pussy," he said hoarsely.

"You disobeyed me, Josh." A soft smile curved her face as Marcus continued to knead, cup and lift her breasts like water. She allowed herself a little mewl of pleasure at the sensation and wiggled her ass in the sand. She chuckled softly at the rumble of frustration, almost a whimper, from her submissive. "If you don't do it again, I will forgive you and let you continue. Will you do it again?"

"No, Mistress. Fuck it, no." There was a primitive fervency in his voice that made it rough as gravel. "You're just so beautiful."

"Then you are forgiven," she purred. "Continue. And I don't need to remind you that you need to ask before you let that bad boy go over."

"No, Mistress."

"Then keep going. You are the beautiful one, Josh," she added quietly, with fierce sincerity as she watched his intent features, the renewed movement of his hand. "You cannot imagine how watching you do this makes me feel. You'd drown in how wet I am. I'm adding to your sculpture already, aren't I?"

His head bobbed once, a jerk, and his breath hitched.

She loved it, loved bringing him to the edge of control with nothing but words and the sight of her spread, aching center. She could have offered Jonathan this, if only he had wanted it. Her vision faltered and for a moment she was uncertain again, almost self-conscious, then she heard him moan.

"Please, Mistress…I need to…"

She used his need as her rope, and pulled herself out of that quagmire.

"Ask me, Josh," and she trembled with the anticipation of it, every vibrating nerve ending screaming at her to unsnap the leash.

"I - want - to…come," he gasped, every muscle of his body flexing with his effort to maintain control. "Please…may I come, Mistress…Please, I can't—"

"Come, Josh." It was merely a whisper from her dry throat.

His name was lost in his cry, a mixture of growl, groan and shout. His cock spurted, the white fluid jettisoning onto the sand pattern on her thighs and mons, overlaying it, intertwining with it, spattering her pussy with his juices, giving her glistening lips a momentary pearlescence as the two secretions of desire met and merged.

His legs buckled and he caught himself with a hand just outside her quivering thighs, the heel of his hand digging hard into the ground as he milked himself onto her body with furious, jerking strokes, the muscles rippling along his working arm mirroring the flexing of his facial features.

Marcus's fingers had tightened on her nipples, shooting sparks of fire through her, proving beyond reasonable doubt he knew his way around the female form. She arched, the climax trying to roll up and over her, drawing tight the lines of nerve endings in her thighs and lower belly, her clit shuddering and her body flushing with the wave. She caught Marcus's hands, stilling them, and made them both watch Josh finish, until his forehead was touching her calf, his rasping breath tickling her convulsing pussy.

Lauren reached out and lay her hand on his hair, a trembling stroke, her excitement communicating itself not just in their combined scents, but also in the erratic motion of her fingertips along his hair line.

"You are magnificent," she murmured. "You please me so well, my love, and Marcus, too."

"Absolutely," Marcus reached forward, along her arm, and rubbed his knuckles along the back of Josh's neck. "Beautiful boy."

"You've earned some cozening," she decided. And Marcus had earned some relief.

Josh lifted his chin a bit, sliding it through his artistry over her hip bone, and looked at her with a heavy lidded tomcat expression that had her suppressing a smile, even as her heart skipped a beat. His hand crept up, over where Marcus still held the weight of her breasts in his palms. Josh's fingers spread over the top of her left breast, the heel of his hand pressing against her heart, his intent expression focused on the response of the organ beneath it. It still tripped at a higher rate, due to the spin of watching his climax, and his lips pressed together, moistening, like a boy did when concentrating on an important task. She fought the urge to arch into his touch. Her tits ached for a mouth, for Josh's mouth. She wanted to be bitten, suckled. She wanted to know what Josh's hands would feel like on them, as Marcus's had been.

A flicker in his gray eyes marked the increase in her heart rate. One finger ventured lower, stroked the tiny bumps in the soft darker flesh of her aureole. "Behave," she said, and the finger slid away. He gave her an unrepentant smile that did not quite dispel the turmoil in that storm cloud gaze.

"I want you to lay on the towel here, next to me," she gestured. "On your stomach, without your clothes. Marcus is going to rub oil into your body. That is," she arched her brow at their engrossed archangel, "if it would please him to do so. I know it would please me, very much, to watch him do it."

"Anything that would please you, dear lady, surely would please me," Marcus snapped out of his reverie with a smoothness she could only admire. "But in this case, I believe my pleasure to serve will exceed yours to command."

At her suggestion, a wary look had stolen onto Josh's face. He eased up into a sitting position, as Marcus shifted. Lauren propped herself on her elbows as he left her to rummage through the duffel for the suntan oil she had seen in there when he removed the food.

The easy familiarity of the moment was leaving Josh in the face of her new command, and she could see his apprehension building. She wanted to keep his cock jumping, that was how a sub was broken down, but the anxiety in his eyes reminded her that there was much she did not know about him. Strong attraction did not bring in-depth knowledge of a person's soul with it. Did he know he could say no? She searched his expression for a clue.

He was damaged, and she had no desire to be responsible for deepening the wound out of ignorance. Some subs were incapable of saying no. Inevitably, the worst of the dungeon sadists would find them. Staff people like Maria kept an eye out for those with a victim mentality, and they were no more allowed to return than the type of Master that would take advantage of their psychosis. They were trouble to a D/s establishment. Jonathan had been one of those hard to recognize, and once he was recognized, it was too late for Lauren's heart.

She pushed that away and concentrated on the man before her, who was *not* Jonathan. Josh's glance darted toward Marcus, but she saw he was not looking at Marcus's face, but his hands, clasping and removing the suntan oil from the bag. Josh was thinking about those hands being on him. She could not tell if his anxiety was revulsion at the thought of Marcus's touch or fascinated concern with his own response.

When she had first gotten into the D/s clubs, she had learned all the clinical terms. D/s was a game comprised of so much pure intuition, it was like a primal tribal dance. As a result, it had to have safe words. Jonathan had not been into safe words. He wanted her to turn him into a wanting, mindless, unfulfilled creature, something almost non-human. As a result, he had almost transformed her into the type of monster that would let a sub offer everything just short of death for a smile from her. That had been his game, and it had needed no safe words, because there was no rescue plan for a terminal illness.

Lauren sat up, heedless of the sand that tumbled to her lap and thighs. She caught Josh's face in her hands as he started to lever himself over her legs.

"Josh," she said softly, brushing a light, tender kiss over his lips. They tasted so sweet it was all she could do not to dwell there. "You know what I think about when I'm scared?"

He shook his head, then remembered. "No, Mistress."

She smiled. "You are so good. I think about butterflies. Butterflies are safe, don't you think?"

He heard the undercurrent, she could see it, but his gaze was puzzled. He knew the game so well, but why did he seem to know so few of the rules?

"When you want to feel safe," she said gently, "If you just say the word, 'butterflies', things will become safer. Do you understand, Josh?"

He did, but she saw uncertainty in his gaze. She tightened her fingers on his face.

"Your pleasure brings me pleasure," she said, in a sharper tone. "I will be very angry with you if you do something you genuinely do not feel comfortable doing. If you are afraid of something, you need only tell me. A Mistress takes care of her beloved."

It had come out before she thought to check back the endearment, but at the heat that flared in his eyes, she moistened her lips, swallowed the emotions that rose up in her, and kept going. "Do you understand?" she asked, more softly. "I won't permit you to hurt yourself for me. I do *not* want that. Are we clear?"

It broke the moment a little bit, put them out of the game and back on equal footing, but that was what was needed. Acceptance came with it, proven in his sudden, easy smile, and the strength of his hands closing on her wrists.

"I'm where I want to be," he responded, rubbing his thumb over the tender skin covering her pulse. "And with the people I want to be with."

Chapter 13

He included Marcus in his glance, eliciting a flicker of surprise in that one's expression. Josh's gaze came back to her face, and rested there for an intent moment.

Her senses dimmed, shutting out the sounds of surf, Marcus's presence, even the sunlight and white sand. There were just Josh's eyes, his sensuous, firm mouth, and the planes of his face.

"Your heart is in your eyes, did you know that?" he murmured, and somehow he had drawn close, so he spoke a breath away from her lips. "I'm not afraid of anything I see there, Lauren."

Something loosened in her stomach and she relaxed. A sub had to be strong to be a healthy sub. There were aspects of Josh that were not healthy. She'd already seen some of the dark places, but he was in possession of the essence of himself, enough to make the conscious choice to trust her. That simple evidence swamped her, made her tremble deep in a place that a hundred vehement declarations of devotion wouldn't have been able to touch.

He brushed his nose along her cheek and then his face and his hands slid away. He rolled gracefully over her leg, giving her a brief touch of the cold wetness of his softened penis on her leg. She gave a short, surprised squeal, which he answered with a chuckle.

He sprawled lazily onto the towel. He was half covered with sand, like a young boy. He adjusted himself on his stomach and crossed his arms just beyond his head. The motion pulled the muscles up along his back, and he pillowed his cheek on his overlapping hands, his face towards her.

She had of course noticed, several times, that he had another tattoo on his back, but this was the first time she had taken the time to do a close study of it. Again, the artist had chosen a sword as the central part of the design, though this one was of a more dramatic size. This sword had been tattooed from the base of his neck to just above the cleft of his buttocks. The hilt was simple, the blade polished silver gray, but from hilt to tip the weapon was wrapped in a barbed vine. Here and there a rose bloomed, perfect in detail, but mostly there were thorns and barbs, stenciled as if pricking his skin in many places, with a tiny black drop of blood here and there. In one place, the drop had fallen upon one of the roses, spreading and staining the pure crimson petals. It was some of the best work she had ever seen, and yet it offended her. Someone had marked what she now thought of as hers, and there was inherent cruelty behind the choice of the artist, as if the intention was to make him feel the sharp dig of the thorns.

The choice of the artist. The impact of that hit Lauren, and she leaned over, trailed her fingers over it. "Your wife was a marvelous tattoo artist," she observed.

Josh flinched as if, in truth, the tattoo caused him pain.

"I'm sorry," she said. He shook his head, but turned his face away. She could have pushed it, but he had given her enough for the moment, on several different levels. She lifted herself into the beach chair. The open sides of the chair were just above Josh's gaze, so that he could turn his eyes upward and see the curve of bare buttock and point of her left hip when he had a desire to do so.

Marcus knelt on his opposite side, and brushed the sand off of Josh with a towel. Then he poured the oil into his hands, rubbing his hands together to warm it. He glanced up at Lauren, gave her a half smile, reassuring but somber, and put himself to his pleasurable task.

Lauren sighed herself as Marcus's long-fingered, elegant hands began to spread the oil over Josh's back, polishing the lean, muscular physique of the naked man beneath his touch.

At the sound of her breath, Josh turned his face back to her, the pain again shuttered in his eyes. Liquid need uncoiled within her, and with studied casualness, her hand dipped. She traced the remains of the sand sculpture Josh had made on her, drawing his eyes there as she dipped her fingers into the small valleys where his fluids had collected, not quite dry, viscous satin to her touch.

He moistened his lips at her motions, and the need tightened, reminding her of how close she had come to orgasm just from watching him above her. However, as much fun as it was to hold his attention with her movements, it reminded her that she had some nurturing to do.

She stretched and pulled the duffel over to her. While Marcus continued his languorous massage, and Josh's eyelids drooped, she made up another small plate of smoked gouda cheese on cornbread crackers, and brought out a bottle of cold spring water, the outside of the bottle wet with ice and its own condensation.

"Something to drink or eat?" she asked her reposing charge. At his nod, she fed him from her hand, watching with a thickness in her throat as he took each small cube from her fingertips, his lips and tongue caressing her with each bite, his eyes never leaving her. She put the bottle of water to his lips often, to replenish his fluids and to be enthralled by the rise of his Adam's apple with each swallow. He lifted his hand to her wrist to steady her hold on the bottle, his eyes promising her…anything.

When he'd had enough, Lauren wiped the corners of his damp mouth with her knuckle. He caught it between his teeth and stroked it with his tongue a moment before releasing her. His gaze dropped as he did so, a flirtatious motion of deference that had the added perk of allowing him to slide his attention over her aching nipples, as hard as any coral forged by the ministrations of water and sun.

"Close your eyes," she commanded, and Josh obeyed, with a slight frown. She was pleased with his reluctance, but she wanted his body to relax, the muscles to go smooth and flowing under Marcus's touch. He needed rest, because she was far from done with him.

His initial tension about Marcus's touch seemed to have melted away. Lauren did not know if it was because her presence gave him the illusion of protection from unwanted advances, or because of the longstanding friendship between the men, and Marcus was behaving himself. Or maybe the environment they had been weaving since the onset of Marcus's card game had made nothing taboo or to be feared, simply experienced. Like being at an amusement park, they knew it was all there for pleasure and enjoyment, and therefore non-threatening, an escape from reality. The intrusion of reality too often could turn pleasure into something as warped as the reflection in a fun house mirror.

After a few more moments, she rose, leaving him under Marcus's capable hands as she strolled naked down to the water's edge. She lifted her arms to enjoy the feel of the warm sun and breeze move along her body.

The island did have magic. She felt decadent, sensual, a creature of sex rather than a woman with tedious emotional baggage. She again felt that sense of being a goddess, standing naked on a sun-drenched beach with a breeze caressing every crevice.

The first wave curled around her ankles, barely kissing her toes with foam before it rolled back, but by the time it returned she had moved up to her thighs into the cool water. She loosed her hair, shook it out so it tumbled down her back. Another step and she was able to lift her feet and roll to her back like a sinuous mermaid, passing her hands over herself to clean off the sand and the arousing evidence of Josh's desire. Her body quivered under her own touch, but she did nothing more than tease it.

She had held Marcus's hands, deferring her own climax. She was on that sharp, sparking edge of sexual arousal, where the body was so suffused with the weight of it that it could balance on the brink, hold to it without going over, as long as the host did not give in to gravity.

The rewards of not giving in grew proportionately with every moment of resistance. Nature taught a person every lesson they needed to know, and Lauren knew lava sealed in the earth grew hotter over time, until the eruption was capable of moving tectonic plates. As she rolled and stroked herself, dipped her head beneath the waves, she felt like molten fire being contained but not cooled by the grasp of the surf, a part of the changing earth herself. The temperature of her inner fires was rising with her play with Josh and Marcus, and she wondered if the eruption for which she was headed could consume the pain and mistakes, burn them away and leave dark, rich soil for new things to take root.

She came out of the waves; her hands raised to twist her hair back up onto her head. Marcus watched her approach, the languorous movement of her bare hips, the water rolling off her breasts, small drops poised on her nipples and thighs, sliding down her neck to pool in her collar bone. She was fully into it now, he could tell by the sinuous way she moved, sure of her power. Though his affections were reserved for men, he had a special appreciation for women Doms. The good ones were in touch with themselves, with the Divine Female within, so to speak, and it showed in their movements and words, the calm coolness of their eyes. She reflected those traits in every aspect of her being at this moment. It was a breathtaking sight, and gay or straight, one had to revere it. Whatever she had lost, she was getting it back.

Josh watched her as well, lips compressing over an audible swallow. Marcus suppressed a smile. "You might close your eyes, mate," he murmured. "She did tell you to shut them."

"It's worth the risk," the man under his hands said, and Marcus could only agree.

Lauren retrieved her swimsuit bottom and stepped into it, shrugging it back up over her close shaved pussy and sliding her fingers along the elastic leg seams to position the garment over the curves of her buttocks, thrusting her breasts out with the movement. She saw Josh looking at her beneath his lashes and let him get away with it. She enjoyed the idea that he would be getting hard for her again, his cock painfully stiff between his stomach and the sand beneath him.

She also liked the way a man's hands looked against another man's skin. Marcus's strong fingers stroked and kneaded their way over broad, glistening shoulders, caressing Josh's hairline. With a sidelong glance at her, Marcus worked his massage down Josh's back, the knuckles turning to knead the dip in the spine, the point of the sword, then his palms smoothed down the tight buttocks.

Marcus traced the inside curve of one muscular cheek with a fingertip, grazing the fine hair there with a nail. Josh's thighs tensed, creating an attractive rigidity to the territory above them.

She studied his face. His expression was intent, aroused, and disturbed. There was a plea in his eyes as he looked at her, but now she knew that he knew he could stop it at any time.

Lauren could see those changes happening in his face. When she had told him about butterflies, and let him say what he wanted, his response - the sexy smile, the reassuring strength of his hands - those things said he was making his own choices. And that was important. The sub had to make the choice to give up choice, and keep reinforcing that for the game to work.

The fact that he wanted her to play Mistress, wanted to leave the decision up to her, meant he didn't dislike how it felt. He just was uncertain. He needed her validation.

She responded to his pleading look with an indifferent, I-want-you-suffering look. She retrieved her bikini top and re-hooked the lower strap around her back. She raised the bra and wiggled her still-wet breasts into it, tying the strings around the neck and then made further adjustments to the fabric, shaping them around her breasts, sliding her hand in to lift them into the correct position for the shelf bra style.

"So, Josh," she gazed down at him, her voice falling like silk, "who is making your cock hard again? Me, or Marcus?" She squatted by his head, making sure her thighs were spread so he could see the way the crotch of the suit barely covered what it was intended to cover. Lauren cupped his chin, caressing the jaw line.

"Who's making it come to attention again? Mommy or Daddy? Don't you dare lie," she said sharply, as his eyes flicked away, color staining his cheeks. "I know the truth, but I want to hear it from your lips."

"Lauren—"

"Mistress," she corrected, tightening her grip so her nails dug in. "Tell me."

"Both," he mumbled, trying to pull his face away.

She clucked at him, jerked his chin back to her, and enjoyed the flash of temper in his eyes. "I didn't hear you."

"I said...both."

"Good boy. Such a good boy deserves a reward."

Josh made a sound, part protest, part involuntary sound of pleasure, and Lauren shifted her gaze to Marcus. He was running an oiled index finger slowly up and down the cleft between Josh's buttocks, his thumb stroking circles at the base of Josh's heavy testicles, revealed by the spread of his thighs.

"Mistress," Josh swallowed, "I can't—"

"I know," she said, her tone softening. "But he'll just touch you. Just touch you. Nothing goes inside. And if it makes you hard for me again, I like that. See?" She slid her grip to his hair, pressed his face closer, brought her crotch up to his nose. "Smell how much you please me."

She felt the stir of air as he inhaled, and his tongue flicked out to swipe his lips, less than an inch from touching her. Her body moistened instantly, and she had to stifle her own moan.

Damn, but this could be tough. Marcus looked at her with amused eyes, but she saw he was suffering in the same delightful way she was.

"See how much we desire you?" she murmured. "How much you are adored, cherished?" She bent, pressed her lips to his forehead, just a light brush. He nuzzled his nose against her cheek. The tears that pricked her eyes at the easy, intimate gesture were unexpected. Lauren cupped his jaw, held him to her a second more in a moment more tender than sexual, then slid away from him abruptly, back into her chair.

She stretched out her legs before him, and lay her hand on the point of his shoulder as Marcus continued his ministrations. Now that he had sharpened the blade of arousal with anxiety, Marcus eased off the more intimate contact, returning to a general massage of the back and buttocks, thighs and shoulders. She was sure the continuous touch, the even, slow circles, would keep his subject stirred. The lull of it would bring Josh's thoughts back to those more intimate touches and the unsettling effect they had on his body.

For she had no doubt Josh had been aroused. Lauren suspected men sometimes longed for a non-feminine strength in a sexual touch, a matching of body power fraught with delightful possibilities.

"I'm not gay," Josh muttered suddenly, shifting under her hand. He looked back at Marcus, challenge in his gray eyes.

"Of course you're not, silly boy," Marcus chuckled. He caressed Josh's jaw with light fingers, his face reflecting his pleasure when Josh did not pull away. "No more than two college girls exploring one another under their nightshirts, trying their first taste of what lies between their thighs. The body has no sexual preference. Our hearts choose who we love; only our minds try to give it a classification. But when we strap our minds down and give control to another," his fingertips slid down Josh's ribs, lingering at the top of a bare hip, "our bodies have free and delightful rein to experience, enjoy, endure. The sensations take over... anticipation, nervousness. What will this feel like? Taste like?"

His voice was soothing, melodious. Lauren was as enthralled as Josh, watching the movement of Marcus's hands, but they stilled at that moment, so that Josh's pensive glance flicked back up to Marcus's face. "I've been your friend a long time, Josh," Marcus said quietly, his eyes serious. "I know what you are, and what you're not. Trust me...trust Lauren, and be still." He shifted his gaze to Lauren. "I believe you indicated you were going to give our boy here a reward for good behavior."

She started out of the reverie his words and movements had woven over both of them. Marcus grinned, though he dropped his attention to Josh and got his hands working on his charge again.

There were grades of Masters, she realized. The most common were probably those like herself, who sought physical and emotional fulfillment. Then there were those like Marcus, who had taken it to an art form, as a man who appreciated art certainly would, honed the game to a level of craftsmanship spellbinding to watch.

She took a moment to enjoy the way he looked, his expression absorbed in the beauty of Josh's body, his hands glistening with the sandalwood oil. Idly she wondered how Marcus would look, slicked down in it, polished like a gem, the same way he had rubbed Josh, and the image was a pleasant one.

There were a million facets of this diamond to explore and cause to sparkle. However, at the moment it was the banked fire in Josh's dark eyes she wanted to bring back to full flame.

"So I did," she smiled. "I'm letting Josh choose. What would you like as a reward?" she asked, tilting her head toward him.

Josh reached out a long, brown arm and laid his palm over her bare foot.

"I want to know about the man who hurt you."

Oh, he was clever. And if it was just cleverness, she could have been angry. But those gray eyes, soft now like a dove's breast, filled with gentle curiosity, were not hiding his feelings. He was interested in her, wanted to know what was going on in her heart. It was something she found she could not deny him. Hell. She suspected she might be unable to say no to anything he asked of her. The ironic double-edged sword of vulnerability in the Dom and sub relationship, where a Mistress might do all manner of cruel things to bring her submissive, and herself, to greater heights of pleasure, but in matters of the heart she was as open as he was, perhaps more.

She wanted to close up. She wanted to say no. She wanted to tell herself it wasn't a problem, that she was on an island in the middle of Paradise, and she would walk away in two days and never see him again.

"His name was Jonathan." It was funny, how little she had said his name aloud since he had left her. It got clogged a bit in her throat, so she had to clear it, and it came out sounding garbled, but she didn't repeat it. Her fingers had tightened on the arms of the chair, but she didn't realize it until Josh's fingertip whispered over her big toe, and she loosened her grip on the grooved plastic.

"I like control, but I'm healthy with it. Control is just a dance; you can lead the dance, but your partner has to know how to match your steps, know when to go left when you go right. A lot of it is imagination, wishful thinking. You only hold power as long as those you hold it over want you to have it."

It helped to work from the general to the specific, like the absurd practice of dipping one callused toe in the water before plunging all the far more sensitive extremities into it. There was a reason that the crotch was the hardest part to submerge without shrieking.

She kept her eyes on the horizon and thought, as she often had, that subs were braver than Doms, ultimately. They obeyed when the Mistress demanded they meet her eyes while they answered a difficult question. She could not have looked at Josh now without the aid of a stereotaxic device.

"Sometimes, someone can be sneaky, exercise power over you in a way you don't notice until you're too deep in a pit to get out. The worst ones can put you there and you think you don't want out, even though you're abandoning everything you value about yourself." She shook her head. "Maybe I should stop."

Josh trickled warm sand from his cupped hand into the spaces between her toes. It made her toes wiggle, dislodge the sand. He repeated the action. It had a comfortable rhythm to it. "I want to hear your story," he said.

Lauren felt his attention centered on her every word, every movement, the working of her throat. Most men didn't look at a woman that closely. Most didn't want to hear anything about a woman's past lovers. To a man, it infringed on his sense of possession, whereas for a woman, it was a way of revealing what she wanted and needed in a lover. She wanted to tell herself that Josh and she really hadn't had time to develop a sense of possessiveness, but she saw the tattoo on his back again, and felt the rise of white anger again at the woman who had inflicted it upon him. She watched the sand roll over the arch of her foot, his fingers hovering just above it. She was lying to herself, protecting herself.

He was a different type of man. For him, intimate knowledge of her past might be a type of possession. It was something Jonathan had never wanted from her, but she had desperately wanted to give him. Josh wanted it, was asking for it.

"I met Jonathan in my favorite club, of course. I played with him. Nothing serious, just safe play. The D/s form of first date. But he was different. He had these brown eyes, these lips... ah, dammit," she closed her eyes, fought the moisture back. "My soul opened up to him like a flower to sun the moment, *the second*, I saw him, breathed him, touched him."

Neither man said anything, and Lauren sat in darkness a few moments, just feeling Josh's touch on her foot, hearing Marcus shift to her other side. She inhaled the comfortable normalcy of tanning oil and the sea and tried to get it to banish the dark shadows that had risen out of her heart the moment she gave voice to the name of her demon.

At length, she made herself open her eyes, watch the horizon again. "I should have known he was an obsession more than anything else, because I felt so damn drawn to him from the beginning. Why would I feel that way about him if he was the wrong person?"

She pushed down the sudden ice of fear in her throat. It was impossible to ignore the similarities in the picture she was painting with what was happening between her and Josh.

She swallowed the shards of glass. "I ignored all the danger signs. He didn't want to meet outside the club, not even for a cup of coffee. I thought he was just being cautious.

"Over time, even when I finally coaxed him into living with me, it should have told me he was only interested in the physical. Especially since that only lasted about a month, and he moved back out. He didn't want anything between us but the game. But he had such a way of making me feel like the center of the universe when I was playing Mistress to him. It's hard to explain, even to myself," she admitted. "I wanted him to fall in love with me as I had fallen in love with him. I assumed it was just something I would have to work harder at to make happen. At my home, he would play, but he gave me nothing more than that. After sex, he was always retreating to the study to work, or having to go out without me. We spent weekends in the dungeons. I devised so many ways to break him down, make him open to me. I'm a good Mistress," a smile touched her eyes as she curled her toe around one of Josh's fingers. "I believe a person plays a submissive because there's something inside they want you to break open." She noted the finger tensed a bit under her grasp. "I did break him open. I thought I opened up every room inside him, made him vulnerable in a hundred different ways. I stroked all those vulnerabilities, collected them to me and cherished them as gifts, the way a Mistress should, and gave him the best of myself."

She raised her arms, caught hold of the back of the chair, bent her elbows and stretched the muscles, tightening her fingers until the knuckles whitened.

"I wanted him more than air," she said, low, her throat choked with it. "Doesn't that sound like a pathetic cliché? All I wanted was to look in his eyes and see that connection I was sure was going to eventually be there. I can't explain now how I got so desperate. I had a full and happy life, career, family. All I lacked was a Mr. Forever, but that wasn't something I was obsessed with having. But I had weak points. A Mistress ultimately has to be as vulnerable to the sub as they are to her, and the sub who knows how can push the right buttons, make the Mistress the slave of her own vulnerabilities. And Jonathan did. Everything I wanted deep in my heart he dangled in front of me, just enough to make me keep grabbing at it. I neglected my work, my life. Every day came to be about getting to the club that night.

"I was going to make him love me," she said softly. "And the D/s game became the chess board, the strategy to make it happen. The more I craved his love, a sincere gesture of intimacy, the more he withheld it. I had never been aware of being lonely, and suddenly I was. I felt inadequate. My self-esteem plummeted and I didn't even notice. It's funny, how someone you love can break you down, take away your identity and recreate you, before you even realize that's what they're doing."

A sun-browned hand covered her left knee and she made herself look at Josh. It took such effort that her eyes felt glassy. He squeezed her, his thumb stroking the protrusion of bone, and his eyes were tranquil gray pools, strong and understanding. She had a sudden urge to crawl into his lap.

"I should say you don't have to go on, but I really want to know."

She tried for a smile, failed, managed a grimace. "You have this image of yourself," she murmured, shifting her gaze to her knees, "as someone competent and smart, someone somebody would like, not because of what you would do for them, but because of who you are. Then you let someone inside, they get your number. They can tear it all down."

Josh understood all too well what she was saying. She could see it in the shadows in his eyes, the flicker of comprehension.

"What happened to end it?" Marcus asked. Lauren tilted her head to look at him. He had drawn close to her chair, so Josh and he were coiled around her like two wolves protecting a member of the pack, their affection and anger for her palpable. She should have felt surprise, but sex, or sexual situations, did tend to create the impression of intimacy quickly, though it was often built on no more than the lust of the moment.

No. She wouldn't let Jonathan make her timid. This was more than that. The bond that had developed between the three of them in less than thirty-six hours defied description, even with the facilitation of their island paradise setting.

"A mirror." She moistened her lips. "One night, as I was getting ready to go meet Jonathan, I realized I couldn't meet my own gaze in the mirror. I had become ashamed of myself, so much that I couldn't face who I was. So I did the hardest thing in my life, because I knew how it would end. I went to the club that night, and told him I loved him, and I wanted more."

In her mind, she was back there, and the pain gripped her, such that she could not speak for several moments. She was vaguely aware of the two men exchanging a concerned glance, some slight movements of their hands upon her, comfort or encouragement, it did not matter.

"He put on this amazed expression," she said, her tone flat as stagnant water. "But there was this little smile around his lips. And I knew." Her voice shook and she clenched her jaw, forcing it to stop. "I knew. He had been playing me from the beginning. True subs don't do that. The whole point is trust. Even if there isn't the intimacy of lovers, there should be the respect of friends. He had used me, twisted me up, and then when I broke, he dumped me. That's what got his rocks off. He had loved having me as a Mistress, but he didn't want Lauren, the woman. He never had. He was a sick, sociopathic son of a bitch and I had been totally gone over him."

Josh rose up on one elbow. With a gentle thumb, he pressed the tear from the corner of her eye, the rest of his hand cradling her face. She shut her eyes, leaned into his touch a moment, let his palm shut out the light so she could focus on the tranquil darkness.

"I stayed away from the club for months after that, but Maria said he never came back after that night. She heard he had gotten some Mistress over at another competing club tied up over him."

She backed away from Josh's touch and he let her, dropping his hand back to her foot.

"I almost went vanilla. I ran from the truth. I wrote off the whole D/s set-up as destructive. Kinky games had destroyed our relationship, destroyed me. But if your blood runs with it, it's hard to shake." A painful smile tugged at the corner of her mouth. "I got over that. As time passed, I realized it wasn't any different than a failed vanilla relationship. He's the guy who says he'll call and doesn't, the girl who says she loves a guy until she finds out he's borrowed the company BMW rather than owning it himself. Some people just fuck with your heads. Jonathan did that to me. It pissed me off, on about ten different levels, because he destroyed my confidence.

"I cried when I saw you with Thomas," she shifted her attention to Marcus. "Because I realized what the difference was between the two of you, and me and Jonathan. You and Thomas cherished each other. You could feel it. You, as his Master, adored him, were enthralled by him as much as he was by you. That's why I had kept hanging in there so long with Jonathan. Like anyone else, I wanted to believe I had found that love to last a lifetime and dammit, I thought endurance would manufacture it. But I learned the most important rule of D/s play; if there isn't already a spark of it between you in the mundane world, it ain't going to happen in a dungeon."

She turned her eyes back to Josh, whose hand was now curled around the arch of her foot. "You remember that kiss, last night?" she asked. It flashed through his eyes, and she nodded. "That's what that was all about."

He leaned forward, and touched his lips to her foot, gently, with an overwhelming reverence. Lauren made a soft sound in her throat, a sound of pain and longing at once. He lifted his gaze, looking at her with warm sympathy in his eyes and something else, something that fanned the spark within her into a shower, like firecrackers going off.

"I would have torn his fucking arms off for you," he said calmly.

It pulled at something low in her gut, something primal and right, and made her reach out and touch his face.

"So," she cleared her throat, tossed her head back, and risked a smile. "This is the moment when Obiwan is supposed to rivet us with some words of wisdom."

Marcus chuckled, though his eyes carried some of Josh's heat. "Relationship games always carry a risk," he managed lightly. "D/s can be dangerous, because it explores the most primitive sides of ourselves. Those involved must have a high degree of trust and a very, very healthy devotion to one another. Like religion, it can be a spiritually enlightening experience, or it can be an expression of psychosis. And somewhere in between, it can be tremendously fun." Gathering his composure around him, he lifted his shoulder in a shrug. "Like chocolate."

Lauren looked at him blankly. "I was following until that moment, Obi."

Marcus glanced up as clouds darkened the sun. Lauren could have lifted her sunglasses, but her eyes still felt too vulnerable and open.

"Imagine how it feels to eat one piece of Belgian chocolate," Marcus suggested, moving to pack up the contents of their basket. "You inhale it, savor it on your tongue. The flavor of it is something that you can choose to let linger in your mouth, building your body's reaction to it, for once you swallow it, it's gone. The pleasure is not in the consumption, but in the sensory experience. To bring it to its fulfilling conclusion, you will eventually swallow it, but the longer you draw it out...ah, the more satisfying that swallow is." He grinned at her expression and pulled a small tin from the cooler. "Bon bon?"

Lauren shook her head at his wicked ways, her mood lightening, and took one. "Okay, is this metaphor going somewhere?"

"Always," Josh predicted.

Marcus shot him a reproachful glance. "Now say you eat another. And another. Somehow, you still want them, you're still cherishing that experience, but the more you stuff in your mouth, the more elusive that sensation gets. But you eat them even faster, without really noticing how they taste anymore. And then, you're sick.

"This is the first piece," he leaned over to Josh, ran a fingertip down the man's throat and along the collarbone.

A flush rose in Josh's face as he made a visible effort to keep himself still. Lauren's breathing hitched, the chocolate melting on her tongue, as Marcus's touch trailed down the center of Josh's bare chest, stopping just above the heart, where his ribs met the surface of the sand. "That's how the game was meant to be played. Savoring, drawing it out, cherishing, never taking for granted the gift that has been given to your senses. You must appreciate it, worship it, even as you run your tongue over it and melt away the outer casing to get to the cream beneath. You hold it captive as long as you can, intending on bringing out its richest flavors before allowing it to explode, and be consumed.

"Jonathan," his lip curled in a sneer, and his eyes flashed back to Lauren, "had a serious eating disorder."

A drop of rain spattered on Lauren's knee. Thunder rumbled lazily in the distance.

"How about we take *lunch* inside?" Marcus offered. He jerked his head toward Josh, a twinkle in his eye.

Chapter 14

෨

They went to the Salerno house. The rain had begun to come down in earnest, their house was closest, and it had the hot water heater the men wanted to check. Isabel came when Josh called, but there were no detours this time. Once depositing them at the Salernos, the elephant vanished into the forest. According to Josh, she was not likely to be seen again until the rain ceased.

The Salerno home was like Lisette's, built to blend into the forest. However, their house had the air of a medieval period country home. The first and second levels had outdoor walking galleries with open archways, rather than porches. The siding of the first and basement floors was done in stonework. Most charmingly, a creek ran by the front of the house, and the head and coils of a bronze dragon rose out of the water, creating the impression of a guarded moat.

Lauren paused at the stairs and turned back, her eye caught by the creature. She went to the water's edge to get a closer look. The dragon's features had been enhanced with different colored metals, the play of light making it into a living, breathing creature. She eased out one canvas toe into the creek, and laid her fingers on the dragon's face, felt the satin curves of the jaw, the rough texture of the scales on the neck, scales that had some movement to them, for they were separately fused, as scales would be. The neck and jaw connections also had a little play to them, so movements of the wind brought slight motions to the dragon's head, increasing the eerie impression of life.

"You're going to get wet," Marcus said, having followed her.

"It's not too bad yet," she smiled and slanted a glance at him. "Have you ever thought about how absurd it is, the way we run inside from the beach when it starts to rain? I mean, we were swimming, immersed in water, and then it starts to rain, so we hunch our heads and flee. This is incredible."

"We need to get inside," Josh called from the first floor. "Unless you two want to drown."

"It's amazing," Marcus agreed, taking her arm to help her step back onto the bank. "Wait until you see what they have in the house."

"So which one of the Salernos is the artist?" she asked, moving toward the stairs.

"Neither," Marcus replied. "The Salernos are New York Italians. Mrs. Salerno is a cosmetic company CEO, and Mr. Salerno is a retired police chief. You feel like you're in an Italian restaurant commercial around them. Lots of shouting, quick-to-anger, quick-to-forgive personalities, devoted to each other in a very practical manner. They have three almost-grown children we've never met. I doubt the kiddies have ever been here," Marcus grinned, a look to his eye that suggested there was a reason for that. He pressed her up the stairs and continued his casual dialogue before she could pursue the mystery behind that look.

"They're not artists, but they're an artist's best friend. They're very generous patrons of three of the artists that have homes here. In the house, well, I'll let you see for yourself."

Marcus's words immediately made sense upon entering the Salerno's large foyer. The interior of the house exploded with artwork. Original paintings, sculptures of all mediums, and pottery work lined the wide corridor. Lauren recognized some of the most well known names in the art world in the styles before her.

Yet the art did not appear to be chosen solely for its market value. There was an underlying theme of unique character, of color and interest to the eye, and the way it blended into the country castle atmosphere. A castle crossed with bourgeois comfort, she amended to herself, as she moved into the sunken pit living area and saw that the center piece of this room was a top of the line La-z-boy recliner, complete with baseball arm cover for a remote and TV directory. There was a pair of worn fleece slippers parked at the base, as if the master of the house was just up getting a beer from the fridge.

"We're going to go down and check the water heater," Marcus said, touching her elbow. "Feel free to wander about. It's a great place."

Josh had already disappeared and Lauren lifted a brow. "He's avoiding me, isn't he?"

Marcus inclined his head. "Regrouping. Trying to piece together those defenses you're systematically shattering. I suspect you won't give him time to do that."

"You bet your ass." She said it with conviction, surprising herself with the depth of it. Marcus grinned and left her to her explorations.

Lauren wandered to the wall of windows and admired the sweeping view of forest and ocean, much like Lisette's home provided.

No, she wouldn't give him much time to regroup. She wanted to get down beneath those shields, find out what he was hiding there and maybe help him heal it.

"Ah, God," she closed her eyes, pressed her temple to the cool glass. Nothing more pathetic than a woman trying to heal a brooding man. The cliché of practically every mainstream romance, and something every woman who reached thirty knew almost never happened. Still, those romances sold millions for a reason. There was a germ of hope in them, the hope that, if they did kiss the frog, he really would turn into a prince. *You just had to believe, Tinkerbell.*

She left the living area and prowled the foyer some more. The Salernos obviously had money to spend on any type of art they wanted, and yet she saw no Van Gogh's or Picasso's.

Everything she saw was an artist established in the past twenty-five years, talent poised on the brink of inevitable genius. On closer scrutiny, she detected another pattern in their choices. Love.

Not in the romance sense, which would likely have been of little interest to Mr. Salerno. No, these pieces reflected the raw soul of love that persisted through every torture the human mind could devise. Lauren touched the sculpture before her with light fingertips. At a distance, it looked like the twisted trunk of a tree hit by lightning, a few jagged edged branches gnarled and jutting from its sides. But when the observer was close like she was, and could study its features, she discovered a sculpture of a man and woman intertwined. They could have been embracing or fighting; it depended on the angle at which one stood, but the overwhelming message was passionate devotion. There was nothing pretty about love, it seemed to scream, but there was nothing more necessary. There was nothing more vital than fighting your way into the soul of another and claiming it for your own.

Lauren smiled at her thought. The catch was, in order for you to claim the soul of another and be happy with the prize, you had to lay yourself just as bare to them. Her touch lingered on the rough-hewn part that was the shoulder of the woman figure, and then slipped away as she turned to wander further down the hall.

At the end, she had the choice of staircases, one going up, and one going down. The latter was where she presumed Marcus and Josh had gone. To her right was a pair of double doors of carved teakwood, rounded at the top to accommodate an elaborately molded archway. Lauren hesitated, then shrugged, turned the polished pewter handles and pushed the unlocked doors inward.

For a moment, she felt just like Julie Andrews.

It was a ballroom, the walls lined with tall arched windows providing a view out to the surrounding forest on two sides, the now turbulent ocean on the third. On the wall space between the openings were gilt paintings in Baroque style, biblical figures, angels in swirling robes, women and men in shimmering dress.

Three glass chandeliers hung from the domed ceiling, each probably weighing more than her Lexus. The floor was polished oak, inlaid with darker pieces to form a starburst design at the center. Chairs lined the wall; brocade and velvet cushioned of course, antiques with carved mahogany backs.

There was a silence to the room, a hush that she could close her eyes and easily imagine filled with the rustle of skirts, men's voices, the light chime of glasses, and a waltz playing in the background. Now that silence was punctuated by the strike of the rain against the windows.

Lauren moved to the center of the starburst and turned slowly, looking at every painting. She tilted her head to discover the ceiling that held those chandeliers was also painted with an array of angels and romantic figures.

When she lowered her eyes, her neck screaming, her gaze landed on one other piece of furniture. Its face had been painted with a cadre of cherubs and positioned between two windows, camouflaged. A smile tugged at her lips and she went to it, pulling open the doors of the tall cabinet.

No need to import the orchestra when you had a state of the art surround sound system. She glanced around and up, but it took a few moments to locate the speakers. The ceiling and wall murals had been painted over their wire mesh faces, screening them so well that the Salernos probably had to keep a location diagram somewhere in case the stereo guys ever had to come in and work on one.

The entire room was a work of art. Lauren had no doubt that masters of the craft had created this fantasy. It was a room that begged for dancing, for music that would flood the room and transport the dancers to whatever mood or mode they chose to embrace. The room's style suggested a sweeping Wagner piece, a light Chopin waltz, or an elaborate Fred and Ginger number, but that wasn't really her style. She wondered what Josh's style would be. At the thought, her lip curved. Lord in Heaven, she was gone over the man.

She squatted in front of the CD player, and looked through the selections in the partition below it. Her finger alighted on a favorite, and a smile crept across her features. She decided she liked the Salernos. She opened the player; laid her choice in it, and then keyed up the track she wanted, setting it for random choice after that. Then she turned up the volume.

The first hard guitar licks vibrated through the room up through the soles of her feet. She turned from the player as John Cougar Mellencamp began to expostulate about his days as a young boy.

She wasn't surprised to find him there, watching her from the arched doorway. Josh leaned against the frame, his arms crossed over his bare chest, his eye glinting with amusement. She twirled, shimmied toward him and back, put in a couple hip-hop moves, flashed a daring smile at him.

The beat picked up and offered the chance to be with a girl just like her.

She worked her way over to him and extended a hand. She wondered if he was one of those men who steadfastly avoided the dance floor, or who had learned just enough to clumsily guide a date through a few obligatory steps and increase his chances of getting laid. She got a quick answer.

He took her offered hand and yanked, spinning her in a tight turn that brought her up hard against him. Before she could get a breath, or her fill of the way his body felt against hers, he twirled her back out again, moving them both into a smooth shag step. She missed her cue on the first round, but when he cycled back to the beginning, she was ready for him. She slid under his arm and flowed along his touch on her neck, as she turned outward, then came back to him again, so that both hands were clasped in his.

It might have been falling in lust up to this point, but at that moment her heart took a tumble in a little more serious direction. She felt the fall, the vertigo. The grin on his face, the sheer enjoyment of playing off each other, the ease with which they moved together. He moved into a Latin step and she was turned so her back was brought up against his front, her hips tucked into the angle of his. His palm pressed into her stomach, and her arm curled around his neck as he rocked and twisted them down and then back up again. She pressed her nose briefly against the warmth of his throat as Mellencamp invited her to sink her teeth in.

She spun out again, laughing, and then he had her by the waist facing him, revolving them around the room in an impromptu Fred and Ginger waltz at a beat that the couple themselves would have enjoyed if they had had Mellencamp's talent at their fingertips. She caught hold of his bicep for balance, and he gathered her closer, his hand dipping low on her back so she was firmly against him.

Lauren looked up into his face. His grin had faded at the corners, the curve of his mouth now more tense, underscored by something in his eyes that stopped her breath and elevated her heart higher than was warranted, even for such stimulating aerobic exercise.

His grip was gentle, but strong enough to tell her he had her captured if he was of a mind to hold her. They were still moving together over the dance floor, the line of his thigh insinuated between both of hers as he switched back into the sensuous steps of the Latin dance, to the mean tempo that called for recklessness and sexual heat. To lyrics that insisted love could hurt in a way that would make you welcome the pain and ask for more.

The kiss was easy, a slight movement to put his lips on hers, but the fire swept through her like the churn of the electric guitars. Somehow, he kept moving, and the sinuous roll of his body against hers, the turn, the steady cradle of his palm against the side of her neck and back of her head, made her totally his for a moment, incapable of balance without him.

The song ended, and the patter of the rain returned. He eased her down and in a finish turn that left some unwanted space between them, but he kept hold of her hand, caressing her fingers and gazing into her confused face. As if on cue, John Cougar eased into the poignant *Ain't Even Done With The Night*.

Josh drew her closer, and she took the step, staring up into his face, aware of only him.

"Joshua?"

Marcus's voice wafted up from somewhere beneath them, calling from within the house.

Josh cleared his throat. "Yeah?"

"Come here a minute. There's a vibration that feels a bit off."

Nothing off about what was vibrating between the two of them, but it was certainly unsettling. Josh gave her a crooked smile as if he heard her thought. He squeezed her hand and left her, his steps light and lithe, slapping across the hall and toward the basement area.

Lauren wrapped her arms around herself, feeling a bit lost, left with the company of Mellencamp's wistful voice and without Josh's heartbeat against hers.

Lord, what was she doing, getting all gooey over this guy she barely knew? It wasn't rebound; she was way too far past Jonathan for that. The terror she had felt on the beach returned, thinking about how instantaneous her feelings were for Josh, just as they had been with Jonathan. But maybe that was the way she fell in love. It was her, not the man. This was a different guy, totally different. She wasn't going to wallow into some psychoanalytical bullshit that suggested she kept choosing the same guy. Josh had shown more emotional reaction to her in thirty-six hours than Jonathan had in nine months.

Mellencamp was crooning that she'd met the boy who would be the answer to all of her dreams. Jeez, Louise, it was just sex games, just fun stuff. She was exploring, dipping her toe back in, just as Maria had told her she needed to do. The island was a safe place to play, because it wasn't reality, it wasn't home.

But it was home for Josh.

What was it Marcus had said? Remember how children played, for fun and for the fate of the Universe at the same time. Maybe this was a game that was always played best or worst when the heart was involved. Everything in between was just candy, where you had to be careful how much you indulged, or it became the desolate vapidity of a one night stand with a faceless stranger picked up out of a smoky bar.

She opened her eyes and found Marcus standing in the doorway. Apparently, they were tag teaming her.

"So have you played much since Jonathan, or is this your first time since then?" he asked, without preamble.

Lauren lifted a shoulder, turned away to cut off the music before Mellencamp drove her to tears. Marcus didn't fill in the gap of silence, except with the pressure of waiting for an answer. She didn't have to give him anything, anything at all. It was her choice. Her choice. She took a deep breath, turned back to face him.

"No. It's been difficult, since Jonathan, even without the guilt. I've been struggling with it. Maria says I've been going through the skydiver process."

"The skydiver process? That's a new term on me."

"No term," she managed a chuckle. "Just a reference point. There was this documentary about a woman sky diver. One day she jumped out, and something went wrong with her chute. It didn't open."

Marcus winced. "Ouch."

"In spades." Lauren came to stand before him. "She didn't die. She was paralyzed, though, and they didn't think she'd walk again. She did, with several years of torture in rehab. For seven years after that she didn't sky dive. You'd think she'd have nightmares about that jump, and she did, sometimes. But most of the times, she said she dreamed about what it was to jump out of a plane and fly, float on the air, and it just be you and whatever amazing Power it is that creates everything. She realized she missed it, too much to stay away from it anymore. So she went up, and started jumping again."

"Incredibly brave or incredibly stupid, depending on your perspective," Marcus observed.

Lauren nodded. "The reporter asked her what she said to her friends and family, anyone who told her she was crazy for going back to something that had almost destroyed her."

Lauren recalled the firm, gentle touch Maria had placed on her face, that confident caress of a Dom as she spoke the woman's words. "'Fate caused the accident, not skydiving itself. I'm not going to shut out the joy because of fear. If I do that, sky diving won't be the end of it. Next thing I know, I'll be afraid of planes, or going out in crowds, or dogs. The fear will take over and I won't be living.'"

"Extraordinary," Marcus murmured. "And this applies to you…how?"

Lauren's lips curved at the glint in his beautiful eyes. "A smart man like yourself could put it together. I've been at the dreaming point. I want to be back in it again, but I haven't been ready. I've been able to watch, but not to play. Now I'm here, and all of a sudden," she thought about Josh, his eyes, his body, the soul that inhabited them, "taking him over seems the most natural thing in the world. God," she laughed, "Maybe we all need to be in therapy. Maybe we're all sick."

"Hardly." Marcus straightened from the doorframe and took her hand. "Since you've got your parachute on, I want to show you something."

"What? Where - "

He raised her brow by putting a quiet finger to his lips, the glint in his eyes turning devilish. She followed him back through the foyer, and he took her out the front door and down a set of winding stone steps from the front gallery. At the bottom, she was enchanted to find herself in a knot garden of dwarf shrubs, complete with a comfortable bench by a gazing pool for contemplation.

A quick glance at his face showed her that this was not what he intended to show her. He pulled her onward, behind the sculpted topiaries flanking the steps, and stopped before a carved wooden door with a weight and style suggesting that it must have graced a medieval fortress in truth. On the protruding claw of a sly looking stone gargoyle mounted next to the door was a ring of iron skeleton keys, as ancient looking as the door.

Marcus directed Lauren's enthralled attention to the carved plaque above the door.

Here there be dragons of the most delightful sort.

She slanted him a glance. He fitted one of the keys and pushed the door open for her.

The door opened into a hall designed like an open courtyard. Skylights and prisms on either side and over the door directed the beams of outside light onto the cobblestone floor. The smell of fresh water focused her attention on a large fountain in the center of the cobblestone mosaic. Her breath drew in, and for an instant, she was unaware of anything but what lay in the center of the courtyard.

It wasn't the fountain itself, though it was beautiful. Dozens of smooth, colored stones formed a mountain down which the water splashed. The pool, with a diameter of at least twenty feet, was filled with more stones and, charmingly, a wealth of new shiny copper pennies that reflected the lights at the base of the pool. There were lily pads in bloom, full white flowers gliding lazily with the disturbance of the water, and the gleaming scales of gold and silver coy sparkled as they swam beneath the surface. Water jetted up from the rim of the stone fountain and curved over, forming rainbows around the central statuary.

It was that statuary that commanded her attention. The bronze sculpture depicted a man and a woman. The woman wore a lovely evening gown, draped low in the back. The dip in her spine and the dimples over her buttocks were defined. The dress was slit up to the hipbone, and as she was in forward motion, one long slim leg in a stiletto heel was visible, the fragile musculature etched out in metal, with the muted sheen of silken skin. Her upper body was turned toward the man. He stood before her, towered over her actually, because she was small, perhaps just over five feet, but he did not look clumsy. In fact, he was elegant and magnetic in a tuxedo with the tie undone; the shirt carelessly worked open several studs. The intensity of the look between the two caught Lauren's breath, as did the riding crop in the woman's delicate hands. The man's hands had been manacled behind him, and those chains, as well as those attached to the cuffs on his ankles, ran to a circle bolt in the base of the statue, which was braced on a platform atop of the mountain of stones. Lauren could almost feel the sexual heat in the gaze the man rested upon his captor. Her gaze slid over the fall of hair over his forehead, the delicate working of the metal that had even accomplished the impression of a five o'clock shadow, lending the captive a dangerous, predatory look.

"It's a J. Martin," she breathed. "I've never seen one…life-sized. I bought a small one at an auction a couple years ago. A merman, bringing a human woman a conch shell with a pearl in it. The beach is done in sand, shards of diamonds, and topaz glass. It's amazing work. I paid a mint for it, but something about his work just…"

"It calls to you, doesn't it?" Marcus nodded, standing close to her elbow. "He gives them innocuous names, like 'The Power of Woman Over Man', so that the vanilla world buys them, calling it pop art, but it's their unconscious that opens their pocketbooks. Deep inside, they know his work is a direct sexual expression of the soul." He took another step up, until his legs were pressed against the fountain wall, so he could get a closer view of the sculpture.

"He's the client I value most. There's no artist I respect more, and to complicate the matter, he's a very dear friend. Though, I warn you, a pain in the ass. All great artists are. He did the dragon you saw out there as well. That's why he didn't want us lingering over it."

Lauren turned and stared at Marcus. Her throat did not respond immediately to the pressure of her vocal cords, and when it did, her voice came out as a whisper. "J. Martin is…Josh?"

"Joshua Martin. One and the same."

Lauren took a moment to digest that. She walked around the statue, examining it from every side. The light that shone through the windows touched all the important details, the expression, the curves, the tension of the bodies waiting, testing.

It made even more sense now. His wife, the tattoo artist. He was not the tattoo type, but he had allowed himself to become a living canvas for some of her more experimental work. Who but another artist would understand the need to marry art with love, to bind art to their other passions? Or bind him with that passion, rather, not only in the work she did with her hands, but by displaying what she had created of him by branding him with it.

"This is even more incredible when there's a full moon. You see things you can't see with the sun. It's almost like their expressions change."

"Marcus…" Lauren stopped before him again, her eyes filled with pain.

"It's the last complete work he's done since Winona," the art dealer said softly. "His home is littered with half finished work, things he started and then destroyed, mangling them in his rage. Artists are psychotic parents, turning on their children when they see only their failures in them, those things they've planted in them themselves, with every sculpting motion. After all, it was their clay to begin with, wasn't it? The artist's hands being the loins from which they sprung, the creations cannot help but reflect the parent's shortcomings, and so the sight of them is so beastly to the artist that he must destroy them. And yet, Josh leaves them there, broken, destroyed, not giving them a proper burial, simply leaving the half finished next to the demolished. His home, his studio, has become someplace he goes to punish himself, an embarrassment," his eyes met hers again, "that he is reluctant for anyone to see."

She put out her hand, touching his arm, her throat aching with the pain she heard in his voice. He touched the track of the tear running down her cheek and she closed her eyes.

"Did he ever bring her here?"

Marcus shook his head. "I think its part of its appeal to him. It's free of her taint."

"You didn't like her."

Marcus nodded. "Something was off about her, I never could put my finger on what, but I know Josh wasn't Josh when he was with her. There was some dynamic between them that had everything to do with sex, a mutual fascination. You called me an Iowa farmboy. Josh came from the city, but he's always had an innocence to him, and an innate goodness. It's one of the things that makes him so fucking irresistible."

He sighed. "I was holding back on you, somewhat, about he and Winona. I honestly don't know what happened, but I was there the night it ended. I know that he called me from a police station because he had been arrested for assault. He had nearly beaten a man to death. I made his bail. The man refused to press charges, indicating it was all a misunderstanding. The prosecutor felt without his testimony, the police did not have a case. Winona came to his apartment an hour or two after we got home that night. She followed him into his room, and they talked. I couldn't hear about what. Then I heard him tell her to get out in a voice I have never heard Josh use. It wasn't a shout, it was more an invocation. It vibrated through the apartment like the voice of God."

Lauren felt the tension in Marcus's voice communicate itself to her vitals. Her fingers curled into her palms.

"She must have pushed it," Marcus murmured, "because next thing I know he brought her out of the room. Well, dragged her out of the room actually. She was trying not to go, but he had her by the arm and was hauling her to the door. She was screaming, crying. He opened the door, flung her out into the hall so hard she hit the wall and crumpled to the floor. She was crawling for the door when he slammed it. I heard it strike her in the head. There was a blood stain there the next day. She wept out there for awhile and then left."

Marcus turned his gaze to Lauren's stricken one. "You've seen him, Lauren. He would never, not in a million years, consider violence against a woman. And yet there it was. He went to the couch, turned on the television. To the cartoon channel of all things, and turned it on, maximum volume. It made the glass in the windows vibrate, but I could still hear her keening, just beneath the noise. Then it got quiet, and he muted it. He turned and looked at me and said he was going to the island. And he hasn't left here since. That was two years ago."

Lauren swallowed, looked back up at the sculpture with Marcus. In every line, she saw what she herself yearned to have, not just the intensity, but the unbreakable bond, the trust. More importantly, she saw it was what Josh yearned for. No wonder the pull between them had been so strong. She slept with his damn statue on a pedestal in her bedroom with a damn spotlight on it like it was her damn nightlight.

"It's time to lance this boil," she said out loud. "Let the wound bleed out and start it healing."

She looked up at Marcus, resolution in every angle of her body, and the expression of her face.

"I couldn't agree more," he said. He swept out his arm toward another elaborate wooden door embedded in the stone wall of the hallway and crowned with a trellis of ivy. "Let me introduce you to the perfect operating room."

Chapter 15

"They have a fortune in toys in here."

Lauren ran her hand over the finish of a spanking bench made out of satin smooth cherry wood and gazed around her, amazed at the array of equipment in the large room. Mirrors lined two walls and the ceiling, increasing the sense of size, though the deep woven carpets scattered on the flag stones, as well as the large potted plants and variety of heavy tapestries hung on the stone walls, made the space more intimate psychologically, if not physically. There were two costume rooms, complete with fully stocked makeup tables and wigs, to dress for play.

"Look at this," she paused by a carousel horse, molded with a thin faux fur that felt much like the animal it emulated. The bowed head, lifted forelegs and bunched hindquarters spoke of a stallion's desire to run free. Marcus joined her, slid his hand beneath the horse's chest. There was the soft hum of a mechanical reaction. Lauren's eyes widened as a seven-inch erect phallus emerged just below the pommel of the saddle. As she watched in fascination, Marcus demonstrated with a touch of another button the way the phallus would undulate in circles or thrust forward and back. Lauren reached out to it and jumped back with a startled yelp and a laugh as the horse began to rock back and forth in an easy simulation of a canter. The ribbed cock continued to thrust, so it was obvious every rock forward would pull the phallus out, and the rock back would thrust it home.

"Want to give it a try?" Marcus gave her a wicked grin.

"Wow." Lauren looked about her. "None of it looks -"

"Cheap? Embarrassing? The rewards of large amounts of money, dearest. You can have sophisticated sex toys that look like works of art, like Chinese netsuke's, instead of tacky little bare tit statues bobbing on a dashboard. Climb on," he urged again.

Lauren flushed, but her gaze crept over the horse. Truth to tell, it was all to easy to imagine how it would feel sliding in and out of her tight passageway. The tissues dampened, just from the thought.

Marcus gave her a courtly bow. "It would be my pleasure to see your reaction, but even more, Josh would be overwhelmed by it. Don't you think?"

Oh, Marcus knew which button to push. She did, too. She ran a hand down the stallion's back haunch, made note of the velvet and rhinestone straps just above the fetlock joints of the horse's legs.

"Maybe you should try it, Marcus," she murmured, sliding around the backside of the horse to him. "Face down," she trailed her fingers up his bare arm, "cheek pressed against that broad rump, your wrists strapped to the hind quarters, ankles to his forelegs," she directed his attention there. "And then I can plunge that rubber cock into your ass until you scream and buck like one of your young men would."

Her body was pressed against his thigh now, and she felt his genitals swell and rise to her words. Marcus lifted a hand to her face, cradling it as she bit his Venus mound lightly, like a cat. "Ah, Lauren, I've forgotten how much fun it is to play with another Dom. Are you offering, my love?"

"No," she grinned. "Just teasing you. You wouldn't enjoy being tied up as much anyhow, and I'd rather make Josh hard as granite."

"I think you accomplish that just by breathing," he said. "But I agree. Shimmy out of those shorts and let's see if we can't give him a good show."

Taking her clothes off on the beach had somehow been less difficult than here in this quiet room, with just the two of them. She would say that being inside made things seem more civilized, but she could hardly call her surroundings civilized. Something unknown and primitive lived here, encouraging primal behavior.

As if sensing her difficulty, Marcus turned his attention to making some adjustments on the horse's controls so that she was not directly under his gaze. Courtesy from one Dom to another, a consideration neither would have given to a sub. In fact they would have enjoyed watching that sub squirm, self-conscious under their attention but obeying nevertheless, shedding clothes on command. A rueful smile tugged at her lips. No one in the dungeons of the Club had ever accused her of being democratic.

Lauren dropped the shorts to the floor, but left on the Brazilian bikini bottoms. She accepted Marcus's leg up on the horse, since her still tender ankle could not manage the task alone.

She was already moist and hot, but she closed her eyes, centering herself, shutting Marcus out for a moment to ease the tension out of her body being caused by her own ridiculous self consciousness. Gay or straight, any man or woman would get turned on by watching another pleasure herself. Marcus would be aroused, not just by watching her, but, as he said, by the thought of how Josh would react to her.

The idea fueled her confidence, and she found the phallus by touch, drawing aside the crotch of the bikini bottoms with one fingernail to allow her to lower herself onto the shaft. She drew in a breath at the sensation of the ribbed rubber sliding along the silken walls within. She slowed her descent, drawing her own pleasure out like a tightened bow string.

"Take me up slow," she said in a breathless voice. She gazed vaguely in his direction, but her focus was inward. "Then I leave it to your discretion. I don't want to go over, though."

Marcus nodded, reached out, and stroked a hand down her thigh. "I can smell you, dearest. It's perfume."

She smiled absently, dropping her head back and closing her eyes, her inner muscles contracting on the phallus even though it had not begun to move. Marcus picked up the remote to the device and backed away, giving the heat around her the space to expand. He went to one of the high backed carved chairs, obviously left there for the relaxation of the Lord or Mistress of the dungeon as they watched the pleasurable tormenting of their victim.

Lauren purred as the shaft began to slowly rotate inside of her. The horse quivered to life, bringing an easy rocking movement that gave the dildo a slight thrust with each rock back. The sleek, faux fur covering made her feel as if it were a horse's flanks in truth beneath her thighs. There was an increase to the humming, and now she felt a vibration beneath her legs, a rippling like the muscles of the beast, that added to the sensation.

Those ripples were being matched from her womb, and she had to clench her inside muscles to keep from helping it along. Instead, she ran her hands over her damp breasts in the bikini top, cupping them in her hands, squeezing, not touching the erect nipples.

She knew the moment Josh came in, looking for them. She heard his steps on the threshold; his voice, dying away on the question as to why Marcus had brought her in here. She opened her mouth on a ragged breath and could taste him. She felt as if she could even detect his own unique male scent, as if all her senses were tuned to whatever frequency he traveled. It made her hotter. It made her want him with an ache fiercer than any pain or pleasure she had ever experienced. She could have him or keep building her desire to have him, and both ideas appealed to her.

She slid her hands up, the friction of skin on cloth riding the bikini up from the bottom of her breasts, so the undercurves were bared. Her hands traveled from there to her neck, her hair, freeing it from its clip, letting it fall down her back. Her body continued to undulate with the horse, her hips moving in slow circles. The muscles of her thighs contracted as she turned her head to open her eyes and gaze upon him.

The greedy desire in his eyes scorched her, shuddered through her body, tightened her grip on the phallus and almost tore a moan from her throat that would have been an open invitation she would not have had the power to revoke.

"Go sit at Marcus's feet," she whispered. "And don't even think of touching yourself. Your hands... your mouth," she punctuated each word with another circle of her hips, squeezing her breasts in her hands, gripping her nipples and tugging so that she saw saliva gather at the corners of his mouth like a starving wolf, "your cock... they're all mine."

Marcus guided him into a seated position at his feet, for Josh could not tear his eyes from her to watch where he was stepping.

Lauren moaned as the control increased the speed of the inserting phallus, which was now glistening with her wetness as it withdrew partway from her and plunged in again. She saw Josh's eyes on it, knew he wanted it to be his organ, and she reveled in his need, let it drive her even higher. The impact of the vibration pressing against her clit increased on each thrust, and she writhed on her mount. Her ass made a soft, slapping noise on the saddle as her movements became more focused, more intense, skillfully brushing the soft rubber against the place inside that sent an explosion of tiny metallic sparks through her thighs and lower belly, through her breasts. She heard the tender sucking noise that a drenched pussy made. Her attention turned back to Josh.

Marcus was stroking her lover's hair fondly, his gaze riveted on Josh's face, fascinated with his response. Josh sat rigidly against his knee, like a wild predator waiting to be released to the attack.

Her body was begging, calling, but she could be as tough on it as she was on any submissive in a dungeon. She knew the benefit of patience, of waiting. Instant gratification was just that - instant. There was no orgasm as intense as one that you had to work for, work for like a son of a bitch, endure being pleasurably teased and teased ever higher. That was not only her intent with herself, but with Josh. She reminded herself she wanted him to come on command, and he would, if she found that threshold, the teetering edge over which it would take no more than a murmured word to push him over. He looked as if he was close to it now.

The look in his eyes was as wild as the spirit of the stallion she rode. In her imagination, she saw herself release him from her thrall. He surged up from his seated position, plucked her off the horse as if she weighed no more than a doll. He would throw her down to the floor, part her thighs and thrust into her with the frenzy of a wild animal, exploding hot and wet inside her.

She shuddered at the thought, a soft cry like a dove coming from her lips. She gave Marcus a quick nod and he pressed the controls immediately, slowing the rotation of the phallus. It slid from her, retracting into the pommel.

"Josh," she said, her voice like thick cream, "Bring me one of those hand towels. And don't you even think about adjusting yourself."

She knew he was enormous, and derived tremendous pleasure from watching him rise awkwardly to go get the towel. He tried to bring it to her clutched in his hand so it fell in front of his groin.

She clucked. "You know better than that, Josh. I want to see you. Put your hand down, and bring me the towel."

He swallowed, that delightful red flush creeping over his neck, and he walked toward her, obviously having some difficulty. She licked her lips and teased a groan from him at the sight of her tongue.

She took the towel from his trembling hand. Under the heat of his intense scrutiny, she ran soft terry cloth over her wet labia, and then delicately pulled the crotch of the bikini back over herself, adjusting it over her swollen folds, smoothing the wrinkles with the pads of her fingers.

The sound he made was so much like a growl that Lauren lifted a startled glance to him. He was very close to her now; so close another step would bring the curve of her belly brushing against his straining cock beneath the denim.

"I have my limits, Lauren," he said, low.

She knew it, could feel the caged beast hurling against his bars, knew how close he was. But she knew just how hard to push, she always had. It was an art form. Jonathan had teased her with what he never intended to give her, and in hindsight she knew he had given her an unintended gift. He had taught her the difference between torture and teasing, sadomasochism and sexual dominance for pleasure. She wanted to tease Josh, arouse him, make him ache for her, but not deny him, or her, not ultimately.

It was a fine line. When emotions got involved, judgment could become clouded, especially when emotions were tied up in shadows of the past. She intended to dispel those shadows, for the both of them.

"Then why don't you cross that line, Josh?" she murmured, pressing up to him, sliding her arms around him. "I'm a little bitty thing, Josh," she crooned. "A man strong like you could overwhelm me in a minute, take your pleasure."

She drew the word out, sliding it over her tongue like something edible. She nuzzled his neck, put the towel back into his hand. His eyes on hers, he brought the terry cloth to his nose, and weakened her knees. He inhaled her scent, closing his eyes.

She was expecting anything. He might snap, lunge and be on her like a wild animal, take her over and leave her no choices to make.

Instead, he opened his eyes, the gray irises brilliant in their intensity. "I'd like to put my nose in the real thing. Mistress."

She ran her knuckles down the side of his face and he nuzzled them. He sucked one finger into the hot cavern of his mouth and swirled his tongue around it, reminding her vividly of his dexterity in applying the skill elsewhere. Lauren met the sudden mischievous glint in his gaze with a stern one in her own.

"You may kneel, then, and put your nose as close as you wish," she nodded. "As long as you do not touch me in any way."

He gave her a charming smile she immediately distrusted. He knelt, one knee, two knees as she hooked one leg over the pommel and spread her thighs for him.

Marcus was still watching them from his chair, his attention rapt, a palpable presence that heightened the sexual tension in the room.

Lauren looked down at the bare brown shoulders, the streaked mane of hair that lay over them. He had a small scar on the left shoulder, maybe from carpentry work. He leaned forward as she studied that scar, and his nostrils flared, taking in her scent. He made a soft, pleasurable sound, and she felt her response leak from her. The bikini did not have a lined crotch, and the bead of fluid slowly rolled down her inner thigh as he watched. He had done no more than breathe on her, heating her like a bellows to a furnace.

"I'd be happy to clean that up for you, Mistress," he said, his gaze latched on its course over her skin.

She swallowed, and her hands trembled at his soft tone, the need in his face. "Just the leg."

She drew in an unsteady breath as his lips caught the bead just above the back of her knee. His hand balanced him on her thigh, his light touch eliciting a scream from her body for more, a scream that got more insistent as his firm lips traveled upward, following the bead's path. He took his time, sucking her dew off her heated flesh with the leisure thoroughness of a lion cleaning his mate's pelt.

When he reached the upper part of her thigh, his tongue carefully licking just below her crotch, the curve of his skull brushed across her mound with every stroke. Lauren's body quivered despite her attempt at control. A soft whimper came from her lips.

His fingers tightened on her knee, even as his raised gaze communicated understanding. He comprehended, as she did, the desperate need that lay beneath the surface of this game. That was the niggling worry that kept her stepping so carefully. They had no way of knowing if they were lost souls drawn together by desolation or destiny. She was terrified of the answer, but the only way to find out was to let go of fear and take the risk.

He shifted his angle. Just a graze of teeth and lips over her quivering clit, his hands sliding up both her thighs. He was showing her what pleasure could be had, the little boy only being a little bit bad...

She bit down on a groan and slid her hand down over his hair as his tongue gave her a stronger, more insistent lick through the fabric, the friction rubbing her aroused pussy. Her fingers dug in, held him still. He gazed up at her, playfulness warring with dangerous mutiny in his stormy eyes.

If she had only seen desire there, she might have given in at this moment. But she saw the fear. He was scared shitless, just like she was, and he thought he could use her body's needs to shove her away from the shadows that lurked within him.

At heart, people were animals, burrowing in holes with their hurts, never realizing they would die in those holes if they did not summon the courage to drag themselves out and let themselves be healed. A rueful smile curled her lip. Physician, heal thyself.

"Back off," she murmured, shifting the smile into an amused disinterest as he obeyed with a reluctance that was echoed in every raging cell of her body.

Lauren eased off the horse. Her knees were trembling. Josh reached up from his kneeling position, steadied her. His hand slid down her waist, over her hip, to her thigh, lingering. He leaned forward and pressed a kiss there. His expression was reverent, passionate, eager, fierce, and she had to stifle a groan of need. Did a Dom just know instinctively when the time was right? She hoped so; otherwise she was going to kill them both.

"Stay there, on your knees," she ordered, and she put some space between them, gathering her composure. She was too good a Mistress to give away her state of mind, however, so her walk around the room to get a breather was a calculated saunter. She lingered by each sexual device, examined them, ran her hands over soft cuffs, the cold metal of steel bars, the polished wood of a bench. Marcus was watching her, too, his face impassive, but she needed no clues from him at the moment and did not look in his direction.

It was a few moments before her body settled enough that she really began to see what was before her, and then she began watching Josh out of the corner of her eye. His gaze was following her, but she noted the tension in those fine shoulders grew more pronounced whenever she lingered at any type of restraint system, anything that would leave the sub helpless to defense against the Dom. A smile curved her lips. Of course. She stopped.

"I want you here," she said.

It was the dominant piece in the room, a device like a St. Andrew's cross, only modified into an H design. The shape allowed the captor full front and back access to the captive, with the exception of a couple wide cross pieces that could be adjusted up or down, wherever the captor chose to position them. She turned to face the kneeling man, and her heart broke a little as she saw the uncertainty, the desperation and fear, in his eyes.

"Will you trust me, Josh?" she said softly. "Trust me to know when to be kind, and when to be not so kind?"

Would he let her hold the cards until the game was over?

She was upping the stakes, and they all knew it. She had crossed the line that was safe for both of their hearts. She was going to challenge him, push him, see how far he would submit to her. She couldn't look to Marcus for approval or disapproval this time. It was between the two of them.

"I trust you," he said at last, his eyes on the ground, as if he was not brave enough to agree while looking at her. His voice was hoarse. "I don't know why. I hardly know you. But I do. Completely."

Then, as if he had given himself a mental slap for cowardice, he jerked his head up, and looked at her.

"I will serve my Mistress's pleasure," he said.

Lauren swallowed a fist size lump of jagged glass, almost crying out at the pain, but an amazing thing happened to it once it cleared her throat. It lodged in her heart, where it was warmed by the simple sincerity in his eyes, the devotion in his voice, and every line of his body. The jagged edges melted, and she felt a complete, tender fulfillment. Someone who trusted her, believed in her, willingly gave himself to her to be cherished and who would cherish her in return. It was the Whole she had wanted to give to Jonathan, but the foundation for it had never been there. The rest of it was always hard work, but the underlying current to give it a chance had to be there. Josh and she had had it instantly. Now they just had to wade through the baggage to keep from fucking it up.

"Then you should cast your eyes down," she reproved, and came forward. She kissed him on the top of his bowed head, nuzzling his hair. His fingers clutched her calves for a moment, hard.

She clucked at him, correcting him, and he removed his hands, bracing them into tense fists on the floor on either side of her feet. "You need to remember manners," she reminded him, and turned, though her heart had tilted at the sheer desperation of his grasp.

"And what is the lady's wish, now that she has her slave's compliance?" Marcus arched a brow at her, rising from his chair.

Lauren paused, and glanced back at Josh, taking him in from head to toe. The bare back, the tight ass, the pink undersides of his bare feet.

"Put him there," she nodded to the St. Andrew's Cross. "I want him spread and cuffed, face forward. Strip him of all his clothes, oil him down." Her gaze watched the muscles knot across his tanned shoulders, in response to her silky words.

"I really, really like her," Marcus sighed happily.

"Turn around on your knees, Josh. Raise your eyes, and look at me," she said.

He did, and he did not look as pleased as Marcus sounded. Lauren turned, walked toward the dressing room. She undid her swimsuit, letting it fall to the floor, and then turned, a Betty Gable pose, just giving him a hint of profile.

"Will you obey me, Josh?" she asked. "All you have to do..." she raised a hand, cupped her breast and stroked its curve idly. "Is say...no."

His nostrils flared, as if he caught the scent of her from across the room. "I'll obey," he managed roughly. "But I'd rather throw you to the floor, spread your legs wide and fuck you until you lose consciousness."

She nodded, keeping her expression unruffled, though need tightened like a fist in her gut at the dark intent in those gray eyes. "Maybe you'll get that chance...if you're good." She smiled. "Or maybe, if you're bad."

She surprised a grin out of him. It eased the tension in his shoulders, and that reassured her. The stress would come back, she knew, as soon as Marcus started following her instructions. She sensed something dangerous down in this dungeon. The setting was almost too perfect; too open to pushing past hard limits, and she hardly knew his soft ones.

She put her hand on the dressing room door, then stopped, turned back. "Marcus?"

Josh had just shed the shorts, and he was naked, vulnerable and beautiful, his back to her. She wanted to go kiss the soft skin between his shoulder blades, run her hand over the small of his back, smack that taut buttock. All in good time. Down, girl.

"Yes, dear lady?" From Marcus's amused expression, Lauren decided he was repeating the question.

"I want him blindfolded. A full head mask, if they've got one. Ears, nose and mouth open."

She closed the door again on his nod, ignoring the alarm in Josh's face.

Chapter 16

"Keep your eye on the ball, girl," she told herself, repeated it in her mind, tried not to let the pain and worry in those beautiful gray eyes unbalance her, deflect her from her intent.

Marcus had told her the purpose of the two rooms, how one was marked for Mrs. Salerno and one for Mr. Salerno, but she had not gone into either costume room when she first came into the dungeon. Now her jaw dropped in shock and sheer admiration for the quantity of choices. There was everything from queen to jungle girl, gun moll to waitress. She wondered if the Salernos ever left it to chance, each going into their respective costume room to choose, emerging to the fun of coming up with scenarios that meshed unlikely pairings such as Queen with rock star, or waitress with overseer.

She turned and surveyed with quiet delight a wall of toys, including a selection of whips, supple and gleaming with regular waxing. She wondered if that was one of Josh's jobs; he and Marcus had seemed to know where the room was well enough. The variety of mechanisms, from the carousel horse to the automated suspension system, would certainly require regular repair and maintenance to ensure the machinery ran smoothly.

She picked out a handmade braided whip, with an extended handle to increase control and accuracy. Silver rings worked into the seven-foot length gave it a liquid movement when she rolled it out. The balance was near to perfect for her, suggesting the whip had been custom made for Mrs. Salerno. A popper of a half dozen thin strips had been tied into the eyeloop at the end, and though the strips were soft to the touch, they were thin and resilient enough to deliver quite a sting. She ran her hands over the instrument and imagined Josh's long fingered hands waxing the plaited surface, rubbing, his brow creased in concentration, his soft hair falling over his forehead and along the curve of his neck, the smooth muscle in his biceps rolling with his movements.

She was stroking the whip as if she was stroking him, and she stopped herself, surprised at the erratic tempo of her pulse, the pounding of her heart. How could he have affected her like this so quickly? But she knew. She knew when she saw his statue in the courtyard.

She experimented with a few flicks, getting used to the feel. She had told Marcus and Josh that once D/s was in the blood, it was hard to shake. When she had been recovering from Jonathan's cruelty, sure that she needed to break her unhealthy addiction to the lifestyle, she had decided to invest in a nicotine patch, so to speak. She had taken bullwhip lessons from an expert who worked at one of the clubs. Her grandmother had always said that to get out of funk, try something different. Lauren was sure her grandmother never imagined the advice applying to her daughter's colorful sex life.

Under John's tutelage, she had gotten quite skillful with the bullwhip. They practiced at his home; in a barn he had converted into a playroom, though it was not so elaborate as the Salerno's. One evening, a young man showed up, one of the subs who waited tables at the club. He was also a staff "Slave" that could be rented by the hour by Doms, if the staffperson felt comfortable with it. He made a good pretense of having just dropped by John's for a beer, but from the stillness in his eyes, and the shortness of her own breath when she looked at him, they had all known it was a lie. John talked her into taking a passing "test", practicing on a live subject. The boy had smiled at her as John spreadeagled and cuffed him.

She had the boy sweating and painfully aroused after ten minutes, with tiny red marks striping his raised arms, straining buttocks, and quivering inner thighs. She had celebrated her graduation with a cold shower, a long session with the detachable multi-setting head, and a hard cry.

The idea of Josh belonging to her, submitting to her so that she could bring him to peak after peak of pleasure, could hear him groan her name, beg for release and then come back for more…she trembled to think of it, and her palms were not the only part of her body with moist crevices at the thought. A man who would submit to her desires as willingly as Josh was a heady aphrodisiac.

That was just part of it, though. The emotions she felt for him were not just interwoven with her physical desires. The physical desire was like a clutched fist of need, trying to grasp something that would last beyond the last vibration of the orgasm. She not only wanted to play with the lion; she wanted to take him home and keep him.

Enough. She shook herself out of pointless reflection. There were other toys on the wall to examine, and she had to get dressed. There was a fine line between building his anticipation and making him wait so long he fell asleep.

Chuckling at herself, she turned to the racks of clothes.

* * * * *

Her heels were sharp on the ceramic mosaic tile as she opened the door of the costume room. She leaned in the doorway a moment, flicking the whip idly around her feet, letting it make mysterious whispering noises against the flagstones. She felt the Goddess take possession of her soul, equally capable of cruelty or mercy.

She found, however, that her less omnipotent self had to use the support of the door jam for a moment or two, as she reminded herself to breathe.

It had taken her a half-hour at the makeup vanity to achieve the effect she wanted for herself, and Marcus had made good use of the time. She was hard put not to moan in sheer tortured delight at what lay before her, a piece of artwork better than anything the Salernos had paid five figures to own.

Marcus had cuffed Josh on the St. Andrew's Cross, strapping three lines of restraints on each limb to severely inhibit movement. Straps bound Josh at the ankle, calf and mid thigh for each leg, and the wrist, elbow and bicep for the arms. Another strap was around his throat, another at his forehead, holding his head immobilized against one of the adjustable cross pieces. Marcus had even added a strap at Josh's waist that threaded through another cross bar, moved to his lower back for support. The result was that he could move very little, if at all. He was totally, magnificently, at her mercy, his body gleaming with the light sheen of sandalwood oil Marcus had slicked onto every expanse of skin.

The head mask was on, as she had ordered, covering all that beautiful hair and his eyes. His mouth was visible and open, nervous tongue darting out repeatedly to wet dry lips. His nostrils were flared, his body tense, straining with the remaining senses to detect her return.

He was afraid, that was obvious, but overwhelmingly aroused. It was the ultimate state of vulnerability, when a Dom could bring pleasure and joy, or prey upon the sub's darkest emotions and fear.

"Jesus Christ, you are fucking beautiful."

It was a reflection of her own thoughts, but after Lauren blinked and focused on something other than Josh, she saw Marcus was talking about her. She had hardly noticed him once she saw Josh, but now she registered that he had had time to get into the spirit of things himself. He had paid a visit to the costume room and changed into the flowing white and gold robe of a pharaoh, open to show a tanned bare chest and loose silken white pants beneath, sheer enough to suggest the dark smudge of his privates and pubic hair. His feet were bare. If she didn't know his proclivities were not for her sex, and if her mind and heart were not so engaged to the man to his left, her mouth would water. As it was, he made an impact on her blood, which was already moving back from simmer into boil.

He smiled, and it was slow, appreciative and feral, one alpha acknowledging the power of another. "You could make a man think about changing teams for a night or two, love."

She laughed, a soft purr of sound, and strolled out, sauntered as if Josh could see her, let him imagine by her cadence the generous swing of her hips, the quiver of her breasts that resulted from the reverberation of her spiked heels with the stone. The ankle wrap she had tightened and left on beneath the supple covering of the boot was holding up well, as long as she kept her movements slow and deliberate.

She sidled up to Josh, one casual step at a time, until she was close enough for him to smell the exotic oils she had rubbed on herself. She drifted a finger along the slippery line of his neck, down his collar bone. "Are you nervous, Josh?"

A quick jerk of his head.

"But not scared of me, I hope." Her voice was soft, sensual, teasing, but with an undercurrent of seriousness. It was so easy to do this, so easy to do this with him.

The faint musk odor of his oil teased her senses and she indulged, her eyes roaming appreciatively over the slick muscles and flanks. The lighting in the room had been adjusted so the recessed spotlights were positioned to reflect off of the glistening thighs. Lauren swallowed at the sight of his stiff cock, so aroused the glans brushed his belly. It had not been oiled, cloaked in only its natural satin-over-steel smoothness, a bit of fluid leaking from the tip glossing the top.

"No, Mistress." It was just above a whisper. He *was* scared, but she knew by instinct it was his own soul, and the shadows that were rising from it, that were frightening him. A Dom had to bring the nightmares out, let them loose, so there would be nothing between Master and sub but trust, and pleasure, mutual devotion.

The thought brought an ache to her throat and tears to her eyes, and she felt a moment of true sadness. This time, there was no familiar sour taste of bitterness, or the taste of Jonathan. There was only Josh, and the pain and desire she felt for him.

She moved closer to Josh, and very gently stroked her knuckles across his lips, framed by the mask. It was a reassuring touch, though her proximity brushed her thighs against his arousal and made them both quiver.

"You know what I think about when I'm scared, Josh?"

He shook his head, then remembered. "Butterflies, Mistress."

She smiled. "You are so good. Just remember that. Okay?"

He swallowed. He was doing that a lot, and she found the nervousness charming, and arousing. She laid a soft kiss on his lips, which trembled under hers with his uncertainty and passion, and she murmured against them. "I'm here, Josh, and I'm going to make it all right. You're going to give me everything, and I'm going to heal it, and put it back inside you. Okay?"

She had no doubt of it, certain of her power, her role, dressed the part, in the right surroundings.

He shook his head, too overcome to speak, and she stepped back from him. "Are you doubting me, Josh?" She allowed enough ice to creep into her tone to make sure he felt the chill as solidly as a touch from her hand. One slight flick, and the whip end coiled around his ankle, just a whispering touch, then it was gone again. He jerked, his breath catching in his throat.

"You will hold nothing back from me, Josh. Try all you want, but you know who is Mistress here. Marcus," she tilted her head toward the other man. He was watching them both, a morass of things she could not read moving behind his expressive eyes.

"Josh is going to find it very difficult to control himself," she warned. "I don't want to have to be too cruel to him. Please put this on him, and make it as tight as he can stand it."

She lifted her other hand, which held a web of straps, and silver chain. Marcus's eyes flickered to it and then back up to her face. She waited. Would he refuse? Josh was his friend, and he had already warned her he would brook no unreasonable measures against his friend. Could he read her intentions?

Lauren took a step, laid the device in his palm and closed his fingers over it, then her hand over his, tightening her grip. *It's okay*, she mouthed.

Whatever he saw in her eyes satisfied him, for he nodded, curled his fingers briefly over hers, and took the device from her hand.

Lauren stepped back so she got a good view of her subject again. "Marcus is going to put a cock harness on you, Josh," she said. "I want to see your cock on display, and I want you to stay hard for me."

"I suspect," his voice was thick, "I could oblige you in that, regardless, Mistress."

She laughed, a light caressing sound that floated close then drifted away. "But it's like a favored piece of artwork, Josh. I want it framed, mounted for my pleasure."

Marcus dropped to one knee and coated his hands with the oil from the bottles he had used to slick Josh down earlier. His hand closed, with gentle admiration, over Josh's erection. Josh jumped, though he was unable to move his hips more than an inch because of the straps holding his thighs apart and his waist immobile. Marcus oiled the shaft as Josh's breath clogged in his throat, his color rising to his exposed jaw line.

"It feels different, having a man handle you, doesn't it?" Lauren asked. She circled to his right, distracting him from Marcus by making him search for her with his hearing and his nose. "A strong touch. His hand is sure of what will pleasure you, in a way a woman can learn but will never truly feel, or understand. She just enjoys when she gets it right and sees your body quiver under her palm, or feels your cock jump under the moist flick of her tongue, inside the deep recesses of her mouth, as she takes you in, sucking, drawing out your response."

Marcus chuckled as Josh groaned and attempted to thrust against his hand, then jerked in shame. Red color rose along his exposed neck.

"My dear," Marcus said, "you are supposed to soothe the beast until you get the cage on him, not tease him into a rage while he's still unfettered."

She laughed, a delighted sound. "My apologies, Marcus." But her grin was unrepentant.

"Laur — Mistress —" Josh's distress was palpable and she shifted gears, made her voice softer. She came closer to him.

"Women are so much luckier than men. We grow up used to touching each other, in affection, and friendship. It's easy to explore one another, enjoy a woman's knowledge of what feels good. Society doesn't give you guys as much of a break on that. We're free to learn from the beginning that just because we can enjoy what a woman can give to us, it doesn't make us a lesbian. Any more than," her finger reached out, stroked the side of his corded neck, "You responding to Marcus's touch makes you gay."

Marcus slid the tunnel of straps over the engorged and slick cock, and Lauren moistened her lips, her fingers curling into a scrape of nails on Josh's neck. Marcus was aroused as well, visible to her eyes in the loose pants. He fitted the straps evenly over the velvet flesh, a noticeable quiver to his hands as he tested the snugness, ensuring the tightness around the scrotum. He rose and moved behind Josh to buckle the harness just below the restraining strap on Josh's waist. The belted waist served the dual purpose of keeping the harness from slipping, and keeping Josh's penis in an erect, perfect angle for sliding into a woman's heat. Marcus's fingertips caressed the small of Josh's back, the dimples on either side of his spine. Josh's breath was rasping, his cock leaking more semen, and Lauren had to stifle her own raging desire at watching them. She wanted to tease him past bearing, and she was heading there rapidly. Maybe too rapidly.

There was a chain attached to the base of the cock harness, with the links dividing into two separate strands that went to the floor. Marcus came back around to Josh's front and fastened the ends of the chain to each link in the cuffs at Josh's ankles. The chain's weight pulled down on the harness and its contents, keeping it at that desirable angle, which made Josh's now half-mast erection even more impressive. Some distraction might be necessary or she suspected he might explode, regardless of the constriction of the harness. Lord knew, she was close enough herself.

"Josh, would you like Marcus to describe what I'm wearing?"

"Yes."

Crack!

He yelped in surprise, not pain, as the popper snapped at his upper thigh, just below his bound testicles. Marcus's head jerked up, having been just below the whip's path. She gave him a playful grin and reined the whip back in.

"Yes, Mistress," Josh corrected himself.

"Good." She drew close again, shifted the whip out of her left hand and kept the riding crop she had been holding with the whip in her palm. She dropped the tip of the crop; let it play a bit beneath his balls. He tried to strain at her touch, and could not. "Marcus?" she asked.

The art dealer bowed, settling in on the step of the dais that held the St. Andrew's Cross. He leaned back indolently; reaching for a glass of wine he had somehow procured, putting the final touch on the look of an indolent, sensuous Prince of Egypt. He took a sip and considered Lauren, who raised her brow, giving him a slight curve of her lips and a coquettish pose.

Marcus smiled. "Were you not so delightfully restrained, my friend, your body would explode at the sight of her."

Lauren strolled onward, her spike heels punctuating his words. She rested the crop on her shoulder and loosely flicked the bullwhip along the stone floor with her other hand, as he continued to speak.

"Your beautiful Mistress is wearing a tight gold dress, some sort of Lycra - cire cross. It has long sleeves and a just barely ass-covering skirt. The cloth of the dress is sheer, woven with sparkles of gold dust. At different angles you can see a momentary shadow of her pubis, the dark press of her nipples, the cleft of her buttocks, but they are tantalizing impressions only, sure to drive a handsome slave mad, trying to look without being caught looking."

Lauren chuckled.

"The neckline of the dress, always the most important thing to a man," Marcus grinned over his glass, "is a straight line from armpit to armpit, just barely above her nipples, and when she takes a deep breath, you see just that faint crescent of mauve over the nipple. I believe she's rouged them to make it more noticeable.

Lauren gave him a nod of pleased acknowledgment.

"She's made her lips wet as an aroused clit, with a burgundy shade. Her beautiful blue eyes are outlined in black and shadowed in gold. The sleeves of her dress hook with a gold chain between the thumb and forefinger like a medieval gown."

Marcus's gaze descended, and his voice went to an appreciative sensual thickness. "She's wearing gold thigh high boots with a three-inch spike heel and a gold chain circling the ankles. She's slicked back her hair and scattered gold dust across it and her cheeks. She's also carrying a very wicked crop, as you felt, and what appears to be a very long bullwhip.

"She's beautiful," he concluded. "A golden goddess." He ran his fingers along Josh's calf, teased his ankle just above the cuff. "Aren't you pleased to be courting her pleasure?"

Josh nodded, a slight movement all that his head could manage.

"You'd like to see her, wouldn't you?"

Another nod. Marcus tilted his head to Lauren, only ten feet away from her charge.

"Maybe in a moment," she said calmly, though she felt far from calm.

Her mother had once told her that the difference between love and all the lesser imitations of it was so startling, so powerful in its contrast, that once she had actually felt it, she would never mistake anything else for it again. Lauren hadn't known what she was talking about, because the perversity of love was, until you experienced it for the first time, there was no way to distinguish it from the other versions.

To have someone so willingly surrendered to her, open to her like this, was something she had never had, and it was so different from how Jonathan had made her feel that she couldn't imagine why she ever gave the sadistic prick the time of day.

She felt an incredible melding of power and tenderness, craving and worship. She had felt it in small doses throughout the past two days, but this was far more. This was utter, voluntary surrender of one human to another, and it humbled her in a way too powerful to explain in words. Marcus had been right. Such trust, such devotion was meant to elicit the heady flood of protectiveness and desire she felt now, the absolute worship for the one surrendering, cherishing their devotion and trust for the gift it was.

To honor it, to find it and keep it, she would have to risk losing it. That was a lesson Jonathan had taught her as well.

She stepped forward, the heel a loud punctuation on the stone floor, like the snap of a starting gun.

Chapter 17

"You must prove your devotion to me first, before you can see me," she said. The edge of the crop drifted along the line of his pectoral. The skin quivered beneath it, and she suppressed the urge to lean forward, bite warm skin and muscle.

He swallowed. Unbound, but bound by her orders, he had shown occasional flashes of humor. Here, he was helpless, focused on her and vulnerable, and she was about to tread into even more turbulent emotional waters. She thought about calling a timeout to be sure things were okay. It might break the tension that was building, tension that might be important.

She glanced down at his stiff cock. The head was full of blood, a flushed cap for the column of black harnessing straps, and she knew there was no doubt she had him in a high state of lust, when the psyche was more open to being pushed. She wanted answers. She had to have them, to be sure she could take them where they both seemed to want to go.

"Okay," he whispered, before she could open her mouth to ask him again.

She came even closer, brought her scent and nearness to him for reassurance. She caressed his bare neck, traced his lips gently with her fingers. She let him catch them in his mouth and suck on them greedily before she took them away and rested them on his bare chest, tracing the moisture he had left on them across his nipple while his breath caught harshly in his throat.

"Tell me what happened, Josh. What happened with Winona to drive you here, to make you hide here?"

His body went rigid. Whatever he had been expecting her to ask of him, it was apparently not that. Marcus's eyes narrowed on her, but after a moment, his expression became thoughtful and he nodded, tentative endorsement of her direction. *Be careful*, his eyes warned.

She knew. She suspected the danger of this path, and knew it all too well herself, and maybe that knowledge was part of why she dared.

"Can you tell me, love?" she turned her hand over, stroking with her knuckles now, more soothing than provocative. Blindfolding him should make it easier for him to speak of it, just as it had been easier to tell them of Jonathan while staring at the ocean, as if they were not there. But she couldn't be entirely kind.

"Tell me. I'm your Mistress. You're not to hide anything from me." Her hand descended, and closed over the harness, her lower two fingers capturing the chain and giving it a sharp tug. He groaned, trying to thrust into her hand, but she stepped back from him abruptly, leaving his hot skin exposed to the chill of her withdrawal.

"Anything," she repeated. "Tell me. If I decide you need to be punished," she sidled up close again, pressed her full length along his body, let his captive cock slide between her thigh muscles. It was like embracing a board; he was so rigid with hunger and heat. "I'll take care of it. Or perhaps you need a punishment now, to remind you who you obey, who you tell your secrets to?"

"A punishment worse than not being able to see you?" He groaned out the question. He tried to fasten his teeth on her throat, but she eluded him with a chuckle and a sharp strike of the crop along his inner thigh, the left one this time, and a quick flick over his testicles. Then she withdrew again. She took her time walking back, five paces, to the throne Marcus had vacated. She turned, took a seat, and considered him, a whip in each hand.

"Tell me, Josh. Tell me what happened. I'm going to sit here in this chair, and wait for you to tell me. Until you do, you will not be punished as you deserve. You will not touch me or suckle my breasts, or get to plunge that steel cock of yours into my pussy. Do you know how wet my pussy is for you, Josh? It's drenched. I could come just by sitting like this, watching you bound on display for me, as beautiful as one of your sculptures."

He made a noise, part plea, part animal sound of pain. Lauren refused to let herself soften, even though she saw concern flit across Marcus's face. She sharpened her tone.

"Tell me, Josh. It starts with one sentence. You said you trusted me completely. Prove it to me."

She watched and waited. It would have been a nice moment to simply indulge herself in the heartbreaking beauty of his restrained body, but the rasp of his breath and the intensity of his internal struggle came off his body in emotional waves that swamped her. She didn't need to see the visual chaos of his expression to know he was in anguish.

She wanted to know who had caused him such pain, protect him, heal it, kiss it away. Forgive him, if he suffered because he had caused pain. She thought she would forgive him anything.

"Start with one sentence, love," she said, softly, so her voice was like the murmur of his own consciousness. "I came here because I couldn't look in a mirror. Why are you here? What eats at your soul, Josh? It's just us here, and there is nothing outside this room."

"I'm a monster." It came out a whisper, but the raw pain in his voice made it even more potent than a declaration delivered in a shout. She heard accusation, judge, jury and conviction in his resigned tone, the sound of someone trudging off to hellfire with no hope of reprieve.

"Why are you a monster? What did you do, Josh? Tell me."

"I... can't. It's too bad."

She swung the whip, snapped it a hair's breadth from his ankle, so he felt the air a moment before the noise and jerked. Even Marcus started, surprised by the force of the move, his look of uneasiness quickly replaced by admiration as she brought the whip back in a sweeping, controlled curve around her calves. She was, for a moment, the image of the unrepentant Lilith, in the garden of Eden with the sly serpent coiled around her body.

"You have been bad, Josh," she said. "Bad for holding back on me, and Marcus, who cares for you so much. So you need to be punished."

She considered him, then rose, came to him. "So you will be," she murmured, a silky purr as she slid one fingernail down the center of his chest, depressing slightly to leave a red welt, scraping a line down his belly, stopping just below his navel. She lowered herself to a feline crouch, her breath heated, tickling just above his glans. Josh's arms became cords of iron, pulling against the restraints, and she wondered if there was anything more erotic than watching a powerful man strain against manacles.

She hoped the Salernos had made the bindings strong. This was no playful dungeon session. There was devotion here, and yes, intimacy, but there was also catharsis, purging and release. There was something painful in the room, and filled with rage, and it wanted its freedom.

She hoped to God she knew what she was doing, because at this point what was happening had taken on a life of its own. The reward might be a leap forward in trust and love, a binding of the souls, or it could destroy them.

They'd both been there, to that point of soul destruction. Now, whether they were fools or hopeless romantics, they were pushing the envelope again to see if they could find in each other what they had hoped to find the time before and failed. The result was going to be fire, but would it be conflagration, purification or resurrection?

"God, you are so gorgeous." She slid the butt of the whip along the inside of his calf, the ticklish indentation behind his knee, trailed it along his inner thigh. She could almost feel the heat pulsing from his captured cock. She coiled the whip behind his leg, tightened the slack so it pressed into his thigh. She leaned in and bit him there, soothing the pain with a warm swirl of the tongue, savoring the warm taste of his skin, the quivering and bunched muscle under her teeth. Her ear brushed his cock. He rasped out her name, a plea. Her eyes lingered on the tight clench-and-release spasms of his buttocks. He could not stop his body from imitating what it wanted to do, the mindless instinct of a dog humping a leg. Instead of amusing or repulsing her, the image increased her own hunger, for they were rapidly leaving niceties behind. Responses were raw, primitive. She wanted those hips pumping, jackhammering himself into her until she screamed. But not yet.

"Tell me, Josh. Why do you need to be punished? What did you do?"

She eased herself back into a straight-backed chair Marcus brought for her, so she could sit closer to Josh, brush her heeled boot along the inside of his calf.

His head lifted, his eyes and cheekbones masked to her, his lips moistening nervously, somehow appearing even more vulnerable for their solitary exposure on his face. "I can't," he repeated, desperately.

She twisted her wrist and the snap end of the crop zapped his thigh just below the bound scrotum, a quick sting, meant to raise the emotional response. He jumped, swallowed, and the quivering in his legs increased. "Please, don't…"

Marcus made a noise, and Lauren gave him a sharp, negative shake of her head.

"Marcus is here, Josh, and I am here. But in the darkness of that mask it's just you, facing yourself. I will take care of you," she reminded him, and this time the whip's touch was a gentle caress, teasing his balls. "Tell me."

His fists remained clenched against his bonds, muscles unconsciously resisting his restraints still, but she knew it was only a physical manifestation of resistance to the chains that held him in his mind. She longed to let him go, but he had to put it in the open between them. It was the sacrifice that all Masters demanded before they allowed themselves to be worshipped. Complete openness, no hidden corners. *Come on, Josh. Let it go, so I can let both of us go.*

"She was a sub. She liked me to really take control." The first words were thick, clotted as if they had to fight their way free of the grip of a festering wound, choked with pus. His lips pressed together. "She wanted me to dress her sexy when we were out, make her expose herself. We'd go to a club and she'd beg me to make her lift her skirt when she was dancing, let other people see her bare ass. She'd usually have me spank it good before we went out, hard with a belt, so it would have red welts on it.

"I liked playing with her, but I was afraid of being too rough. She could drive me up, make me get so savage with her. She wanted it that way, but... I enjoyed how much she got off on it."

Marcus's eyes flicked to Lauren. A frown flitted across his brow, but she shook her head, putting a finger to her lips and he sank back down on the dais near Josh's feet.

The mask would let him talk inside his head, temporarily push away his surroundings. The outside became the inside, and emotions not normally allowed the sight of day became irrepressible, because sightlessness and being helpless turned you inside out, made shields and controls impossible.

Lauren had watched many subs fall apart. A slave was supposed to have no secrets, expose his or her fears, worries and longings to the Mistress, and the Mistress would address them as she saw fit. It was the way the game worked. It was that automatic vulnerability, impossible to avoid, that gave the Dom such a dangerous edge, that made D/s walk so close to the darkness.

Marcus removed his hand from Josh's ankle, recognizing, as she did, Josh's need for an isolated dark void of space into which to spill the weight on his soul.

"So she got off on you doing all this. Why does that make you a monster? It sounds like you were a good Master."

"She didn't know anything about the clubs at first, just knew she wanted me to tie her up and whip her. It made her come all the time...in the beginning. She didn't really know about the other stuff you could do. I found out about those for her, because I knew she'd like them, and because, I liked them, too."

"It made you hard, didn't it?" she murmured, bending forward and rubbing her fingertips over his constricted organ, eliciting a moan of pleasure, another whispered plea that she ignored. "So you did what she wanted."

He nodded. "Anything. But some things I just couldn't...she wanted me to leave marks, permanent ones, and when she saw how much it bothered me, she wanted me to do it even more. And if I didn't want to do it, she'd take me to the clubs and make me watch while some other Dom did it, make me give her to another Dom."

"Did you like that?"

"Yes...no. It hurt, in a strange way, but it always got me off. It just felt...wrong. But I liked it," his fingers dug into his palms, so fiercely they left marks. She saw the flesh whiten and inflame around the puncture. "I fucking liked it," he repeated, not as emphasis, but as accusation. "It made me hard as iron. I wanted to pull her out of his hands and pound into her, but it was like rage...it felt wrong. I couldn't do it, though I was supposed to be in charge. It hurt," he repeated, confused, arguing with himself.

Lauren swallowed, feeling emotions of her own rise up. A bad feeling was growing in her and she saw it reflected in Marcus's eyes. Did she really want to hear the end of this story? No, she didn't, but she would. She had to.

She pressed her knee against his left leg. She laid her hand upon his thigh.

"So what happened?"

"I just...I did everything she wanted, but it never seemed like enough. I stopped working for awhile, because I was pouring all my energy into new things that I thought might turn her on. It was like..."

"Being strung out on drugs," she finished for him, remembering.

"Yeah..." he swallowed, and his hands eased, twitched a bit. "One night, we went out to dinner together. Just a regular thing, though I did the usual things. I made her wear something sexy I really liked, no panties so I could play with her pussy under the table. She liked me to make her flash the waiter, you know, lean forward over the menu so he could see everything, but she didn't push as much of that, not that evening. She seemed really affectionate, not real pushy, and I could focus on her, enjoy her. But I noticed that night...we didn't have much to talk about.

"I realized we had gotten away from what it was that had brought us together and now it was all about sex. That night felt better, though," he added wistfully. "It was more like us again. I had my arm around her, and through most of dinner, she cuddled against me and seemed happy with me, like she was pleased with me, and that felt good. It had been awhile since I'd felt that way."

Hadn't it been so similar for her, never feeling as if she had pleased Jonathan, always anxious, on edge, not caring about career or personal identity any longer, too keyed up to think about the destructiveness of it? It shamed her to think of it now, how she signed herself over to him, who she was, with barely a murmur or qualm. It was also frightening how she had done it, with no real sense of having done so. She had just hungered for acceptance, self affirmation, because she lost the ability to give that to herself. She had let Jonathan take it away. She and Josh, two insecure people with low self-esteem, uncovered and stripped bare by two people who needed to degrade them to feel worthwhile themselves.

It was pathetically formulaic and painful to see the mirror, but she was strong enough to look. She held the cards now, and had been holding them, since she became true to herself again and said the words that made Jonathan walk away. Now she just had to figure out what the winning hand would be for Josh.

"Tell me what she did." Her spike heel slid against his instep, depressed slightly, just enough to cause another slight red mark, a warning. "Don't keep me waiting, Josh."

The threat laced into the warm promise was a potent mix. His erection, waning a bit from the fluctuation of his emotions, jumped, began to swell so the straps bit into the tender skin again, and he groaned at the discomfort.

She knew the torture of desolation and desire mixed. It tore the senses apart and the shields down. She hoped he didn't need a further push. Marcus was a still presence somewhere to the left of her, and she could feel his tension.

"We left the restaurant," he said after awhile. "I had my arm wrapped around her. She nuzzled against me, then took my hand, pulling me into the shadows between two buildings so we could embrace. She was shy almost, where any other time she might have begged me into the alley in broad daylight and pleaded with me to use her where anyone could walk by at any moment and see her. But she wanted tenderness, and it...God, it was wonderful. I practically swallowed her, pushing her back against the bricks, but just to kiss her, hold her, feel her holding me.

"I didn't think about how unsafe it was where we were. I was supposed to protect her, and I didn't even think about it. Something came at me out of the shadows. I was so stupid, not thinking about how we were in a not-so-great an area, though the restaurant was a nice enough one. Letting her pull me into an alley, for Chrissakes, and I was supposed to take care of her…" his lips curled in a sneer of self-loathing so bitter Lauren could taste it on her own tongue.

"There were three men. They tore us apart and two of them grabbed me, knocked me around a bit, but mainly forced us deeper into the alley, forced me to my knees and held me there while the other one shoved her onto her back in the filth of that alley and yanked up her skirt. He hit her in the face, split her lip…"

He pressed his head back against the cross, his jaw clenching. Lauren didn't move, fighting every urge she had to keep from touching him in comfort or speak soothing words. The wound wasn't open yet. Blood had to be free flowing for it to cleanse itself.

"She was crying, crying my name as he rammed into her. And I lost it. She belonged to me. I was supposed to take care of her, but, no, no, NO. That's not it."

Lauren watched, her own eyes anguished, as moisture trickled from under the mask, curved under his jaw. His voice became brutal, unforgiving.

"For the first few minutes, I didn't even try to do anything, because I was getting hard watching them do it. I was getting off on it, because it was so much like what we did. She liked the rape scenes."

Lauren shifted, her eyes locking with Marcus's.

"I was fucking enjoying it, as if I was watching a Dom get rough with her to torture me, for not being enough. And," his voice broke, "I thought…she's finally…finally getting what she deserves." He choked on a sob. "I fucking *thought* that, I remembered that like I was some kind of diseased redneck wifebeater. It was that, not her being raped, that tore it loose inside me. I lost it."

A quiver ran through his shoulders, a tensing like a cramp.

"Josh —"

"No," his face contorted. "Let me feel it. I deserve it. I became filled with so much rage; ten guys couldn't have held me. I rolled and kicked. I fought them with whatever I had inside of me, three years of unfulfilled passion, fueled up emotional fucked-upness. When I yanked the guy off her, I remember his eyes going wide, looking at my face, and he tried to say something, but I busted his mouth with my fist before he could. I was sticky, sticky, spraying blood on her, and then she was on my back, trying to pull me off, and then the police were there...the police were there."

He stopped, breathing hard, tears dropping off his chin onto his heaving chest. Lauren shifted, rose.

"Don't take it off," he snapped out. "I don't want you to see my face."

"Okay," she said softly, laying her hand against the side of his jaw.

"Don't," he tried to jerk away, but the bindings didn't allow it. "I don't want you to touch me."

"Well, that's just too bad, because I'm going to." She rubbed her hand along his jaw, stroked, kept stroking as her other hand laid along his rib cage, soothing the ulcer of emotions.

"Please," he choked out. "I'm not...that's not all of it."

Lauren raised her head and she sensed his eyes searching for her face. She nodded, stepped back and let him hear her sit before him again. "Tell me all of it, Josh," she said sternly, though her throat ached with his pain.

"One of the guys was critical." His voice was weary now, almost dead. "The other was pretty messed up. I had just knocked the third out. The messed-up one was still coherent enough to talk, and he did, because he didn't want to go to jail for rape, especially since he wasn't a rapist." Josh swallowed, and his voice broke.

"He was just doing what my wife had paid him to do."

Chapter 18

Cold insinuated itself in her vitals like a doctor's invasive instrument. "Josh," she whispered. "Oh God, Josh."

Abandoning anything but her feelings, she sprang up and removed the mask, unbuckling it and pulling it off so she could see his anguished face. He turned eyes to hers that were overflowing not just with tears, but the black despair she had detected in small doses since they had met. Was it really less than two days ago? She snatched up a towel, wiped away his tears, blotted his running nose with tender fingers.

"Don't untie me," he said quietly. Marcus stopped in mid-motion. "I don't deserve the consideration."

He leaned his head back, closed those hopeless eyes. "I didn't know that at first," he murmured. "They separated us. She told the police everything," his eyes opened, went back to Lauren, his chosen confessor, and the detachment in his eyes stirred her, so at odds with his exposed physical condition. "She didn't want her friends to go to jail, or me. When the cops came in and started asking me questions about our... lifestyle, it floored me. Where the hell had that come from? Then I looked at their eyes and knew.

"It was a fucking game. A game she had engineered. She wanted to get off on me being helpless while she was raped, which of course wasn't rape. I didn't tell them anything, didn't make any attempt to defend myself. I wasn't protecting her or them, I just couldn't speak. Everything shut down and I was just inside my head, looking over our whole relationship, everywhere we had taken it, a spiral to hell. We kept going round and round the same subject that fascinated us, deeper and deeper into what had resulted in that dark alley. The police, the way they looked at us. The sick fantasies of bored yuppies while people got robbed or murdered out there, real crimes.

"One of them considered me a lowlife, perverted freak and it was obvious he considered the whole situation a waste of the taxpayer's money. Probably thought they should just shoot the lot of us. The other was more sympathetic, but it was all pity. He had this look, like I was some guy who had been sexually abused as a child, to explain why I was so fucked up now. Like I was some lost little kid that needed a mommy to take me home. And then she showed up to do just that."

Lauren wasn't sure he was even in the room with them anymore; his gaze was so far deep into himself. She could feel Marcus suffering, they both were, but Josh was not going to stop until it was done, now that it was out in the open.

The muscle in his jaw clenched. "Her eyes were shadowed and bruised, her lip split. She looked a little scared by it all. I don't know for sure. I was so messed up that night, I couldn't have said what she was feeling. She got me to the car, started to say something, I don't know what. I just handed her the keys, walked away, didn't look back. I felt like a worthless, dirty piece of shit. Everything shut down, you understand?" His head turned toward Marcus, focused. "I called you.

"When I got home," he said dully, "I stank of blood, sweat, the jail cell, and my own shame. Winona came over, of course. She followed me into my room, closed the door. We looked at each other then, and for just a moment, I had this pathetic glimmer of hope. There were tears in her eyes, and she was trembling. I thought, for just a second, she knows just as I do, that we went too far a long time ago. I cared about her. I didn't have much more than sex with her, but there was a basic attraction between us that could have been more. For just a second, I thought we were about to step on the right side of the line. Then she knelt in front of me and asked me to punish her.

"Jesus," he shook his head, "The rage just took over, and I couldn't control it. I threw her out of the apartment. When I was dragging her, she pushed against me, and her nipples were hard. It turned her on. She couldn't see even then, she couldn't tell the difference between games and real life, or maybe she didn't want to."

He swallowed, shuddered. "I came here. It was quiet enough, and simple enough, for me to put some pieces back together. The things that let you get up in the morning, go through the motions. Eat, drink, sleep, crap. But here I am, playing games again at the first opportunity. It's like, you don't go to hell, it just keeps chasing you down." At Lauren's stricken look, he closed his eyes, shook his head. "No, that was wrong. I didn't mean that, not about you.

"I did the same thing you did. I questioned whether the cop was right, if we were just a bunch of sick freaks. If this wasn't a game, but a scream for therapy. But then, here, where it's quiet, and I could think, I saw it was just the same thing as being gay."

His eyes opened, turned to a surprised Marcus. "There's too many who are, for it to be something unnatural. There are so many who are drawn to D/s. It's in the animal kingdom; you see it all the time. Dominant and submissive is a way of life, and we are animals, we can't escape it, shouldn't want to. We would probably be a lot less fucked up if we acted more like animals, accepted things, and stopped trying to run the world. D/s is part of our instincts, part of what we are, but the question becomes, how far do you indulge it? We don't have 100% animal instincts, and nothing can fuck you up like half-assed instincts meeting overblown intellect.

"Is this okay?" he glanced down at himself, a slight trace of amusement in his tired, tear-streaked face. "It feels okay," he said thoughtfully. "But when is it too much? Will I enjoy this now, and then let you be raped in an alley, get off on it?" his attention turned to Lauren and the amusement disappeared. "Nothing she did changed that I had that thought, when I believed she was being raped for real. People playing D/s games are okay, but what I did, what I thought, was twisted. I took the step from sex to brutality without even blinking. Some people can handle it, some can't. You can, Marcus can, but I'm not one of them. For me, it turned into a power trip, and a dangerous one. I know now it's a game others can play, but I can't. I shouldn't be here, shouldn't be doing this." He shook his head. "You're right. Take them off."

Lauren met his rational gaze. Too rational. "Are you sure?"

"Yes. Let me go. We need to stop this. I need to stop this."

She considered him. "I don't know if that's the right thing to do."

"Were you listening?" he snapped, making her jump with his abrupt venom. "You don't... you're fine, you're perfect," he closed his eyes, averted his face as she stepped closer, "You're perfect," he said raggedly. "It works for you. But I'm a monster."

"No," she shook her head.

He jerked at the right arm. "Listen, let me go. I don't need to argue it, I just need to go."

"To run."

"Yes, to run," he snarled. "What do you care? Let me go!"

"No," she repeated, sure of herself now. She stepped back and loosed the whip from its coil again.

Josh stopped, stared at her. "What?"

Lauren wet her lips, shifted her weight to one hip so the fabric shimmered, giving him a brief glance of the body beneath. "You heard me well enough. You need to stop running from the truth, Josh. The real truth." Her voice had become cool, authoritative, and his attention seemed divided between incredulity and apprehension, shifting between her face, the whip and the displayed delights of her body.

"Let me go," he said between gritted teeth, and yanked against the cuffs, hard enough that the cross proved it had indeed been designed to hold a strong man, for the wood did not groan and the manacles did not allow him to budge the slightest amount.

He was there, bound for her intentions, until she deemed otherwise. It made her hot all over, especially now that she could see the paved road to hell clearly. There was one last exit, right before the pit of flames, so close to the precipice they might be scarred by the damning heat. Or purified by it, depending on how right she was. She took Josh's advice, and followed instinct.

"You like to play, Josh," she said, her voice becoming almost gentle. In contrast, the whip arced up, slashed across his ribs. He gasped, cursed.

"Your crime," her voice rose over his feral growl. "is not in holding back, but in pretending to be what you're not. You liked seeing her thrown to the ground, because that's exactly what she wanted you to feel."

"No," he shook his head.

Lauren sidled closer, sliding her breasts against his abdomen and chest, brushing her pubic bone against his erect and bound shaft.

"Look at me, Josh. I wanted you spread, and tied." She ran the handle of the whip up between his legs, lodged it firmly in the crevice between leg and testicles, making him feel the pressure against his scrotum. "You *are* spread, and tied.

"I wanted your cock restrained so you couldn't come until I said so." Her hand closed over it and he groaned, unable to do more than accept her caress, for the straps allowed him no room for movement. "It is. You can't do anything without my permission. You want to fuck me, don't you?"

He stubbornly looked over her shoulder and flinched when the crop cracked on his flank. She wasn't holding back now. She made sure it hurt, and his teeth bit down on his bottom lip. There was a raging light growing in his eyes and she wanted it in flame. She wouldn't let him retreat into the coffin of his guilt. Not this time.

"Tell me, Josh. You want to fuck me, fuck me hard. You want to feel me writhe beneath you, cry out; rake your back and ass with my nails. But you won't."

She seized his chin in one hand, forced his eyes back to her face, those nails biting into his jawline. "You can't. You can't do it without my permission." She leaned in, her lips touching his ear, which was turning a dull red. "I have to tell you it will bring me great pleasure. I have to order you to do it. You have to make sure it is what I want, because you tremble to please your Mistress. It pleased her to twist that in you."

"No," he said, but there was a grain of uncertainty in his rough voice, the shift of his eyes. Lauren seized that grain. She let the emotion creep into her own voice, her fury with the unknown Wirona.

"She made you abuse her, made you fuck her hard, rape her. She enjoyed the violence, but more than that, she enjoyed watching it make you think you were sick. She hurt you, Josh. She used you. Your unconscious knew it all the time. Why do you think you were always twisted up in knots?" His neck tensed, as if he would pull away from her grasp, but he couldn't, and her hand wouldn't let him.

"You wanted her to feel pain that night, because she betrayed you, Josh. Don't you see? You were never the Dom. *She was.* She was your Mistress. She was supposed to take care of you, love you."

The rage swelled up, and the hurt, and he did manage to jerk from her grasp, causing her nails to slice across his skin. "No," he snarled, struggling so she saw red lines of welts just below the cuff lines on his wrists, proof of his strength. He could not get free, but he could destroy himself trying. "No, no, no!"

Lauren jumped back as one of the links popped on the manacle. Fortunately there were three holding it to the wood. His nostrils flared at her, his gaze flashing victory at her retreat.

Lauren's eyes narrowed. She stepped back up to him. Her hands could be as gentle as a mother's when she so chose, but she wasted none of that softness now. With brutal efficiency, she reached around Josh, jerked open the tongue of the belt to the cock harness, freeing it from his waist. She pulled the ass strap back between his legs and stripped off the full rig, the force of the jerk and the straps pinching the tender skin.

She stepped back, deliberately brought the harness to her lips. The tip of her tongue touched the strap that had been closest to the head of his cock, and she tasted the salty substance that had wet the area there. She tasted it, as delicately as she might sample a hors d'oeuvres at a cocktail party. Her hand with the whip dropped, her fingers curling into the dress. She eased the tight, clinging fabric up, up her hip until her shaved pussy was exposed, just the bottom point of it.

He watched her, fury, fear and lust warring in his gaze, tearing him apart within and without.

Her own insides were being tormented by his struggle. A good Mistress watched the body language, the shift of the eyes, the light sheen of nervous sweat, the state of the cock, to determine what the sub wanted, what would bring them the most pleasure. In so many ways, it was the Dom serving the sub's needs. If the Dom lost sight of that, she took the risk of moving into megalomania, and imposing what she thought was best for the sub. How could she not doubt herself at a moment like this? Lauren was sure even the unflappable Marcus was having second thoughts about what had started under the guise of a playful card game.

When it boiled down to it, she had to go with her instinct, and her feelings. And she wanted Josh. Wanted him, heart, body and soul, and to do that, she had to bring him to her honestly.

She let the harness drop and faced him, her crop held to one side, the whip to the other, her breasts jutting and proud, her chin lifted. Challenge and denial were in every angle of her posture.

"Marcus, let him go."

The man, a somewhat dumbfounded witness to the charged tableau before him, jerked as if someone had just pulled his strings and reminded him he was part of the play. "What?"

"You heard me. Let him go." Her eyes met Josh's furious ones, flashing with equal parts venom and Viking lust. "Come after me, Josh. You want to prove me wrong? Prove you'll take what you want, that you like hurting women, like watching them be raped. Big pussy."

"Lauren—"

"Do it!" she cut Marcus off. As the man pressed his lips together, but moved to comply, she took several steps back, not in retreat, but in preparation, her hip cocked, eyes never leaving Josh's. The lion tamer waiting for the lion to bound into the ring.

He did not disappoint. As Marcus freed the last arm cuff, the art dealer tilted his head, started to murmur something. Josh's attention never wavered from Lauren. He jerked at the manacle the moment Marcus slid the catch from the strap, and yanked his hand all the way free. Josh shoved Marcus aside, sprang off the platform and came at her, his cock hard and ready, his eyes flaming with dangerous intent.

The whip snaked around his thigh, coiled. She jerked, loosing it, and spun him off balance. He recovered fast, faster than she expected, dodging her next strike, but she feinted left and snapped the weapon with a turn of her wrist. She made contact, along that beautifully sectioned abdomen, and raised a bloody welt. She had been taught how to inflict all levels of pain with the whip, the discomfort intended as a stimulus to pleasure. This time she went for pain, to add fuel to his rage.

He was furious, as angry as she had ever seen a man before. To see a young, powerful male in that state was not only impressive, but terrifying, especially since she had made sure all that rage was centered on herself. She watched his eyes calculate his next move and knew he would take her down with it. She wasn't that fast in these heels, or that strong.

She lashed out again, and he took the sting of the braided rope on the forearm, twisting his wrist so he coiled his flesh in its grasp and gripped the weapon in his fingers. He ripped it out of her hand in one brutal and effortless move.

She didn't back away, but watched him charge forward. There was no time for doubt now. She dropped her arm to her side, and let the lion spring upon her.

They hit the stone floor, with her under his hard, roused body. His knee jammed between her knees, spreading her to insinuate his body between her legs. The dress rode up to her waist, as her thighs were pushed up to accommodate his muscular torso. His cock teased at her wet folds, the blunt head a breath away from the decision, as unbearable a taunt to his virility as anything her words could provoke. She smelled the musky oil on his body, felt its slippery touch along the insides of her open legs.

She did not struggle, or move. Lauren could not hide the pulse leaping at her throat, the simple animal response of bringing the full force of an enraged creature upon her, but she kept her gaze on his, tried to remember how to breathe.

He was breathing hard enough for both of them, a harsh, rhythmic sound in his throat. The gray eyes were concentrated slits, his jaw flexing with the emotions he wanted to exercise upon her. His bruising grip left her wrist and his hand came up into the field of her vision. His fingers closed on her throat. They were trembling.

It was a silent, tense moment. If she closed her eyes, the heat coming off that sleek male body and the need of his cock pressing into her could become the searing, greedy touch of hellfire.

She didn't close her eyes, but she did replay the memory of the last few moments in her mind. Then she slowed it down, replayed it again. Any fear or doubt she had left her.

Being thrown down on cold stone tile should have knocked the wind out of her, bruised her skin, jarred the bone structure beneath it. Any or all of those things would have happened if, when they had fallen to the ground, he had not caught her about the back with one arm, slowed their descent so he had taken the brunt of their impact on his forearm. As a result she did not have a bruise or mark on her.

They hadn't missed the exit, though it had been a near thing.

She cocked her head, her brow raised in silent question. His arms continued to hold her, his body quivering with his need, but even so close to her moist gates that her wetness was pooling against his heat, he would not push through that barrier, though the desire to do so would have been unbearable to resist to almost anyone.

Slowly, her lips curved in a knowing, gentle smile.

"You see?" she said softly, raising her own hand now to touch his rigid, suffering face. "You can't do it, Josh. You can't take me against my will. Not just because you're a submissive at heart. Not just because I didn't tell you that you could. You're a decent human being. You're a good man, who got his mind fucked over by a woman who has problems. Just like Jonathan did with me."

His brow furrowed, the rage dying back, but the pain still in his eyes.

"It's that simple, then?"

She would have reached up, stroked his head, if she were not afraid any movement would betray her weakness, and she would pull him into her before it was time. Instead, she turned her head so her cheek pressed into his.

"If we let it be." She eased her legs down a bit, then felt safe enough to stroke through the strands of his hair and run a finger tip along the side of his nose, under one confused eye.

"You're not a Dom, not a Master, Josh," she said. "You've never even been close. You're a submissive. A gorgeous, incredibly sensual submissive that any Mistress in her right mind would cherish forever. You were doing as your Mistress told you to do, and she used you cruelly. I won't let you blame yourself for anything, Josh, except maybe for not recognizing it sooner, because you are an intelligent man. Your only crime is in denying your own worth, because she made you doubt yours. A Mistress doesn't do that, Josh.

"She stripped you down, made you vulnerable, exploited and brought out the aggression in you that's in all wild male animals," she smiled, raking his bare chest lightly with her nails and enjoying the flare it raised in his eyes, the instinctive jump in his cock that caught her breath in her throat. "But then," she sobered, gentled her touch, "instead of cherishing that vulnerability, turning it into pleasure for both of you, she used it to abuse you."

"I thought," he murmured, his throat thick, "like you did. I thought it was the games, the games that screwed us up."

"Games can," she agreed. "You play for pleasure, not for power, but power is such a base element of playing that it's easy to make it go bad, in the wrong hands. But I think…" and she thought of Jonathan, and knew her next words were the truth she had been struggling to understand herself, "Dominant and submissive exist in all relationships, whether they role play it or not. What protects people when they play is love, and the trust that comes with it, when it's real."

A sigh raised and spread that delightful expanse of chest against her breasts, and he laid his forehead down on hers, a gesture of tender weariness that undid her. She stroked his hair, cupped the back of his head to hold him there while she pressed a series of small kisses along his jawline, and her arm crept around him and held as he closed his eyes tightly and the pain shuddered through him and through her, binding them and cleansing them both.

"I'm sorry," he murmured at last, nuzzling her cheek.

"Well, you should be," she slanted a smile at him, her body aching for him, but her heart soothed by the ease she felt relaxing his muscles. "What kind of man treats his Mistress this way?" She traced his bottom lip, "You've been very, very, bad."

He chuckled, but his eyes were serious as he framed her face in his hands. "You risked too much. I could have really hurt you."

She shook her head. "I knew you wouldn't. I just knew it."

"You should have stopped. You really pissed me off."

"That was the plan. And," she gave him an impish look. "I couldn't."

He frowned. "Why not?"

She tilted her head up, saw Marcus sitting on the lowest step of the dais and eyeing them with an appealing combination of relief, confusion and arousal. She also noticed he held a police baton in his hands. He had been ready to intervene if needed, if she had been wrong.

"Ye of little faith," she teased.

He rolled his eyes, made a dismissive wave at her. "Not a doubt in my mind," he said dryly.

"Tell him why I didn't stop, Marcus."

The art dealer sighed. "You never said anything about butterflies, you moron."

Chapter 19

Lauren could not prevent a reflexive gasp and arch as Josh chuckled, vibrating his semi-erect member against her. His eyes darkened and he moved, just slightly. "Something I can do for you…Mistress?"

Her rebellious submissive. She managed a suitably unaffected look, though her body fairly screamed an affirmative answer. "Many, many things. But first, your punishment. Marcus must put you back on that cross." Her finger traced a path, albeit a trembling one, down the center of his chest, "I intend to torture you."

"What if I disobey?" he leaned down, bit her throat, and she moaned, gripped his shoulders.

"I would have to punish you severely," she drew the last word out several more syllables than proper English required, as he rubbed his knee along the inside of her thigh. So close…

She caught his hair and tugged, hard, eliciting a yelp, and made him meet her eyes. "You will obey me, Josh, because I am your Mistress. Now, get up, and go back to the cross, because I want to see you walk that fine ass of yours back across the room and lick my lips over it. And," she didn't ease her grip, "you'll straighten my dress first, with your teeth, so you'll smell how much pleasure you bring to me."

"Cruel bitch," he said, with a smile that trembled at the edges and twisted her heart. He eased up, leaving her missing his weight, but quickly drove that from her mind.

He bent to her thigh, running his tongue over the taut muscle and making her squirm before he took the hem in his teeth and tugged. His chin and jaw scraped her sensitive skin, as he went back and forth, to the outside of each side of her hips. The wet heat of his mouth fastened on her skin here and there until he had the skirt worked over their flare and tapering down along her thighs. She rolled to one hip to help him, giving him an unimpeded view of her bare ass, and enjoyed his huffed, frustrated breath.

When he rose, his cock was fully recovered, and it was all she could do not to touch herself to relieve some of the aching pressure. He looked at her with such yearning, she almost broke again, but she managed to make an imperious gesture, an order to go back toward the cross. He nodded, acknowledging the command, but with a deferential dip of his head, he bent, slid his arms under her, and lifted her to her feet, straightening the dress with respectful hands, smoothing the fabric from waist to thigh. As she looked up at him, unable to tear her eyes away from his face, he focused on her hair, tucking it back up into the pins she had used when she slicked it back from her face. Taking care of her.

He held her face in his hands a moment, his thumbs along the jumping pulse and fragile bones of her neck. He did not say anything, but Lauren was not aware of silence. A hundred words and emotions were expressed in that look. She thought it might be the first expression on Man's face when he was first created and the whole world was a new place, with so many mysteries and wonders, places of dark and light.

He released her, turned and walked back across the room, his body moving gracefully. He stopped before the cross and hesitated only a moment before he allowed himself to be once again stretched out and strapped in. It made her eyes sting, his trust.

However, sentiment was swallowed by even stronger emotions as she watched the process of restraining him. The adjustment of hip, the tightening of his stomach, the flexing of muscles as his arms were extended. Marcus buckling the straps over his spread, muscular thighs, framing his arousal. She had him stop before he restrained the neck and forehead. She wanted Josh to be able to move his head this time.

"Cock harness, my lady?" her Egyptian assistant queried, his dark hair whispering along the white silk of his robe as he turned his head toward her.

"No, not this time. I intend to make use of it."

She came back across the floor to stand before Josh, strutting, slow, her hips swaying with her steps. His eyes drank in the sway of her body, the quiver of her breasts, the hard points of her nipples. Last time he had been blindfolded. Now he did not have to imagine.

"Ten lashes, I think," she tapped her foot. "And if you handle that well, then you'll get a reward. Do you think that's fair?"

His hands closed into fists again. The shadows still lurked in his eyes, the residue of opening a festering wound to bleed, and she intended to wash it clean once and for all with pure, healthy lust.

"Ask me for them, Josh," she murmured. "Tell me you want my punishment."

Josh nodded. "Anything to please you, Mistress." And his lips curved up in a way that speared straight to her vitals. "Anything."

"Insolent creature. Perhaps I'll make it fifteen."

He was hard as a rock when she landed the first blow, licking the area just above his hipbone. The shuddering reaction of his skin was almost the same as if she had caressed him.

He kept his eyes locked on her, and she didn't make him cast his eyes down. She liked to see the fire build, passion destroying pain. The shadows were being chased away by an excruciating combination of pleasure and pain, a tug-of-war that was bringing a flush to his face and chest with every strike. It was as alluring as the red glow she was bringing to the skin on his thighs and ass as she switched from one side of the cross to the other. The whip snapped, pulling blood to the surface of sensitized skin.

Strike fourteen, and he was panting, his eyes filled with the light of the wild animal again, only violence wasn't what he had in mind this time, she was sure. She caught the rattail end of the whip around his shaft on the last stroke, tugged before she loosed it. Even as he jumped, a male, defensive reaction, fluid leaked from the tip. He was ready to detonate, every muscle quivering and possessed by the savagery brought by mindless desire, and she had brought it to him.

The thought of that was almost as stimulating to her as the thought of what she wanted to do with that cock.

"What do you think of our beautiful man, Marcus?" she asked, coming closer. Josh strained against his bonds toward her.

Marcus was watching Josh, almost as fascinated as the bound man was with her.

"He's the most beautiful thing I've ever seen."

"Mmmm. Would you like to fuck him, Marcus?"

That snapped both men's attention to her. Lauren stepped up to Josh, aware of the charged tension that filled the air between him and Marcus. She laid her hand along Josh's cheek, made him look into her eyes. "What do you say, Josh? I've always wanted to ride a man with another man inside him." she leaned in, licked his jawline and let him strain to nibble at her temple. "I think it would feel absolutely incredible."

Marcus drew close to Josh's shoulder, meeting her gaze over the tanned curve of skin and muscle. His hand touched Josh's nape, a whisper brush down his spine. A shiver ran through Josh, but it did not appear to be one of revulsion. He brushed his lips against her face and she let herself be nuzzled as Marcus bent, and gently kissed the line of Josh's shoulders where neck and collar bone met.

"You must answer your Mistress, Josh," Marcus commanded quietly, and Lauren felt her already warm blood stir as she heard some of the Master enter Marcus's voice. "Tell her what you desire."

Josh turned his head. Lauren's hand lay on his bare chest, playing there, her hips rubbing inside his thighs, brushing his excited groin.

Josh met Marcus's gaze and something deep, lingering, was considered. "If it will bring my Mistress pleasure," his attention came back to Lauren, "then I want Marcus to fuck me."

There was still too much shuttered behind those gray eyes. She curled her hand on his neck, tightened her grip.

"It will bring me pleasure, Josh, only if it brings you pleasure," she responded. "Do you want Marcus inside of you?"

Josh gave a half-deprecating laugh. In a slight motion that took both his captors by surprise, he laid his forehead briefly against Marcus's close temple. "I believe he always has been, in one fashion or another."

Despite the seriousness of the moment, Lauren felt her cheek muscles quiver at the utter shock that crossed Marcus's normally self-possessed features. Josh might have appreciated it as well, except the admission had flustered him, and he had lowered his gaze, a light flush rising in his cheeks.

The shyness, and deference, stoked the fire in both of his admirers. Marcus's hand came up, cupped Josh's jaw, his thumb making a firm stroke over the other man's cheek, and when Josh's eyes lifted, Marcus pressed a brief kiss on the other man's lips, his brilliant green eyes locked with storm gray. No tongue, no physical outburst that might send Josh into a panicked retreat. She had to admire Marcus's restraint. After such an admission, she would have wanted to gobble him up whole.

Marcus lowered his hand, caught hers, and drew it forward. He curled her fingers around Josh's cock and the man groaned at the squeezing pressure of her heated skin.

"I'd like to see you stroke him while I prepare myself for our beautiful boy, if it suits you, my lady." he said. Not a command, not from one Dom to another, but a request she was more than willing to grant.

She nodded. "I'll be right back," she whispered, touching Josh's jaw, and turned her back to him, bending over the close chair. She coiled the whip on the seat. When she straightened and turned, Josh's eyes lifted.

"I could almost see your pussy," he murmured. "I'm glad you came to the island."

She smiled at the disjointed thoughts and touched his face, his neck.

"Me, too." She ran her hand along his arm, over the three straps that held it there above his head. "Are you comfortable?"

He chuckled, glanced down. "Not entirely."

She wrapped her other hand around him, and slipped back into a Mistress's role with the ease and joy as if she had been born in a dungeon with whip in hand.

"Good," she murmured, rubbing her breasts against his bare chest, drawing his eyes to the gather and stretch of the fabric as the full curves lifted to accommodate the pressure. "Do you like being uncomfortable for me, Josh? Do you like being so hard so long for me?"

"If it makes my Mistress wet to see me so," he made a futile attempt to catch her ear in his teeth when she rubbed her cheek against his.

"Bad boy," she chuckled, giving his cock a hard squeeze that brought something close to a whimper from him. "But I think you know your Mistress too well. We'll have to punish you for that, won't we, Marcus?"

Marcus had emerged from the dressing room with a green glass bottle. His lithe movements toward them shifted the open white silk robe, emphasizing and framing his chest, hard stomach and even harder cock, clearly molded by the soft material of the gathered pants.

Lauren heard Josh swallow. Her hand rested on his collar bone, so she felt the pulse jump.

"Butterflies, Josh?" she asked.

His eyes tore from Marcus and came back to her. "No," he managed.

"Good. You tell me, you tell us, if you get them, at any point." She flattened herself against him and captured his mouth in an open, hot kiss. She fisted her hand roughly in his hair and moved in, straddling his erection, sliding his aroused member along the slick channel of her clit and labia, rubbing. He rocked forward, just the small amount his restraints permitted, and groaned again as she moved over his sensitive head.

She felt like groaning herself. His brief contact on her clit was unbelievably powerful, her response as close to an orgasm from just a brief touch as anything she'd ever had. The friction of pulling off of him, going over that thick ridge of the glans, was worse. She had to tighten her grip, steady her breathing.

Fortunately, her captive was distracted from pressing his advantage. Marcus had moved around them during the kiss. Lauren smelled the exotic scents from the bottle of oil as he uncorked it. Josh went rigid, and there was a shift in his eyes, apprehension.

"Sshhh," Marcus made a gesture only Lauren could see, and she nodded, sliding her arms around Josh's waist. She turned her hand over, accepting the small pool of oil into it, the texture slippery like her own fluids.

"Just some lubricant, dear one," Marcus murmured and laid Lauren's hand, palm down, in the indentation right above Josh's buttocks.

Lauren let the liquid drain onto his skin. At Marcus's guiding touch, she slid her oiled fingers down along the inside of the curve of Josh's ass, then deeper, letting the oil follow the impression of her fingers. It flowed over and into the tight opening that fairly radiated Josh's tension. She ran her fingers around and over it, and transformed the tension of fear into the strain toward release, his breath beginning to grow rapid. She was pressed full against him, her head lifted to watch what she was doing, and she gasped as he sank his teeth into her jugular. It was a non-puncturing grip, but strong all the same. He sucked harshly on her skin. The lack of finesse tightened her own nerves, a spiral from breast to groin. She turned her head to dislodge his mouth but recaptured his lips in a damp kiss.

Her hand slid up the small of the back, and Marcus's touch smoothly replaced hers. His long fingers fondled Josh's buttocks, squeezing, a stronger, more masculine touch that she was not sure Josh noticed immediately, due to the seamless transition dance of their hands and her efforts toward keeping his attention on plundering her hot mouth, fused on his.

Marcus had changed the music when he went to get the lubricant, and the beat was building again, a deep drum rhythm at once complex and primal. It vibrated through the floor, through the soles of Lauren's feet, tingling in the contact between her palm and Josh's shoulder and neck. She pressed herself even more tightly against him, now holding his head still with her touch so she could nibble on his neck.

"I want to touch you," he muttered against her cheek.

She smiled, which did nothing to dispel the raging, aching need in her own eyes, a need as much emotional as physical. "Tough," she whispered, with a slight catch in her tone. "You'll wait for me to take you."

"God," his breath exhaled in a rush as she worked the dress up with her movements and rubbed herself along the top of his engorged head again. "Please...I'm going to explode."

Marcus had loosened the drawstring of the silken pants and they pooled around his ankles, revealing an impressive erection rising out of a curling thatch of black hair.

"First, you take Marcus," she caught his shoulder in her teeth, channeling the shudder that rippled dangerously along her skin into the fierceness of the bite to gain some control of herself, "Then, I take you. But if you come when Marcus goes in, you get nothing but my whip," she nipped sharply on his nipple and he gasped, "on your adorable ass."

"I can't..."

Lauren glanced around his arm and saw Marcus removing a condom from his robe.

"You better," she said without a break, covering Marcus's muted rattling of foil. "Because my pussy is dripping for you. Feel that," she rubbed it along his length again and managed a strangled chuckle when he let out a noise, part animal, and part inventive curse. His muscles strained so hard against his bonds she could see the flesh reddening around the imprint of the straps again, hear the material creaking to contain him. "Tell me you won't come."

"I won't." He fisted his hands as she slowly, slowly slid herself up his length again. "Jesus, fucking...Lauren, stop..."

She paused, let him feel the rippling through her sensitive tissues, revealing how close she was herself. "Marcus."

"I'm here, dearest." He moved up behind Josh. He was somewhat taller, so when he moved Josh's hair aside to kiss his exposed neck, he only had to raise his eyelids to meet Lauren's gaze. His arms lowered, his hands coming to rest on Josh's hips, his long, strong fingers caressing the lines just below the restraining strap on his waist. Josh's thigh muscles tensed in a fascinating display of virility that Lauren admired as she slid away from him, standing back a step to lock eyes with him.

"Remember," she said softly. "You can't come until I say so. Forget, and you'll feel my whip." She moistened her lips, watching his glazed, frantic expression take in every curve of her body, the jutted hips, the tilt of her tight breasts, the light play of her fingers along her thigh. She inched the fabric up, up again exposing only the very tip of what she was offering him, a cloven fruit, the ripe, succulent inside exposed to his gaze, just out of reach.

Marcus's eyes were very green and alive, and yet very much in control. It could not help but elicit the greatest admiration of another Dominant, or make a sub go weak with obedience. Lauren thought she could have simply stood back and watched him with the quiet joy of watching a master of any type of art work his magic.

His chest pressed against Josh's shoulders. "Lay your head against my jaw," he ordered, the command delivered in a voice like a sensual caress. Josh obeyed, tilting his head. He bucked, startled, when Marcus's hand reached around, closed around his cock.

While Josh had thus far demonstrated an amazing level of control that she suspected was the result of a successful artist's discipline, Lauren knew that what Marcus was about to do could in fact cause Josh to explode, despite his best efforts to hold himself back. The only thing that might prevent it was the fact this would be a virgin fuck, so to speak. His nervousness, and the unusual feel of it might combine to keep him from losing the grip.

"Easy, love," Marcus crooned, tightening his grasp in delightful conflict with his soothing words. "Mustn't disobey your mistress. What a fucking, gorgeous tight ass you have. You want me in it?"

Josh nodded, one jerk of his head. "Tell me," Marcus said sharply.

"Yes." Josh was panting and Lauren saw a convulsive ripple under Marcus's slowly stroking fingers, resulting in a small explosion of fluid. A slight smile curved her lips and she picked up her whip. Josh's eyes jerked to her. "No," he protested. "I won't."

She nodded, flicked it around his feet. "I know you won't, Josh. You'll take every inch of him, but you'll save all that for me, won't you?"

He nodded, almost beyond speech. He wasn't going to make it, despite his best intentions. Lauren thought if she had touched herself at this moment she would go off herself. Lord in Heaven, she had never had the opportunity to experience the sexual high this type of power could bring, power based on trust and emotional bonds. What she thought she had with Jonathan did not even compare.

"You need the harness, Josh."

"I don't, Mistress," he promised her, a fierce light in his eyes. "Only for you. Please don't. I'll wait for you."

Her heart tugged at the ragged fierceness in his voice. His vow was like a knight's oath of absolute fealty and protection to his lady, a promise fate could easily overturn. But it was not the success of the vow, but the intent of it, that mattered.

"I didn't make it a question, Josh," she said.

Marcus removed his hand, and Josh groaned as she retrieved the harness and buckled it around his shaft. Se made it tight, holding in all the juices that wanted to flood themselves in her. Lauren stood back, fondly caressing the recaptured cock with her fingers as he twisted and squirmed in futile torment. She couldn't wait to feel his orgasm explode inside her.

"Take him, Marcus," she said.

Marcus's grip had risen to Josh's shoulder during her ministrations. Now his fingers shifted, closed on Josh's throat. His gaze on hers, he drove himself in, his fingers tightening, creating pain with pleasure.

Josh cried out, a guttural noise close to a scream as the sensation swept from prostate to scrotum, nipples to cock in a wide, sweeping tidal wave. Lauren watched with wide eyes and parted lips as Marcus slid out, then back in, a slow rhythm that took the wave down, then built it back up, and up. The music of Josh's rasping breath mingled with the hard slap of male flesh against male flesh, the bass of the music playing, and she felt light headed. She kept her eyes on them though, physically unable to look away.

Josh began gasping, then moaning, then he was snarling like an animal, his eyes locked on her face. Marcus pumped harder into him, whispered into his ear. Both men were sweating now, all muscles straining. They were like two powerful stallions, too mesmerizing to express in words.

Josh flung his head back against the wood piece behind him, but she didn't think he even registered the blunt impact. Marcus's skillful strokes were teasing the bundle of nerve endings within in the manner intended to drive a man to release. For Josh, it was a drive to insanity, an explosion for which there was no release in pressure. He jerked futilely in his bonds and spoke Marcus's name, a snarling plea.

Marcus gave a harsh moan, his fingers flexing, and emptied himself. He sank his teeth into Josh's shoulder, drawing blood, but Josh's head lay tense and helpless against him.

His aching, needy eyes fastened on the clear fluid trickling down her thigh, her involuntary reaction to watching them, and she knew they had waited as long as they could bear. It was time to reward them both.

Chapter 20
ಸಿ

She came forward, his tormentor, his temptress, the center of his universe. The whole world narrowed to her face, her body, her scent.

He let his apprehension go with both hands, all his fears of doing something wrong. Winona had given him those fears, because he had disappointed her so often. Lauren's touch, her voice, her eyes, they all said that he could do nothing wrong with her except turn away or hold back his desires. He was under her control, directed by her commands, but more than that, he saw in her aroused eyes her immersion in him as he was immersed in her. There was no detachment, no sense of distance.

She had taken an enormous risk when she hadn't untied him when he demanded it. He remembered the way her hand had trembled, not out of fear of his rage, but out of fear of taking the step that would lose his trust, and destroy the bond they had sensed between them from the beginning. That was what this was about. Something far deeper than two people who had known each other for such a short time should be experiencing, but deeper nonetheless. He could hope desperately that she would stay when this was over, let him learn more about her, cherish her. But, even if she didn't, he could give her his absolute devotion now.

They were all adults. They all knew sex, really good sex, could make the mind manufacture bonds and emotional involvement where there was nothing but lust. But sometimes sex was more than that, a transcendent experience where everything was stripped away except the bare soul, and a person found a permanent resting place for his heart. He saw it in her. He didn't have to know anything more about her than he did at this moment to know it, to be sure of it. If he lived through the unbearable pleasure of the next few moments, he was never letting her go.

With Marcus still hard and warm inside him, she slowly inched the dress up her hips, bringing the hem sliding up her thighs, a millimeter at a time, and then past the crotch. He saw the closely cropped area around her pussy, the short hairs curled around the opening moist with her arousal, and then she came to him.

Marcus was moving again, slowly, keeping ripples of sensation going and attempting to defy the laws of nature and keep himself in an erect state, even after emptying his own seed. Apparently, he'd had some experience at it, for as he made some sinuous, circular movement of his hips, Josh could still feel him, feel his cock getting a bit stiffer, taking up more room, teasing him again.

Lauren slid the chair she had used closer and stepped up on it, bringing her breasts to Josh's eye level for a moment. She leaned forward, pressed the nipples pushing up the stretched cloth against his forehead, squashing the soft full part of the curves beneath it against his eyes, his nose, let him inhale her, strive to taste her. She was lifting the cross piece behind his shoulders, lifting it over his head and then re-anchoring it there.

She used the bar to lift her legs off the chair, hook her knees up onto his shoulders and slide in, spreading her thighs before his face, bringing her wet center an inch before his mouth and resting her ankles on Marcus's shoulders.

"Eat, Josh," she commanded.

His mouth took possession at once, tongue plunging into the wet musk of her, a sound of pure animal pleasure rumbling like a growl in his throat. Lauren cried out and her skin rippled around his tongue, gripping it, in a small, squeezing pre-orgasm. She was close, and the only thing he wanted more than to fuck her was to hear her scream with release. His lips worked double time, sucking, kneading, tongue flicking, thrusting, until she was writhing on his shoulders, gasping, and he groaned in reaction to it, and to Marcus's thrusts.

He gave a frustrated oath as she pulled back, her body quivering and glistening with sweat under the glitter. Her expression was one of total hunger now, though, and he knew she was not going to leave him denied. She brought her legs down, slid her grip to his shoulders, and clasped her thighs around his waist, so her ass was brushing his cock. He saw her gaze flick to Marcus and then made a noise of pure joy as he felt Marcus loose the waist strap and pull the harness off his cock, without breaking his own rhythm.

She braced the sides of her spike heels along Marcus's hips.

"Yes," Josh murmured, every cell of his body roaring for her. "Please."

Her nostrils flared, taking in the smell of herself on his lips, glistening with her fluids. She lowered herself onto his erect cock which, despite the slightly off angle, easily routed itself into her slick wetness as if it knew it was coming home.

Down, down, she went down on him inch by wonderful inch, and it almost overwhelmed him. God, she felt good. She was everything. So, perfect, so right. It sounded inane, but it was true. She wrapped her arms around his shoulders, lifting her body so she was pressed against him from neck to joining, coupling her hips even closer. Marcus kissed her cheek, and then Josh's temple.

"Now, Josh," she murmured. "Fuck me, now."

He wanted to hold out, wanted to build her as high as he could before they both leapt, but it felt too good.

She rocked her hips, forward and down once, and the animal swept over them all.

* * * * *

She had never had the actual flood of a man's climax stroke her over. Fire seared through her, burning everything else away and leaving only him. His scent became her air, his body the solidity of the earth beneath her feet, his orgasm a flood of fire jetting into her womb, and the slick sweat and oil making it possible for their coupled limbs to move in a tidal rhythm, higher, higher.

Tantric sex focused on delaying physical release as long as possible, to build its pressure to heights overwhelming in their power. All she had done to keep him waiting, herself waiting, now exploded through the dam of restraint. His bindings became the anchor onto which they held to keep from being swept away.

She swallowed his fierce cry of release into her own mouth and gave it back as his cock slid rapidly back and forth across the taut strings of her nerve endings and ignited a symphony of response.

Emotion became pure physical, and her body bowed back, a raw scream tearing from her throat as the climax took her, too much to take. She was as helpless as he was to the overwhelming force of it, her juices flowing over him, her muscles gripping him, milking him inside her, squeezing every drop of his release into her body. He said her name, over and over, and his mouth was wet and open on her sternum as he sucked on her, muttered against her, touched her in the only way his bindings allowed.

They both cried out as Marcus came again, and they were all carried forward on the wave of this additional climax, thrust into sensation so strong it was almost pain. She could not hear what she was crying out, but it was blending with their own words, a simple primal chant as old as the stone beneath their feet. She inhaled the smell of sex, of men's bodies, her own musk, and thought she was going to lose consciousness.

She might have done so, for it seemed a long, long while before the pounding surf eased and gave way to a smooth, rhythmic movement of smaller waves. The soft ripples deposited her back into the sands of reality, the warm, wonderful reality of Josh's body, his closed eyes, hair damp at the temples. She was collapsed upon him, clinging to his neck, her trembling legs still somehow holding onto him, perhaps because Marcus was holding onto her calves.

She opened her eyes to a burning sensation and saw the reddened tips of her fingers, where they had dug savagely into the wood of the cross.

Marcus looked somewhat like an angel that had wrestled with a demon. However, he was the first to become a bit more in tune with the world around them. He slid gently from Josh, easing her legs down. He took care of his aftermath with one of the moist towelettes available on a built-in shelf next to each of the room's devices. Lauren tried to keep the tile floor from sliding out from under her wobbly spike heels by gripping Josh's shoulders for balance. He cracked open an eye to look at her.

"If you've a mind to remove these…Mistress," he made it a husky caress that trailed up her spine like fingertips, "I can help hold you up."

"Or collapse to the floor with me."

He chuckled, acknowledging the truth of her words, and planted a lingering, fierce kiss on her temple. She cupped his head, holding him there, her eyes as tightly shut as his for a moment.

"God, that felt good," she murmured, surprised when tears choked her voice. "Thank you."

"Likewise." He lifted his head, a tender stroke of his nose against hers. "I'd really like to hold you."

"Oh! Sorry," she smiled, somewhat unrepentant, and tugged off the leg straps, amazed at the ease with which the buckles unsnapped, when they were so resilient when locked. She smoothed her fingers over the deep red welts on his arms, leaned forward and placed her lips there. His other arm curled around her back, folded her to him as he moved off the cross and sank down to sit on the dais. She went down with him, sitting on the step below, her body folded between his bare thighs. The wetness of his cock pressed against her side. He laid his head over hers.

"I really like you, Josh."

He chuckled against her hair, and she lifted her head to look up into his eyes. Both of them were grinning foolishly. "That's not what I meant. I mean... aside from all this, I really like you. You're someone I'd like to get to know better."

"I think you probably know me better than most people ever have," he tucked a curl behind her ear, "and," he lifted a shoulder, "I don't know why it is, but two people can be together five years and not know how to love each other, cherish each other, and others can do it," he glanced at his wrist as if a watch was there and slanted a glance at her, leaving the thought unfinished.

She swallowed, uncertain what to say, not sure if she needed to say anything, because the idea was at best a fragile miracle that words might destroy.

"I know," he nodded, as if reading her thoughts. "I'm not talking about the kind of love people have after twenty years, where they can finish each other's sentences. That takes work, and time. But I think all those relationships start with something more than just a flash of lust. You feel like you could just sit and look at that person forever. You just want to be near them. I felt that...feel that, with you.

"But you don't need to do anything about it," he added quickly. "I mean, it doesn't obligate you to me. You have a life, and this is just —"

She placed a finger on his lips. "Don't," she said quietly. "Don't start playing those games. You trusted me with those straps on, trust me with them off. We'll figure it out. I want to be with you, too. Just," she traced the firm lips with a finger. "Just shut up."

He cocked a brow, and then gave her a slow, sensual smile that reminded her that expression was all he was presently wearing.

"Yes, Mistress," he replied.

She heard Marcus give a weak chuckle as Josh's lips took hold of her mouth, and all her senses, once again.

Chapter 21

॰๑

Marcus had to leave the following morning. Josh and Lauren followed him down to the wide beach, clean and white in the light of late morning. It was a day that begged to be whiled away, gazing at the surf from a reclining position in comfortable beach chairs.

Lauren felt something tighten in her chest when she saw the charter boat. It had already dropped anchor and a dingy was making its way toward shore. Marcus looked very different in a golf shirt and perfectly tailored slacks. He wore an expensive gold bracelet, Italian shoes, and his hair was carelessly styled to fall in lustrous waves to his shoulders. He looked every inch the urbane New Yorker, but his eyes, moving over the two of them, held a warmth and wistfulness that was a reflection of her own desire to hold onto the special bond they had forged here.

It had been one of the most incredible emotional and physical experiences of her life. She suspected it would rate among the top ten for Marcus. At least for now, until he garnered other experiences to knock it down the list.

The thought curved her lips in a smile, and loosened some of the tight feeling. She left Josh's side and put her arms around Marcus, lifting onto her canvas sneakered toes to brush his lips with hers. His hand caught in her hair and he held her there against him a moment, savoring the sensual pleasure of bodies and lips touching, recalling experiences shared. He eased her down and she smiled at him. "You keep those boys up in the Big Apple in line, you hear me? And if you need any help..."

He chuckled. "You'll be the first. You'll scare their cute little asses off. Maybe," he looked away, then down, an unusually vulnerable move for him, then his eyes lifted and found hers over his sunglasses. "I might call Thomas, see what he's doing these days."

She squeezed his hand at her hip. "You do that. Don't let him go, Marcus. Not if he's the one."

He nodded, touched her cheek, then looked over her head at Josh. She stepped delicately out of the space between the two men. Marcus moved forward, hugged Josh close. It was the embrace of good friends, brothers, and something that did not need definition. Josh held him just as firmly, his fingers tightening on Marcus's back. Lauren thought she heard a murmured, "thank you", before both eased back, looking a bit choked up by the moment.

Men. Such softies. She smiled on them, felt the warmth of the sun, and thought today was the most beautiful day in the world. More importantly, tomorrow and the next day could be even more beautiful. There were no limits to the possibilities of life.

"I have a parting gift for the two of you," Marcus said, reaching into his travel bag. He gave them an enigmatic smile as Lauren came to Josh's side.

He pulled out the deck of cards that had started their adventure. The deck had been divided in half and each portion tied charmingly with sprigs of forest greenery and gold satin ribbon, probably stolen from one of the corsets from the costume room. One of the fragrant white blooms that grew wild on the island was woven into each sprig.

Marcus took their hands, pressed the cards into their respective palms, and held them there, linking the three of them in a circle.

"I will be interested to see who is holding the cards next time we meet," he said quietly, looking between them. "But I suspect we all know that when it's done right, you don't keep score." He flashed a wicked grin. "It wouldn't be half as much fun otherwise, no pun intended."

Josh lifted a brow. "I don't know if I should be touched by your sentiment, or figure you're saying I'm dealing with half a deck."

"No more than the rest of us, dear boy," Marcus chuckled and laid a hand alongside his neck, squeezing. "That's why you have to find the one with the other half. Maybe you have. I surely hope so." He smiled at them, then released Josh and embraced Lauren, pulling her close again. Lauren held him hard to her heart for a moment, overwhelmed by her emotions, and by what he murmured in her ear. However, being Marcus, he refused to leave her with tears.

She was chuckling as he pulled away. Marcus shouldered his carry on, and headed down the beach toward the waiting dingy.

"What did he say?" Josh asked, taking her hand.

Lauren linked her fingers with his. "He said he anticipated getting some lucrative creations from his favorite artist very soon."

Josh shook his head, turned, and lifted his hand in response to Marcus's wave before the art dealer stepped into the boat. "Mercenary bastard," he said affectionately. "So what else did he say, before that?"

Lauren looked down at their entangled fingers, then up at him. "He said not to let you hide here all the time, to make Isabel share you with the world a bit."

"And what did you say?" His neutral expression guarded his feelings, giving her the freedom to say her mind. That shuttering told her all she needed to know. Warmth bloomed inside of her.

"I said I wouldn't leave without you, however long it took."

"You need to be a doctor, Lauren," he said after a moment. "You have a gift for healing."

She nodded. "I might at that. There's a clinic on the main island. It needs a doctor more than a wealthy clinic in Atlanta. Lisette has tried to talk me into working there before. I can practice there for awhile, until you and Isabel decide you want to be somewhere else. Is that what you want?"

He looked away, but she caught his chin, brought his face back to her.

"Don't look away when I'm speaking to you. Tell me what you want, and be truthful. Or I'll know." She put enough edge in her voice to get a responsive flash in his eyes, a visible flush of heat on his body, but in her eyes there was something softer, warmer, and it was that he answered.

"I want you. I want to be with you." He reached out, drew her to him, slid his hands up the soft skin of her arms. "I'd like to get to know you better, learn everything about you, make you happy, take care of you. I'd rather," he swallowed. "I don't mind being with other people, but... physically, I'd prefer not to share you."

"I've always been a monogamous type of girl," she responded, her voice thick with emotion at his shy vulnerability, the hope in his voice. It told her they still had a ways to go to heal all the pain Winona had inflicted, but they had taken the most important step. She arched a brow at him, letting him see the healthy humor in her gaze.

"A possessive submissive?" she teased. She laughed when he made a fierce face and gathered her firmly in his arms, underscoring his point. "Well, I don't know. You'd have to work really hard at pleasing me."

"Yes, Mistress," he murmured, nuzzling her neck, his tongue teasing her skin so her muscles became loose and flowing like the cool waters rushing over their bare feet. Her hand gripped his shoulder and she lifted her head, raised her palm to his face, traced the cheekbones, the sensual lips.

"All those things you said," she murmured. "I want to be the same, do the same, for you. Give you inspiration."

"You're already doing that," he bit her neck and she shivered.

"Then let's go to your house and see if we can help you finish some of the things you've started."

"It's a sad place."

"We'll fix it. Do you want me?"

He looked down at her, the wild reckless passion of the artist in his eyes, daring her to tame him, begging her to try. It almost made her smile.

He molded his palms to her hips with the care and reverence he would clay, his fingers grazing her bare hipbones where the shorts and top parted. He slid his hands back, let the thumbs meet, and cupped her buttocks, pushing her into him, against his hard arousal.

He bent his head, pausing just a whisper above her ear, breathing upon it.

"More than air."

The combinations of sensual intent and raw vulnerability in the whisper pooled like liquid chocolate in all her senses. She slid her arms around his neck and brought his head down for a kiss that had the searing heat of lava deep beneath the earth. The mere movement of his lips on hers loosened everything within and without her, including her grip on Marcus's cards.

The cards hit the sand, the loose binding giving way, allowing them to be picked up by the ocean breeze. They were lifted and spun in all different directions, the sea, the sand, the dunes and forest beyond, and against their legs and ankles.

Lauren melted into Josh's kiss, felt his body melt into hers, and decided to let Fate hold the cards for this hand.

* * * * *

That night, they slept on his deck. Josh rose up on an elbow, watching Lauren as she slept. The moonlight on the waves below them reflected in the glittering strands of her loosened blonde hair.

"My little dominatrix," he murmured with soft, fervent affection, and a smile for them both. He bent, pressed a light kiss to the corner of her lips, just a taste of endless possibilities, and then lay back down beside her, gathering her close, protecting and protected, and found peace.

Also by Joey W. Hill

ಐ

eBooks:
Afterlife
Board Resolution
Chance of a Lifetime
Choice of Masters
If Wishes Were Horses
Make Her Dreams Come True
Nature of Desire 1: Holding the Cards
Nature of Desire 2: Natural Law
Nature of Desire 3: Ice Queen
Nature of Desire 4: Mirror of My Soul
Nature of Desire 5: Mistress of Redemption
Nature of Desire 6: Rough Canvas
Nature of Desire 7: Branded Sanctuary
Snow Angel
Threads of Faith
Virtual Reality

Print Books:
Afterlife
Behind the Mask *(anthology)*
Enchained *(anthology)*
Faith and Dreams
Hot Chances *(anthology)*
If Wishes Were Horses

Nature of Desire 2: Natural Law
Nature of Desire 3: Ice Queen
Nature of Desire 4: Mirror of My Soul
Nature of Desire 5: Mistress of Redemption
Nature of Desire 6: Rough Canvas
Nature of Desire 7: Branded Sanctuary
The Twelve Quickies of Christmas Volume 2 *(anthology)*
Virtual Reality

About the Author
✽

I've always had an aversion to reading, watching or hearing interviews of favorite actors, authors, musicians, etc. because so often the real person doesn't measure up to the beauty of the art they produce. Their politics or religion are distasteful, or they're shallow and self-absorbed, a vacuous mophead without a lick of sense. From then on, though I may appreciate their craft or art, it has somehow been tarnished. Therefore, whenever I'm asked to provide personal information about myself for readers, a ball of anxiety forms in my stomach as I think: "Okay, the next couple of paragraphs can change forever the way someone views my stories." Why on earth does a reader want to know about me? It's the story that's important.

So here it is. I've been given more blessings in my life than any one person has a right to have. Despite that, I'm a Type A, borderline obsessive-compulsive paranoiac who worries I will never live up to expectations. I've got more phobias than anyone (including myself) has patience to read about. I can't stand talking on the phone, I dread social commitments, and the idea of living in monastic solitude with my husband and animals, books and writing is as close an idea to paradise as I can imagine. I love chocolate, but with that deeply ingrained, irrational female belief that weight equals worth, I manage to keep it down to a minor addiction. I adore good movies. I'm told I work too much. Every day is spent trying to get through the never ending "to do" list to snatch a few minutes to write.

This is because, despite all these mediocre and typical qualities, for some miraculous reason, these wonderful characters well up out of my soul with stories to tell. When I manage to find enough time to write, sufficient enough that the precious "stillness" required rises up and calms all the competing voices in my head, I can step into their lives, hear what they are saying, what they're feeling, and put it down on paper. It's a magic beyond description, akin to truly believing my husband loves me, winning the trust of an animal who has known only fear or apathy, making a true connection with someone, or knowing for certain I've given a reader a moment of magic through those written words. It's a magic that reassures me there is Someone, far wiser than myself, who knows the permanent path to that garden of stillness, where there is only love, acceptance and a pen waiting for hours and hours of uninterrupted, blissful use.

If only I could finish that darned "to do" list.

I welcome feedback from readers - actually, I thrive on it like a vampire, whether it's good or bad. So feel free to visit me through my website www.storywitch.com anytime.

ಐ

The author welcomes comments from readers. You can find her website and email address on her author bio page at www.ellorascave.com.

Tell Us What You Think

We appreciate hearing reader opinions about our books. You can email us at Comments@EllorasCave.com.

Why an electronic book?

We live in the Information Age—an exciting time in the history of human civilization, in which technology rules supreme and continues to progress in leaps and bounds every minute of every day. For a multitude of reasons, more and more avid literary fans are opting to purchase e-books instead of paper books. The question from those not yet initiated into the world of electronic reading is simply: *Why?*

1. *Price.* An electronic title at Ellora's Cave Publishing runs anywhere from 40% to 75% less than the cover price of the exact same title in paperback format. Why? Basic mathematics and cost. It is less expensive to publish an e-book (no paper and printing, no warehousing and shipping) than it is to publish a paperback, so the savings are passed along to the consumer.
2. *Space.* Running out of room in your house for your books? That is one worry you will never have with electronic books. For a low one-time cost, you can purchase a handheld device specifically designed for e-reading. Many e-readers have large, convenient screens for viewing. Better yet, hundreds of titles can be stored within your new library—on a single microchip. There are a variety of e-readers from different manufacturers. You can also read e-books on your PC or laptop computer. (Please note that Ellora's Cave does not endorse any specific brands.

You can check our website at www.ellorascave.com for information we make available to new consumers.)
3. *Mobility.* Because your new e-library consists of only a microchip within a small, easily transportable e-reader, your entire cache of books can be taken with you wherever you go.
4. *Personal Viewing Preferences.* Are the words you are currently reading too small? Too large? Too… ANNOYING? Paperback books cannot be modified according to personal preferences, but e-books can.
5. *Instant Gratification.* Is it the middle of the night and all the bookstores near you are closed? Are you tired of waiting days, sometimes weeks, for bookstores to ship the novels you bought? Ellora's Cave Publishing sells instantaneous downloads twenty-four hours a day, seven days a week, every day of the year. Our webstore is never closed. Our e-book delivery system is 100% automated, meaning your order is filled as soon as you pay for it.

Those are a few of the top reasons why electronic books are replacing paperbacks for many avid readers.

As always, Ellora's Cave welcomes your questions and comments. We invite you to email us at Comments@ellorascave.com or write to us directly at Ellora's Cave Publishing Inc., 1056 Home Avenue, Akron, OH 44310-3502.

Discover for yourself why readers can't get enough of the multiple award-winning publisher Ellora's Cave.

Whether you prefer e-books or paperbacks, be sure to visit EC on the web at www.ellorascave.com for an erotic reading experience that will leave you breathless.

CPSIA information can be obtained at www.ICGtesting.com
Printed in the USA
LVOW07s0105171214

419124LV00001B/121/P